ALSO BY NATHAN NIPPER

Life on Christmas Eve: A Novel

AMERICAN INHERITANCE

a novel

NATHAN NIPPER

A POST HILL PRESS BOOK
ISBN: 979-8-88845-566-1
ISBN (eBook): 979-8-88845-568-5

American Inheritance:
A Novel
© 2024 by Nathan Nipper
All Rights Reserved

Cover design by Conroy Accord

Post Hill Press
New York • Nashville
posthillpress.com

Published in the United States of America
1 2 3 4 5 6 7 8 9 10

For my wonderful sons,
Graham and Heath.

ONE

I never really hated America as much as Bob thought I did. But I was really mad at it. So was Bob. Turns out we had that in common. It's basically the only thing we had in common.

I had never met Bob, even though he is my grandfather, until the COVID pandemic was in full swing in 2020. The reason we'd never met was simple—my mother hated him. Based on Mom's sparse but noxious input about her dad while I was growing up, my image of him was a cross between Ebenezer Scrooge and Darth Vader, a crotchety villain brooding from a dark mansion somewhere in Virginia. She mentioned once when I was little that he lived in Virginia, and for some reason that stuck in my mind. So, Virginia always held a menacing connotation for me, bolstered in later years when I learned about slavery and the Confederacy. Then my image of him evolved into a mix of Scrooge, Darth Vader, and Robert E. Lee, with Confederate stars and bars on his shiny black helmet.

I was in undergrad when Charlottesville happened, and it seemed to confirm the state's toxic status—in my mind, at least. When I saw video of those neo-Nazi tiki torch bearers, I scanned the crowd, half-expecting Darth Grandpa to be in the mix. Such was my dim view of this mysterious figure who, despite being my grandfather, had no bearing on my life whatsoever.

I never expected anything from or wanted to have anything to do with Bob. But he is a very wealthy man. And very wealthy men usually get what they want.

I'm Tom Brock, twenty-five years old, and a graduate student at San Francisco State University where I'm working on my MFA in playwriting. Actually, I technically finished my coursework on campus last fall, before COVID hit. Now all I have left is my thesis project, which is a full-length play. I started working on it in January. It's called *Latchkey*, and it's semi-autobiographical, about a kid growing up poor with his single mom. I got a decent rough draft of Act One done. Then COVID struck and the world went to hell. That was more than a little distracting, so it slowed my progress. At least that's my excuse. Truthfully, it was a convenient distraction because I was very much stuck on Act Two—like, the words "Act Two" were all I'd written.

I live in a way too nice three-bedroom villa on a quiet, tree-lined street roughly halfway between San Francisco State and Stanford. I never would've been able to afford a place like that on my own, but I lucked into being the third roommate to friends Skylar and Darren. They'd already been renting the house for a couple years as grad students at Stanford. About a year ago, their third roommate moved out and while they were hunting for a replacement, I happened to meet Darren at a performance of Eugene O'Neill's play *Long Day's Journey Into Night*. He had a friend in the cast. We made pretty easy conversation, I guess, and a few days later, Darren had me over to check out the house and meet Skylar. Skylar was cold and intimidating, which as it turns out is her regular operating mode. But somehow, I didn't annoy her sensibilities too much and soon found myself on the hook for $1,675 a month in my share of the rent.

I survived off the fumes of my massive student loans and a couple of nearly maxed-out credit cards. That way, I wouldn't have to get a job and could concentrate on getting through grad school faster. That was the strategy, anyway. But since I was no longer enrolled full-time, yet still had to finish my play to complete my degree, I felt my own doomsday clock rapidly counting down. The funds were running out and banks would be coming to collect on those loans sooner than later (I didn't know exactly when and was afraid to look it up). Four years of undergrad at private Reed College to get my degree in political science. Now, three more to get my MFA. Seven years of student loans totaled somewhere in the vicinity of deep shit. Or something like $250,000. I didn't know the precise figure because I was afraid to look that up too.

I had no immediate prospects for paying back $250,000. I started dreading all this back when I was at Reed, and it's what eventually drew me to democratic socialism. I mean, think about the absurdity of this situation: we live in the most filthily, opulently, obscenely rich nation in the history of the world.

And we say to our youth, *"You too can gain access to these obscene riches. All you must do to buy passage is earn this holy grail of a college degree."* Then we give them the easiest kind of free money to do it, they earn the holy grail degree, and we say, *"Now, time to pay up!"*

And the youth are like, *"Wait, how? Where's the living wage, much less one that will cover my loan payment?"* When you think about it, it's really like a twisted new form of slavery.

Well, I'm fervently anti-slavery. So, during my last year at Reed in 2016, when Bernie Sanders came along, he suddenly became my abolitionist hero. He knew what we were feeling, knew how bad it sucked, and he was mad as hell about it. I loved that. I loved his passion for sticking it to the billionaires, making them pay their fair share of taxes and all that. I loved his "healthcare is a human right" stance because, of course it is. Why *wouldn't* the richest society in history provide free healthcare for its people when it can easily afford it? And I absolutely loved his idea for free college and canceling student debt. So, I did a little local volunteer work for the Bernie campaign in 2016, you know, before the Democratic Clinton machine totally screwed him out of the nomination.

My 2016 experience helped me land a gig last year in Bernie's Bay Area campaign HQ. Still not a paying gig, but it got my foot in the door. If Bernie could swing the nomination this time, maybe I could graduate to a paid role. Then Bernie wins the White House, cancels my student debt, and we're off to the races. Okay, maybe that was a bit too much of a win-the-lottery strategy, but it was all I had.

Just before the pandemic came along and ruined everything, I was settling into a solid daily routine. Wake up around 8:30 a.m. Stretch and head out the door by 9 a.m. for a five-mile run. Shower. At my favorite coffee shop by 10:30 (it's my favorite mainly because it's within walking distance of my house and I don't have a car) where I worked on my thesis project play for a few hours. Then I'd get a ride from Darren or Uber it over to the Bernie campaign office by 2 p.m. Raid the snack room, answer phones, enter data, hand out bumper stickers, make copies, and fume with my coworkers over the latest campaign trail outrage until 6 p.m. Then call it a day.

That was life until the South Carolina primary. Then Michigan and Florida. And suddenly, just like that, Bernie was done—beaten by… *Joe Biden*? I mean, it was insanely demoralizing.

Wednesday, April 8, was the last day of the Bernie campaign. After hugging and tears at the office, people made plans to commiserate over beers at someone's house later that night (a bar wasn't an option due to the pandemic). Gathering in a big group was also technically a no-no, but people planned to do it anyway. I had just slung my bag over my shoulder and pushed in my desk chair for the last time when Nicole semi-startled me with, "You going to this thing?"

Nicole was the office vixen who wore bright lipstick colors and too-tight everything. Multiple times she caught me checking her out as she retrieved pages from the printer.

"I don't know," I stammered. Her eyes seemed to want me to say I was going, but then I was always bad at reading these situations. "But, I think probably, yeah."

"Okay, guess I'll see you there," she said with an arched eyebrow.

I watched her saunter away and my heart ascended to my throat. I'm still caught off guard most of the time when women express interest in me. Not that I'm unattractive. I'm 6'1" with long, wavy dark brown hair, dark brown eyes, a lanky strong build—you know, respectably toned without looking gym-rat ripped. I've had several reliable female friends over the years affirm my decent looks. Yet I'm still surprised when a girl I think is hot thinks I've got anything to offer.

The Uber ride took forever to get to a house in Cupertino, and the fare was way more than I cared to spend on something like this. It would only be worth it if things went somewhere with Nicole. The COVID situation made me nervous, of course, but it's amazing how libido trumps COVID so easily.

The party was like a rowdy wake—one part mourning the death of Bernie's campaign, and one part giant, booze-soaked tirade against Joe Biden, establishment Democrats, Donald Trump, Republicans, and Fox News (not necessarily in that order). The loudest, drunkest voice was a burly guy I barely knew named Austin, holding court at the kitchen's island. He had a scraggly red beard and wore a red bandanna to keep his wild hair out of his wilder eyes. He was jittery, sort of bouncing to the beat of the hip-hop blaring from the living room.

"We're doing it all wrong, man," declared Austin to the crowded kitchen. "There's no such thing as candy-ass revolution, know what I'm sayin'? You can't reason with *MAGA*. You can't reason with Biden or Pelosi or Schumer. You can't reason with *Trump* or McConnell. You think Castro achieved revolution with votes? Nah, man. It was boots and Glocks. That's what it's gonna take."

"Yeaahh!" The kitchen audience egged him on.

Were they serious? My socialism is a lot more Sweden than Stalin. Besides, weren't guns the other side's thing?

"Boots on necks and Glocks in faces. That's the only thing they'll pay attention to, man," yelled Austin, holding up a finger gun and taking aim. "That's the only way to make the change. You want real revolution?" He dropped the thumb hammer of his finger gun and recoiled as if firing it. His audience cheered lustily.

I stood just outside the fray and finally locked eyes with Nicole as she leaned against a counter in the kitchen. She smirked, then walked briskly toward me.

"I've had enough of this shit," she said leaning toward my right ear. "Wanna get out of here?"

I did, though it was considerably uncool to step out of the hazy, noisy house and have to admit to her that I had no vehicle. I pulled out my phone to order us a ride. She grinned condescendingly.

"Come on, Junior. I've got a car."

Nicole talked way too much. We finally started making out on her living room couch, but she kept pausing to rant about how Bernie was never the right vehicle for the revolution. She said he was useful for advancing the socialist ball, but it would take an army of younger, smarter, more charismatic candidates like Alexandria Ocasio-Cortez to truly achieve the revolution.

"Bernie's a cartoon. He's harsh and old," she explained. "A cartoon with his heart in the right place, but not the messenger to rally the whole working class."

She paused the making-out for long enough interludes that I'd think we were never going to advance bases. But then she'd dive right back in. Until another Marxist thought struck. She said something about "the list." I was just about to inquire about this list when she made it clear that she meant the list of anyone who opposed the revolution. An *enemies* list.

"You can't reason with asshole Republicans," she brooded.

I mumbled semi-agreement with her just to keep things going. Honestly, she kind of scared me a little. I haven't been with that many women, but Nicole appeared to be my first openly communist one.

The next time she came up for air, I tried a subtle shift in topic to try to head off another ten-minute diatribe: "So, are you going to work on the Biden campaign now?"

She sat straight up and gave me a long death stare.

"What?" I asked, innocently.

"Are you serious?" She stood and glared down at me. She did not appear to be playing. It was the first time I noticed she was wearing black, military-style boots. I hoped she wasn't also packing a Glock.

"Yeah, I mean, you said it's got to be a long-game revolution."

"Joe *Biden*? Get the hell out."

"But…"

"*Now*."

She pointed at the nearby door with her right arm emphatically extended.

"Okay." I tossed my hands up and exhaled incredulously as I got off the couch, stepped to the door, and let myself out. I heard her quickly lock it behind me. I guess "Joe Biden" was her trigger phrase.

Fortunately, my phone was still in my back pocket, so I was able to order a ride home. More money that I really couldn't spare flushed down the toilet. Total wasted evening.

The driver on the way home yapped about Governor Newsom's hypocrisy, COVID tyranny, COVID treatments, and all kinds of out-there crap. By the time I finally got home, my anxiety was boiling over. Fortunately, I had some weed left, so I smoked awhile on the back patio and tried to calm down.

The morning after the deflating Nicole experience, I sat staring at the blank page on my laptop. I just wasn't feeling it. And the more I didn't feel it, the more I got freaked out about never finishing the play.

Part of me was terrified of being officially done with grad school because what would I tell people that I do? I've been a student for over seven years, and it was such an easy social cover-all. Working on my MFA got me out of things a lot of times ("Oh, I *would* help out with that thing, but I've gotta get to class."). It sounded semi-impressive and purposeful. What would I do after this? My funds were depressingly low. One of my credit cards was pretty much maxed out. The other had maybe $1,800 left on the limit. I had just enough student loan money to cover two more months' rent. Worst case, I could probably move back to my mom's in Aberdeen, Washington. But I didn't really want to do that. My mom, Amber, is kind of a basket case and always has an awkward boyfriend around.

In avoiding my play, very different inspiration struck—a rant that I quickly turned into a blog post. The plight of my generation, the lie we've been sold known as the "American dream." The injustice. The racism. The climate fear. And now, the pandemic terror. A lament for the end of the Bernie campaign. How he was screwed by the billionaire establishment (again!). A treatise on the overdue necessity of democratic socialism in the US. How Bernie *must* be offered a cabinet position in the Biden administration, and how Biden must adopt *all* of Bernie's platform. (It's the least he could do since Bernie graciously stepped aside in the race.) How this is the *only* way forward for the new Democratic Party with my generation so obviously clamoring for change. Then I turned my sights on the evil dictatorship of Donald Trump.

I felt *alive*. I quickly published it to *Medium* and posted on all the socials. Then I made lunch and waited for all the likes, hearts, and shares to roll in. I felt certain I'd nailed the zeitgeist. This one was surely destined to go viral.

Two hours later, I had three likes and zero shares. Not exactly the game-changing stuff of legend I had in mind.

But unbeknownst to me, I apparently had one reader on the other side of the country who was about to drastically alter the course of my life.

TWO

It was a hot Wednesday afternoon in early May. Not that it mattered. I had nothing going, nothing to look forward to. Nowhere to go thanks to COVID. On most days I essentially hate myself, and that day the sudden hate wave was more crushing than usual. I daydreamed about killing myself. How bad could it be? I'd have a few friends who might sort of miss me for a while. But they'd get over it within a couple weeks or less. Probably less. I wouldn't really categorize myself as suicidal—I'd never actually attempted it or even come close. I'd say I'm suicide *curious*. I mean, who among my generation isn't at this point?

It was 4 p.m. and I laid on my back in the backyard. No sunglasses, my eyes closed, the sun absolutely searing my face. But I didn't care. Smoking a joint, trying to even out, trying a half-hearted end-run around the idea of killing myself. I had been lying there just a few minutes when I heard the back door open and someone step into the yard.

I opened one eye in time to see Darren toss one of those stiff cardboard mailers toward me, which landed softly in the grass within my reach.

Darren must've thought I was rather pathetic—aimlessly smoking a backyard joint in the middle of the week with nothing going, no prospects. It *was* pathetic. Darren had prospects. He was on track to finish grad school by the end of the summer. He was going to be an economics professor, which sounded astoundingly boring to me. But at least he had momentum. He was dating a woman who went to Stanford with him. I was alone, staring into the abyss.

I slowly sat up and read the name above the return address on the mailer: *Robert G. Brock.* It took a long moment for the name to register. When it did, I got mild goosebumps. He was the grandfather I'd never met.

I ripped open the mailer and pulled out a very official-looking letter on expensive-feeling paper. *From the Desk of Robert G. Brock* read the letterhead across the top. The letter was brief and to the point. I was invited to visit my grandfather's home in Virginia to discuss terms of a "potential inheritance." No inheritance amount was mentioned, but I read the line about twenty times because my mind was racing so hard.

I didn't know much about my grandfather, but I knew he was super rich. He had started a chain of convenience stores or something. But we had no relationship whatsoever, so it couldn't be much of an inheritance. But what if it was? Then I had the sinking feeling that it could just be an item, like a watch or an old boat or something. That's probably all it was. But why would I be invited to discuss "terms" if it was just an item? And what did it mean by "potential" inheritance?

I was invited to meet with him at 3 p.m. on Tuesday, May 26, which I found oddly formal and specific. That was two and a half weeks away. If interested, I was to call the phone number listed to arrange travel details.

I pulled out my phone and looked up Robert G. Brock. The G apparently stood for "George," and he apparently went by "Bob." He was the founder and CEO of Liberty's, a chain of restaurant/ convenience store/gas stations with locations in Virginia, Maryland, Pennsylvania, the Carolinas, and Georgia. Google claimed his estimated net worth was $200 million. And he was apparently a big Republican donor. Of course. Because there aren't enough of those already in the world. And of course, the universe would have me be related to one.

I went to my bedroom, closed the door, and dialed the phone number from the letter. A very professional-sounding woman answered. She introduced herself as Kathy Montgomery, Mr. Brock's administrative assistant. I thought it was a real rich-old-white-guy move to delegate a conversation with your grandson to an assistant. But part of me was glad he didn't answer the phone. What would I even say to a grandfather I'd never met?

I gave Kathy my email and she said I would receive a flight confirmation by the end of the week. Then she asked if I had any questions. I wanted to blurt out, "How much is the inheritance?" But I tried to play it cool instead. As a result, the great mystery of the inheritance tortured me for the next two and a half weeks.

As soon as I hung up with Kathy, I briefly considered calling Mom, but she would lose her mind at the prospect of me meeting Bob. And I couldn't mention any inheritance to Mom because she'd probably have an aneurysm. I was probably kidding myself to even hope that this would end up being anything.

My flight was a very early one from San Francisco to Norfolk, connecting in Chicago. After landing, I ordered my own ride and hoped I'd either be reimbursed for it by this mysterious grandfather of mine, or that he lived nearby and the ride wouldn't cost that much. Neither option panned out. It was at least a forty-five-minute drive.

My driver turned off a rural two-lane highway onto an expansive property of open pastures dotted with trees and surrounded by solid white fencing. We continued up a long, curving, paved drive past green fields in which I counted three horses. I expected the driveway to end at a Southern plantation–style mansion with Greek columns. Instead, the car stopped in front of a large, single-story, mid-century ranch house. It looked nice, but much more modest than the mansion I'd created in my mind as a kid. Beyond the house lay a sparkling inlet of Chesapeake Bay. It was an amazing property, and all I could think as I got out of the car was that I could have grown up visiting here. I had been deprived. This was practically criminal.

Just after I rang the doorbell, a smiling woman opened the door. "Hi, Tom?"

"Yes."

"Nice to meet you in person. I'm Kathy, Mr. Brock's executive assistant. We spoke on the phone."

"Yes, hi."

She extended her hand and I felt like my progressive COVID social mores were being tested, and likely undermined. I was wearing a mask; she was not. I reluctantly shook her hand.

Kathy looked middle-aged (though I'm really bad at guessing ages), with straight, shoulder-length brown hair, and very formal in a blouse, skirt, and heels. As she invited me inside, she said, "Mr. Brock will be with you in a few minutes. Before your meeting, he would like you to take this assessment."

She handed me a clipboard with a pencil and stapled set of papers beneath the metal clamp.

"Uh…okay," I said, somewhat amused, as I accepted the clipboard.

"You can have a seat here, if you'd like." She gestured toward a wooden bench that was set against the wall in a wide hallway that fanned out in both directions from the entryway. "When you're finished, just bring it to my office right down there," she said, gesturing down the hall to her right.

"Okay," I said, feeling more than a little confused. This was *nothing* like how I had ever imagined meeting my grandfather for the first time.

I sat on the bench and heard a man's voice, then laughter, from down the long hallway to my left. Was that my grandfather? My stomach sank a little and I felt a surge of anxiety. *What was I doing here?*

I took the pencil and glanced over the top page of the packet on the clipboard. There was no heading or any other information, just numbered questions. I flipped through the packet—five pages with ten questions per page, front *and* back—one hundred questions total. What the hell was this?

Question number one: *What is the supreme law of the land?*

Question two: *What does the Constitution do?*

I shook my head, then glanced down the hall in each direction. Was this a joke?

Question three: *The idea of self-government is in the first three words of the Constitution. What are these words?*

I sighed deeply. What was this, some kind of manipulative political litmus test? It was already super annoying. I scanned some of the other questions: *Who makes federal laws? How many justices are on the Supreme Court? Who wrote the Declaration of Independence?*

This was extremely stupid. But I closed my eyes and tried to refocus—if there was any money involved in this potential inheritance then sure, I could jump through the hoops and take Bob's dumb test. I took a deep breath and returned to question one.

An hour later, I finally finished, or at least scribbled some sort of answer for all one hundred questions. I walked the clipboard down the hall and held it up in the open doorway.

"All done?" Kathy asked.

"Finally," I replied, hoping she noted my irritated tone.

"Great, thank you," she said cheerily as she stepped out from behind what looked like a very tidy, organized desk and took the clipboard from me. "He'll be ready for you in just a few more minutes."

This had more inexplicable delays than a doctor's office visit. I returned to my wooden bench and scrolled social media on my phone. After another quarter hour or so, Kathy reappeared, carrying my test.

"Okay, Mr. Brock is ready for you. Right this way."

My stomach flipped again as I stood and started to pick up my duffle bag.

"You can just leave your bag there if you want."

I left my duffle by the bench and followed her down the hallway in the opposite direction from her office. She opened the door to reveal a large study, and sitting behind an ornate wooden desk was my grandfather, Robert G. Brock—Bob.

"Mr. Brock, this is Tom."

A half grin formed on the right side of Bob's lined face.

"This is my grandson, huh? Wow. You're taller than I thought you'd be."

He was older, paler, and frailer looking than the photos I'd seen of him in my cursory online search a couple weeks back. But I didn't say anything. My tongue was temporarily paralyzed.

"Tom, nice to finally meet you." Bob rose slowly from his fancy ergonomic chair and extended his hand across the desk. Another handshake—*really*? I shook his hand, forgetting to try to match the potential alpha maleness of his grip. Predictably, he totally did the alpha male grip thing, squeezing the life out of my comparably soft-clay hand.

"Thanks for making the trip," he said, sitting back in his chair. "Please, have a seat."

I sat in one of the two upright leather chairs facing his desk as Kathy handed him my test booklet. He immediately began skimming it.

I studied my grandfather for the first time. He was fair-skinned, mostly bald, with his remaining crown of solid gray hair shorn down to a buzz cut. He wore rimless glasses on his slightly hooked nose. His face sort of reminded me of a less-menacing Dick Cheney, which was not a helpful comparison for someone I was already inclined to dislike. His face was wrinkled and tired. I realized I had no idea how old he was. He wore a plaid collared shirt with the top button undone and a white crew-neck T-shirt underneath. I noticed a framed photo on his desk of he and (I assume) my grandmother. If I remembered correctly, she had been dead almost as long as I'd been alive.

Kathy left the study and closed the door behind her. Awkward silence descended like a sudden fog. I squirmed in my seat, glancing around at the built-in dark wood bookshelves filled with books and mementos. There was no computer on his desk, just papers, file folders, and a phone with lots of buttons, like the kind you see in corporate offices. Framed memorabilia, photos, and awards adorned every spare section of wall space that wasn't covered by bookshelves. There was a faded, presumably battle-torn American flag behind glass. A small sign on another shelf read, "*Hippies use back door.*"

"You can take off your mask," he said casually.

"Excuse me?"

"Your mask. You don't need it in here. I don't have any COVID symptoms."

"I'd prefer to just keep it on."

"Why? I'm not sick. I'm not worried about catching it from you. We're a few feet apart, so..."

"Yeah, I'm fine with wearing it."

"Just take off the darn mask, okay?" he said, chuckling, his voice the slightest bit edgy. "You don't have to do the political mask theater for me. I'd kinda like to actually see my grandson's face for the first time."

I shook my head, annoyed, before finally removing the mask. I did not like the principal's office vibe of this meeting so far.

"Thanks," he said. "Can I get you a Pepsi?"

His abrupt change in tone was jarring, but I *was* thirsty.

"Uh...sure."

He set my test booklet on his desk and rose from his chair with a grimace, as if it pained him to stand. He was a little shorter than me and had a slightly protruding gut, but overall seemed reasonably trim for an old man. He gingerly walked a few steps to his left to an old-fashioned Pepsi machine in the corner of the office by a large window.

"I always preferred Pepsi," he remarked.

"Me too, actually."

"Whaddya know? Some common ground," he said, glancing at me with a half grin.

I'd never seen anything like his Pepsi machine, an antique, surely fifty years old or more. He opened a slender vertical hatch revealing several circular slots, each holding a glass-bottled Pepsi. He pulled out two bottles, deftly pried off their metal caps on a hook on the side of the machine, and flipped the caps into a small wastebasket on the floor. He handed me one of the bottles.

"Thanks."

He slowly made his way back around the desk to his chair and as he sat, he asked, "So, you know why I had you take this test?"

"I do not."

"Any idea what this is?"

"No clue."

"I didn't think so. This is the US government's citizenship test."

"Okay," I said hesitantly as the principal's office vibe returned.

"You failed it."

"Hmm."

What can I say? It was a tough test.

"You scored a fifty-three. The government's official passing grade is just a sixty. Actually, it's kind of ridiculous—people who apply for citizenship don't even have to take this full test." He held up the test booklet for a bit of emphasis. "Government gives them all these questions ahead of time to study. But their actual citizenship test is just *ten* of these questions. Could be any ten out of the hundred, so they have to be prepared for all of them. It's an oral exam. And they just have to get six out of ten right to pass and become an American. Pretty easy. A little *too* easy if you ask me."

I didn't ask him.

"It appears that you don't know enough about your own nation to qualify as a citizen," he continued.

I shrugged. "I mean … I really doubt most people could pass it just getting ambushed like this."

"Unfortunately, you're probably right about that. You know, the Founders counted on an educated and engaged populace to make this self-government experiment work. And a religious populace too, as John Adams said. America only works if people know the basic mechanics. That's why it's falling apart now. You don't think that's a problem, citizens not having the slightest clue how their government works, how we got here, the basic American story?"

I casually shrugged again. "I'm not sure it really matters."

"Oh, it definitely matters. A *lot*. You were working on the presidential campaign for a bozo whose aim is to fundamentally change our form of government, but you can't pass the basic citizenship test? There seems to be a disconnect."

I silently wondered how he knew I'd worked on the Bernie campaign.

"If it was up to me, people would have to pass the citizenship test to be able to vote," he said as he adjusted his glasses. "Unfortunately, it's not up to me."

"How's that any different from all the other voter suppression crap that Republicans always try?"

"Requiring someone to show an ID is not suppressing the vote. You used to have to do more than that just to rent a video. That's why all this vote-by-mail stuff is total bull. It's ripe for rigging and fraud, just the way Democrats prefer their elections. Blaming it on COVID is mighty convenient. People can still go to the grocery store and touch all the same stuff, but they can't go to a voting booth in person? Come on."

"It's always Republicans trying to suppress the vote. Why would you want fewer people voting unless you think you're going to lose every time?"

"Why would you need to mail a ballot to everyone, including dead people, unless you think you're going to lose every time? Now, back to you flunking your citizenship test…"

I grinned and took a swig of my Pepsi.

"You find this humorous?" he asked, narrowing his eyes at me over the top of his glasses.

"I find it pretty irrelevant. And weirdly confrontational."

"Well, let me tell you why it's *very* relevant."

He picked up another sheet of paper from his desk.

"I recently read your blog post where you wrote, and I quote, *'The age of the unfettered capitalistic white patriarchy is over. And not a moment too soon. Their racist regime left in its cruel wake a debris field of poverty, injustice, and misery. America is long overdue for a new nation, one guided by the oppressed, the colored, the working class, the queer, those that embrace science.'* I can't go on—'bout to throw up in my mouth." He paused briefly and looked at me. "That's some grade A bullcrap right there. I especially like the part when you gripe about your generation's student loan debt and how you can't find jobs with a living wage. Like someone *forced* you to get a student loan."

I just set my jaw and looked at him, trying not to blink in the radiation of his cold stare.

"Two-hundred-thousand-dollar education and you can't pass the citizenship test," he said. "I'm just curious how you seem to think you're qualified to diagnose and prescribe for a nation you apparently don't even know?"

"I grew up in America, so I'm pretty sure that qualifies me to have something to say."

"Seems to be a trend with you millennial-Gen Z-ers—plenty to say, all the time, but don't even know enough about your own country to qualify as a citizen. One of the hilarious things about your generation is how you think you're the first humans to discover that life's tough. And the whining about it all—it's extra annoying 'cause you've got phones surgically attached to your hands so you can broadcast every up-and-down emotion twenty-four seven. Your phones are like talking mood rings."

What is this geezer's problem? I wondered as I blurted, "Dude, did you just invite me here to ream me out?"

He ignored my question.

"So, it's my understanding that you did not take a single course in US history post–high school. Is that right?"

"How do you know that?"

"According to your transcript, you graduated from a college that doesn't require one American history or civics class. That oughta be illegal in the United States. But that's par for the course with these Marxists running higher education. Indoctrinating kids to hate their own country. I'd say their master plan is working."

"How the hell did you get my transcript?"

He ignored my question again by perusing the sheet of paper in his right hand as he casually sipped the Pepsi in his left.

"I understand you have no car. Significant student loan debt. Is it true you smoke marijuana?"

"What? I mean, sometimes, yeah, for my anxiety. It happens to be legal where I live. But what are you reading? How do you know all this?"

"Private investigator."

"You *spied* on your own grandson?" I exploded. "Isn't that illegal or something?"

"No. I did not spy on you. A private investigator *investigated* you."

"Okay, that's…this is insane. Totally creepy. I mean, you can't do that. You can't just go digging through my trash. We have privacy laws. *Jesus!*"

"Uh, I'd appreciate it if you'd refrain from using the Lord's name in vain."

"What?"

"You just used 'Jesus' as a substitute cuss word."

"Yeah?" I shook my head. "Whatever, man."

"I'm serious."

"I believe you think you are."

He glanced at my apparent rap sheet again. "I don't remember seeing anything here about you being such a smartass."

I couldn't take it anymore.

"Look, I'm pissed, alright? How'd you feel if you were dragged across the country to meet a total-stranger long-lost relative who's apparently been spying on you, and immediately makes you feel like you've been indicted? This is some weird shit and I'm done."

I clanked my half-empty Pepsi bottle on his desk, stood, and took a firm step toward the door.

"Well, you've traveled all this way. Don't you want to at least hear about the twenty-five million dollars?"

I got a chill on the back of my neck that seemed to rush to my brain and almost made me shudder. I paused and glared at him. Was he serious? I couldn't tell.

"Come on back and hear my proposal."

I hesitated at the door. Did he really say *$25 million*? Defying what I thought were my better instincts, I trudged back to the chair and sat.

"So, what are your summer plans?" he resumed.

He didn't seem to have any questions I could answer without feeling completely inadequate.

"I'm not sure yet. I mean, I've got to finish my final grad school project. After that, I was thinking maybe take some time off."

He chuckled condescendingly. "So, what's your plan for this time off then?"

"I don't know. Clear my head. Figure out what I want to do. I, uh…"

"You don't want to be a playwriter?"

"Yes, I'd like to be a *playwright*, but you know, those jobs aren't exactly like working in IT."

"Have you started sending out résumés yet?"

I just shook my head, bracing for his next barb.

"I mean, you should've started that six months ago," he continued.

I wondered if this is what it felt like to have a dad. I was not a fan.

"You know, you don't exactly have any moral currency to be doling out advice to me *now*. Maybe, *maybe* if we had some sort of actual relationship. But we don't, so…"

"Okay, well…bottom line is, you don't have much in the works currently. So, my proposal might be good timing."

I sighed and narrowed my eyes at him.

"I am prepared to offer you a potential inheritance of twenty-five million dollars even." He paused to gauge my reaction.

I tried to keep a poker face, but I'm pretty sure my eyes betrayed my rapid pulse and racing mind.

"However…in order to earn this inheritance, you would need to complete a lengthy trip around the US to various sites that I've selected, and complete a few tasks along the way. As long as you complete the full itinerary, the money is yours."

We stared at each other for a moment. He wore a self-satisfied grin, then cocked his head to the side as I debated what to say.

Finally, I asked, "Like, where would I have to go? What do you mean by 'lengthy?'"

"You'll have to find out. That's part of it. If you agree to the deal, *then* you get the itinerary."

"But I don't really know what I'd be signing up for."

"You'd be signing up for twenty-five million dollars."

"But what's the catch? What is this really? I mean, you never wanted to have anything to do with me my whole life, so why are you doing this now?"

"That's not exactly true. I wanted to have a relationship with you and your mother. But *she* didn't."

"That's not how she sees it."

"Well, that doesn't surprise me." He took a deep breath, removed his glasses, and held them up toward the sunlight streaming in from the large window by the Pepsi machine. He squinted and examined them. Satisfied, he put his glasses back on and looked me in the eye. "Tom ... I'm a very wealthy man. But I'm also a relatively old man and I want to take care of some things before my time is up. That includes giving you your inheritance. I'm not so petty that I want to cut my closest male relative out of the will, even if you were essentially cut out of my life. You look like you've got a question."

"Well ... why the weird strings attached, then?"

He laughed and leaned back in his chair for a moment. Then he folded his arms and leaned forward, his elbows resting on the desk.

"I love this country to my core. What God has allowed me to achieve, building my company, it couldn't have happened any other place on the planet. But loving my country seems to be putting me more and more in the minority. 'Patriotism' has become a dirty word. Frankly, by the sound of that blog you wrote, you're lost, son. *Socialism?* Really? That is just ..." he paused, glancing momentarily at the ceiling fan. "Well, for starters, it's *idiotic*. And it's an insult to every American who has bled for this nation so you can have unprecedented opportunity. So, I'd be derelict in my duty as your grandfather if I didn't try an intervention."

"Wow." I shook my head at him, but I couldn't maintain eye contact with his smug stare. "So, that's what this really is? Some kind of Republican MAGA conversion therapy? No thanks. And by the way, I'd say you've already been pretty derelict in your duty as a grandfather."

I got up and left his office this time. I made it to the bench and grabbed my duffle bag. Who attaches strings like that to an inheritance? Did he really think he could turn me into some Red State cultist just by sending me on some patriotic propaganda tour? He clearly did *not* know me.

THREE

I hadn't even made it to the highway from Bob's house yet, and I was already doubting myself. What kind of dumbass walks away from $25 million? Then again, I could not participate in his effort to soothe his conscience. That's all this was—a last gasp effort to cover twenty-five years of guilt for driving away his daughter and having no relationship with his only grandchild. That's it; I made the right decision. This was just some sick rich man's game. And I refused to play.

I ordered a ride on my phone and sat on a shady patch of grass to wait. A few cars trickled past, but otherwise it was a quiet, peaceful spot. You could really hear yourself think, which meant I was flooded with even more doubt about my principled stance to walk away from $25 million. The money *would* serve *some* practical purposes, like solving my crippling fear of figuring out what to do next in life. I wouldn't have to stress over getting a job. I could wipe out my crushing student debt. I could buy Mom a brand-new car, any car she wanted. Hell, I could buy her a house. My whole life, she had only ever rented—mostly crappy apartments. Now she lived in a small house in a janky neighborhood in Aberdeen. I'd enjoy changing that.

I could write plays. I could even bankroll my own production. I started talking myself into this bizarre venture. How bad could

Bob's road trip be? Whatever it was, I could surely suck it up for a couple weeks to earn $25 million.

Just as impulsively as I'd stormed out of Bob's office, I suddenly canceled my ride and started the long walk back to Bob's house. Every step of the way I grew afraid that I'd already blown my chance at the fortune. Bob didn't strike me as a second chance guy. I'd never forgive myself if I screwed this up.

By the time I made it back to Bob's office, I'd been gone forty-five minutes. My stomach was in knots.

"Twenty-five million's pretty hard to walk away from, huh?" asked Bob.

"Yeah. Kind of," I replied with a hint of shame in my voice.

"So... are you saying you want to accept the terms of the deal?"

"I guess so."

"Now wait a minute, you don't say you 'guess so' when we're talking about this level of transaction. I'm gonna need something a little firmer."

"Then *yes*. I accept the terms of the deal."

Hearing myself say those words aloud made me loathe myself even more. This went against so much that I believed in. I essentially hated the rich—how could I even remotely consider *becoming* one of them? Inherited wealth is the worst kind, one of the disgusting foundations of the white patriarchy. The ability of whites to pass down generational wealth is what helps keep black people and other minorities in perpetual oppression. I knew all of this and now I was about to become part of the problem, just another cog in the white supremacist machine. How could I show my face around my friends ever again?

"But, one question, like, will you be covering my flights and hotels and stuff for this trip?"

"You won't need 'em. You've got a hotel room on wheels. I'm gonna let you borrow my RV."

"Huh?"

"Yeah. Did I not mention that part before?"

"You *do* know there's a pandemic going on right now? Not the best time to be roaming the country."

"Ah, you'll be fine. As long as you quadruple-mask, keep eighty yards' distance from folks. You'll survive. Besides, you'll literally be traveling in a protective bubble. This will be a lot safer than hotels. And just to be clear, to get the inheritance, you've got to finish *every* last detail of the itinerary, no matter how long it takes you."

"You're not going?"

"Nah. No, I'm too old and grumpy. Besides, this is *your* quest."

I smirked and crinkled my brow. "This is not usually how an inheritance works."

He smirked back. "Well, twenty-five million dollars is a heckuva lot of money. So, I'm gonna need to see a little effort."

I resented his tone but tried to calm myself by focusing on the end goal. My phone buzzed in my back pocket and I pulled it out to check.

"Oh, and one other thing," he continued, "your phone stays here."

"What?" I glanced up at him. He had to be joking. "No."

"Yes. It'll be locked in my safe for the duration of the trip."

"No, that's crazy."

"It's not crazy. And it's part of the deal."

"No, this is like, *harassment.* You can't just hold my stuff hostage. A phone is a lot more than just a phone now."

"Oh, really, Captain Millennial? Please, tell me more about this phone contraption. Can it send telegrams?"

"You don't really understand how that would actually turn my life upside down."

"Actually, I do. I'm probably saving your life. Social media's like brain crack to you people. And just like real crack, it kills. Kills your soul."

"People will think I'm dead."

"No they won't," he waved his hand dismissively.

I rolled my eyes. There was clearly little use trying to reason with this fossil. Not that I wouldn't still try. "But what about emergencies and stuff?"

"That's part of the fun. And challenge. You'll have to figure it out."

"If something happens to me, I'm going to sue you for even more money."

I was thirsty after my long, balmy walk, so I picked up my half-empty, now-lukewarm Pepsi from his desk and took a drink.

"I do actually have a life,"—that was an exaggeration, but he didn't need to know that—"so, how long is this going to take?"

"Oh, I figure it'll probably take you no more than a month."

I was in the middle of another drink when he said "a month," a notion that made me choke on the soda. I coughed, and rolled *$25 million* over and over in my mind like a mantra to try to calm down.

"Does your RV have GPS?" I wondered.

"Nope."

"Then how am I supposed to…do you have a US map?"

"Of course."

"Well, can I borrow it?"

"Nope."

I folded my arms and looked out the window at the bright green pasture. I loathed him wielding his rich man superpower against me. This is what they do best, manipulate with money. I also hated that it was so hard to resist. I craved the financial security he was offering. And I hated myself for craving it. I briefly considered trying to bargain with him, maybe taking less money in exchange for not having to complete his nefarious road trip. Then again, I really wanted the full amount. Damn, greed was making fast work of me.

"So, what's it going to be," he asked. "Are you all-in?"

"Okay." I took a deep breath before saying, "Yes."

He grinned, stood, and extended his hand across the desk. I reluctantly shook it, trying to give a firmer grip this time.

"So, do we need to put any of this in writing?" he asked.

"I don't know. I mean, I don't guess so."

"Don't be foolish. *Of course* you want it in writing! You *always* get it in writing!"

I'd barely met Bob and he already had a knack for making me feel totally dumb. He sat in his chair again and picked up a paper-clipped document from his desk.

"I had the contract drawn up, so read that carefully and see if you have any issues," he said as he handed me the document.

I pretended to read the contract very carefully. I *did* read every word, but my mind was a tornado of conflicting emotions and the unknowns of this mystery road trip. Not to mention the anxiety over the thought of trying to drive an RV. I'd never driven anything larger than a Toyota Camry, so this could be a huge problem. The contract seemed straightforward to my untrained eyes. I seriously resented the stipulation about leaving my phone but what choice did I really have? Rich dudes gonna rich dude, I guess.

Another stipulation required me to call Bob after each stop on the itinerary so we could debrief the experience. I glanced up from the contract and asked, "How am I supposed to call you after every stop without my phone?"

"Guess you'll have to figure it out."

I just shook my head in silent reply. After a decent five minutes of my contract concentration charade, I said everything seemed acceptable and we signed two copies of the document: one for me, and the other went back in a folder on his desk. Immediately after the signing, he picked up a small cardboard box from the floor behind his desk, stood, and handed the box to me.

"Here's your itinerary," he said.

The box's top flaps were open, revealing several VHS tapes and a manila folder. I peeked inside the folder, which contained multiple printed pages.

"Oookay," I said, slowly and skeptically.

I rummaged through the tapes in the box and could see each one was labeled with a handwritten number.

"Start with Tape One," he explained. "Gotta go in order."

"What is this?"

"They're recordings of me explaining where you need to go for each stop along the way. Background, history, important things I want you to know. You have to watch each part all the way through. No fast-forwarding."

"And how exactly am I supposed to watch these?"

"There's a VCR in the RV. Should still work."

"If not?"

He just shrugged with a faux bewildered look on his face.

"I'll just have to figure it out," I sarcastically answered for him.

"You're catching on."

"You know, we have amazing new advancements in video technology," I said, glancing inside the box.

"Well, I don't have time or desire to keep up with all that stuff. When I buy something like a video camera, I take really good care of it, and it lasts me a long time. My VCR camera still works. It's the only thing I had on hand, so I used what I had. It's called being resourceful—one of the many things I hope you glean on your journey."

I counted five tapes in the box. "Geez, how long have you been working on this?"

"I don't know. A while. So, you ready to check out the RV?"

"What, *now*?"

"Yeah, let's go." He was already halfway to the office door. "Daylight's burning."

I followed Bob through his spacious living room, past worn leather furniture and a large stone fireplace, out some French doors, and onto a flagstone patio. As soon as we stepped outside, two large German shepherds bounded toward us. One of them immediately lunged at me, pawing my legs. I froze and put up my hands as if in a holdup. I'm *not* a dog person.

"Limbaugh! Get down!" said Bob to the dog trying to get acquainted with me. Fortunately, Limbaugh did as he was told, but the other dog promptly replaced him, nudging its nose where I'd rather it didn't.

"Rush, quit that!" commanded Bob. He gave Rush and Limbaugh vigorous face and head rubs, and afterward they trotted beside us at a more respectful distance.

"So, how is your mother?"

The question caught me off guard, just like most of his questions that afternoon. "Uh...yeah, she's fine, I guess."

"Does she know you're here?"

"No. Not yet."

"Takes a lotta hate to keep a grandson away from a grandfather for twenty-five years."

I couldn't tell exactly whose hate he was referring to. His? Or was he blaming Mom? I had only ever heard Mom's side of things of course and had no reason to doubt her version as definitive.

"You could've reached out," I challenged.

"Well...your mother, she made up her mind a long time ago. She's at least as stubborn as me. Did she ever mention me when you were growing up?"

"Maybe a couple times."

I didn't really want to get into this. It was *their* war. I was just a civilian casualty.

"Well, what'd she say?"

"I remember her saying you're an asshole."

"Figures," he said with a disappointed sort of grin.

The wide, paved driveway from the front of the house continued around to the back where it ended at a huge, detached garage/workshop with three separate retractable doors. Bob pressed a keychain remote, and the right-hand garage door began clanking upward. Daylight slowly revealed the RV and...it was a total letdown. Not exactly what you would expect from a multimillionaire. Between the VHS tapes and this monstrosity, I sensed a trend with Bob—this was not a guy who splashed much cash on toy upgrades, like, *ever*.

"There she is," he declared triumphantly once the tall garage door opened all the way, allowing a full view of the dingy silver RV in all its non-glory. "1979 Airstream Excella. What do you think?" he asked enthusiastically.

"Uh...I think I should've asked to inspect this before I signed the damn contract is what I think."

"True. No backing out now." He grinned. He walked toward the narrow door on the passenger side of the RV. "I'll pull it out."

He stepped inside the RV and slid into the captain's chair behind the wheel. The giant tin can started without too much fuss and he eased it out of the garage until the RV's bumper was clear of the door. Then he turned off the engine, stepped back onto the pavement, and tossed me the keys. Naturally, I fumbled his toss and had to pick them up out from under Limbaugh's inquiring wet nose.

I walked cautiously around the Airstream, feeling overwhelmed. It looked complicated. Just above the bumper on the right, "Corps of Discovery" was written in neat script with yellow paint, which was now badly chipped. I continued my amateur inspection of the exterior which had a blue stripe around its entire midriff. Finally, I pulled the latch on the door located around the middle of the passenger side of the bread-loaf-shaped contraption. I stepped inside and was greeted by the scent of musty fabric mixed with traces of corn chips and spearmint chewing gum. It was like stepping into a 1970s time capsule. What had I gotten myself into?

Between the driver and front passenger chairs was a console with a small TV/VCR combo sitting on top. Behind the driver's seat was a small couch that folded out into a flat bed. Directly behind the front passenger's chair was a "dining" area, with two facing swivel chairs and a tabletop that could be folded up and stowed. Immediately beyond the couch on the driver's side began the galley with short counter, cooking range, sink, and mounted microwave. Just to the right of the RV's door was the miniature refrigerator. Continuing back past the fridge was the main "bedroom," I guess, which consisted of another, larger couch that also folded into a flat surface for a "bed." Finally, just beyond the couch/bed was the bathroom, complete with a tiny sink on the right, miniscule toilet in the middle, and somehow, a slim shower stall on the left.

Bob stuck his head through the open door and asked, "Everything look good?"

"How would I know? I don't know how any of this twentieth-century stuff works."

"The manual's in the front console. I checked."

That wasn't reassuring.

"I probably still have some tapes in here if you wanna borrow," he offered. "Got some Tom Clancy somewhere."

Who the hell was Tom Clancy? Probably some redneck country artist. *No thanks.* I stepped out of the hot, stuffy space back onto the driveway.

"Okay, so, ready to take off?"

I honestly thought he was joking. He was not.

"What, right *now*? I mean, what about…I don't even have clothes and stuff."

"Maybe just buy some on the way. You're gonna be able to afford it, you know, assuming you complete everything."

This was all happening way too fast for me to process. Is this how he did business? At light speed? Is this what made him a *good* businessman? Whatever it was, I didn't like it. I wiped the sweat off my forehead and dried my hand on my jeans. I looked over the entire length of the RV and sighed. Maybe it *was* best to get going right away, so I could get this whole thing over with.

"Okay. Well. I guess I'll just, uh, look through the manual first," I said.

"I'll leave you to it then."

Bob left me with the RV and returned to the house with Rush and Limbaugh on his heels. I climbed back into the RV and located the manual in the central console. Then I started the engine and mentally crossed my fingers that the air-conditioning was still functional as I flipped the switch. It was…not as forceful an airflow as I'd prefer, but enough to stave off heatstroke. There was also a small fan mounted behind the driver's seat that still worked.

After about half an hour with the manual, I summoned enough courage to attempt departure. It all felt rather dreamlike, in a bad way, as I reentered Bob's house and returned to his office to get the "itinerary" VHS tapes and my duffle bag. I also required several minutes with my phone—first, to text Darren and Skylar that I'd be gone for a few weeks on a trip. I told them I was "reconnecting" with my grandfather. They didn't know the history there, so I didn't bother explaining further. I tapped out some quick social media posts indicating I'd be offline for a few weeks. Then I thought of Mom. I started a text to her, then deleted it. Too hard to explain in a text. And I almost called, but then I didn't want to hear her rant about what a horrible idea this was. I didn't want to catch her in a mood. So, I put off calling her. I'd wait until I'd been on the road a couple days.

As I powered off my phone and handed it over to Bob, I felt sure I was forgetting to do something. I also felt utterly exposed without it.

Bob walked me back out to the RV. I loaded in my bag and set the box of VHS tapes in front of the console between the front chairs.

"Well, good luck," he said from the RV's doorway.

"Thanks."

"I meant to ask you this earlier. How would you sum up the American experience in one word?"

Once again, this guy's questions confounded me. I scratched my head and glanced down for a moment, thinking. Finally, I looked at him and said, "Oppression."

His jaw clenched and he made a scoffing sound. He hung his head, then twisted his neck to the right and scrunched up his face in a hard wince. "I was afraid you'd say something like that. Well…safe travels."

FOUR

I pulled VHS tape number one from the box and pressed the power switch on the dusty, ancient TV/VCR combo machine. Somehow, it seemed to work, and a blue screen appeared. Inserting the tape triggered a mechanical memory—I hadn't used a VCR since I was a kid.

After several seconds of flickering, flashes of random recorded TV programming, and lots of static lines, Bob appeared in decidedly low definition. He was apparently sitting on one of the leather couches in his living room.

"I'm gonna go out on a limb and reckon you don't truly know what it means to be a political conservative," he began. "Especially after being fed a lifetime of anti-conservative propaganda. So, here's what I believe. Being conservative is being in favor of limited government. Believing in individual freedom. Believing in and upholding the law, our Constitution, the greatest freedom document in the history of mankind."

I rolled my eyes and made so many exasperated sounds in just the first thirty seconds of his video that I decided I would have to seriously chill if I was to survive this polemic.

"I believe in states' rights. California has no business telling, you know, Florida how to conduct their affairs. I believe in property rights. Free enterprise. Low taxes. Minimal government regulation of business. I believe in *all* of the Bill of Rights. Strong national security. I believe in school choice. Total energy independence. Sensible environmental protections. I believe that patriotism and love of America is appropriate and should be encouraged. I believe there's value in our Judeo-Christian heritage. And I believe in being colorblind. Affirmative action oughta be abolished. Equality of opportunity? Absolutely. We should strive for that. But a special leg up based on something that happened to your ancestors three hundred years ago? That's ludicrous *and* unfair. Equality under the law, like the Constitution provides. Not this new equity crap. Equity is this new code word that *sounds* like equality, but it's not. It's just a new quota system based on race and sexuality. It's glorified discrimination."

"Oh, geez. Racist much, Bob?" I yelled at the screen.

"When President Reagan was about to leave office—this was 1989—he gave a final TV address from the Oval Office. And he talked about what we need is to develop 'informed patriotism.' He said we have to teach history based on what's important instead of what's in fashion. It's probably safe to assume you've received plenty of the fashionable history. Reagan's warning was about losing our American memory, which will erode the American spirit. Well, he got that one *exactly* right. So, that's my wish for you on this trip—informed patriotism. Or at least that you'll get the informed part, and then you can decide for yourself on the patriotism."

My mind was pretty made up on that one. Even the word *patriot* made my skin crawl.

Bob finally got around to assigning my first destination: Washington, DC. I stopped the tape and turned off the TV. I could listen to the rest later. I had a ton of logistics to figure out first.

I buckled myself in behind the wheel and eased the RV into drive. Fortunately, I didn't have to back up at all or else I would've taken out Bob's garage for sure. It was what I imagined driving a tank must be like. I started to sweat just pulling it through the driveway, around the side of Bob's house and on past the white-fenced fields to the nearest highway. When I finally reached the highway, I had no idea which way to turn and no voice-of-Siri to guide me. I decided to turn right because it seemed easier, and just hope for the best. I would drive until I hit civilization, then try to figure out how to get to DC.

Turning onto the two-lane highway was hairy. I got up to thirty miles an hour and it seemed reckless. I was either skirting the edge of falling off the road on the right, or veering into the other lane on my left. The road felt way too small. Every time an oncoming car approached, I winced, expecting death by head-on collision.

As I swerved my way down the road, it occurred to me that I'd been set up to fail in this fishing boat of an RV—that way Bob wouldn't have to pay me $25 million. He could say, "*I wanted to give him the inheritance, but the pansy millennial socialist just couldn't hack it in the real world. Couldn't even drive a forty-year-old RV!*" Then he'd guffaw with his Republican shooting-club buddies and raise a Scotch glass to capitalism. He was obviously a cold-blooded madman.

It took the better part of an hour, but I finally nosed my way to civilization—my first accomplishment of this peculiar quest. My second accomplishment was finding a gas station. The fill-up cost made my eyes water: sixty-two gallons for $116. Plus, I had to buy a US atlas inside the convenience store. Making June rent was going to be a huge problem.

Getting the RV up to sixty miles an hour on Interstate 64 felt like I imagined it would feel getting a World War II bomber off an aircraft carrier: terrifying.

I followed signs for Williamsburg, hoping there would be a store, somewhere I could buy some clothes and stock up for the trip. Miraculously, I found a Target just off the interstate on the right, which meant I could glide into its parking lot without the death-defying stunt of a left turn.

I bought two pairs of shorts, two pairs of jeans, a pack of socks, a pack of boxers, and five gray V-neck T-shirts. Between the change of clothes in my duffle and the new stuff, I hoped to get by with doing laundry once a week on the road. I bought food—lots of cereal, ramen, frozen burritos, and plenty of Yoohoo (it's one of my vices). I also sprang for a burner phone. Bob's contract only specified no smartphone, so technically I was in the clear. Besides, the phone was the cheapest, bare-minimum thing I could find, which meant it could only make calls.

In the parking lot as I loaded my stuff into the RV, an old man sized up the silver breadbox Airstream Excella as he put away his shopping cart.

"Nice RV there," he said. "Old school."

His declaration startled me, but I mumbled, "Thanks." He said something else that I didn't catch, but I asked him if he knew anything about an RV park nearby. He did, because he happened to be staying at one. His name was Hugh Evans, and he eagerly gave me directions. Then he overshared about every aspect of the park, its amenities, and the greater Williamsburg area.

Fortunately, my first RV park experience was only about fifteen minutes away and they had an open slot. I paid the seventy-five-dollar overnight fee for the RV pad and hookup. I'd been on the road less than three hours, and I was already hemorrhaging money.

I managed to park the RV on the pad, relatively straight, and without plowing through the adjacent picnic table. Hugh Evans showed up later and helped me with the hookups, which was cool. But then he rambled on and on for another half hour about how COVID came from a Wuhan lab.

Eventually, I shirked Hugh and collapsed on the couch bed in the "bedroom" in the back of the cabin. I used some rolled-up clothes for a makeshift pillow because I forgot to buy one at Target. No sheets or blanket either. Epic fail.

I slept surprisingly hard and woke up with harsh sunlight seeping in around the edges of the RV curtains. I had a horrible crick in my neck from my terrible clothing-pillow.

I dug out Bob's ancient 1980s (or maybe '70s?) coffee maker from one of the galley drawers and plugged it in. Making drip coffee was one of the few skills I'd learned early in life from Mom. She had often required me to pull coffee duty on hangover mornings. I thought I'd set up everything correctly but when I pressed start, the old machine hissed, sputtered, and managed to squirt coffee essentially everywhere but in the pot. I scrambled to contain the damage but ended up unplugging it and dashing the whole thing into the sink. Then I had to waste a third of my only paper towel roll sopping up the mess on the counter and floor.

After that poor start, I sat down with a large bowl of Life cereal to watch Bob wax poetic about George Washington on the video.

"Most Americans don't fully appreciate how fortunate this nation was to have him as our first president," said Bob. "It was a divine appointment too. That doesn't mean he was a saint—none of our leaders are saints, with the possible exception of Calvin Coolidge."

Bob laughed lightly at himself after the Coolidge reference. I didn't get it.

"What I like about Washington is that he was a farmer and solider first. He wasn't a glory hound. He didn't like the spotlight. He was humble and a very private man, always private with his emotions. But he cried at the official farewell to his military officers. He was a hard worker, intelligent. Loads of perseverance and self-control. He was loyal and bound to his duty, even though he didn't really want to be in charge of the Continental Army."

I poured another round of Life as Bob continued his Washington brag session.

"Probably nothing reveals Washington's character more than setting the precedent of serving only two terms as president. He could've easily served the rest of his life if he wanted. By the same token, maybe nothing reveals the *rotten* character of Franklin D. Roosevelt more than the fact that he scorned precedent and got elected *four times*. He would've kept going too if the grim reaper hadn't stepped in."

Note to self—Bob apparently hates FDR.

I didn't know most of the stuff Bob rattled off about George Washington, but I knew the one thing about him that canceled out all that other stuff: he owned slaves. It was like Bob was reading my mind because next he said, "Now, every progressive and Marxist college professor, and smart-aleck college kid, loves to fixate on George Washington being a slave owner."

"Uh, how could you *not*, Bob?" I sputtered at the screen with a mouthful of cereal.

"And look, of course it's terrible that he owned slaves. But within the context of his time and culture, it's notable that he *did* evolve on the issue and seems to have come to regret slavery. For one thing, as president he signed a bill banning slavery in the new territories opened up during his administration."

"White mansplaining. Not a good look, Bob!" I exclaimed at the screen again.

"And in his will, he freed his own slaves. He was the only slave-owning Founding Father to do that. I know, that doesn't appease the cancel culture mob who are hell-bent on prosecuting the past. But it *was* a step in the right direction. Washington wrote, '*I can only say that there is not a man living who wishes more sincerely than I do to see a plan adopted for the abolition of slavery.*'"

As if Bob's Washington defense wasn't annoying enough, he explained that at each stop I had to read—out loud—relevant quotes that he'd selected for me. Even worse, he said I had to have a witness listen to me read the selections aloud, and then sign and date the page. I dreaded that requirement. I picked up the manila folder of readings for the entire road trip and flipped through them. I groaned because there was a ton.

FIVE

When some of the iconic DC landmarks first came into view as I drove up the George Washington Memorial Parkway, I couldn't fully indulge my visual curiosity as I labored to keep the yacht of an RV in the lane. Driving the behemoth would take a lot of getting used to.

I lucked into a parking space that was probably designated for buses since there were three of them occupying the spaces to the left of mine. But the lot was clearly marked "Public," and I didn't see any signs prohibiting RVs, so I just parked and hoped for the best.

I had a whole list of monuments Bob required me to visit, so I started with the one closest to where I parked: the Martin Luther King, Jr. Memorial. I followed a long wall engraved with MLK quotes to a block of grayish stone, which Bob said on the video symbolizes the "mountain of despair" from a line in MLK's "I Have a Dream" speech. Sliced neatly out of the center of this "mountain" and shifted forward on the plaza is the "stone of hope." I walked around to the front of this stone and looked up at the heroic visage of MLK protruding from the rock, wearing suit and tie, arms crossed, and holding a rolled-up speech in his left hand. It's a powerful monument in its own way, and I felt sacrilegious for thinking this, but the statue looked to me like a Marvel Comics rendering of the civil rights icon. And that bothered me a little.

I positioned myself right up against the stone on MLK's left-hand side and gazed out across the Tidal Basin. Bob said the MLK statue's gaze was purposefully aimed *away* from the Thomas Jefferson Memorial on the opposite end of the Tidal Basin. He said MLK is looking away because Jefferson was a slave owner. That seemed entirely appropriate to me, but Bob wasn't having it. On the video, he said both men were deeply flawed, that they both had adulterous affairs. Bob insisted the statues should be looking squarely at each other, symbolizing grace over America.

I wandered back to the wall of quotes behind the statue and began reading. As I stepped toward the fourth panel, I saw her for the first time and froze in my tracks. She was a radiant woman, maybe close to my age. She removed her mask and took a long drink from a disposable water bottle. Fair skin, her cheeks strawberry-flushed, her dark brown hair in a ponytail. She wore a light gray T-shirt, blue athletic shorts, ASICS running sneakers, and a backpack. She seemed absorbed in the quote. She smiled to herself, a simply beautiful smile, and slowly shook her head (presumably at the quotes). I caught myself staring at her. As stupid as it sounds, I was in love, very suddenly and inexplicably. I longed to know everything about her.

I slowly closed the short distance between us and paused a few feet from her. She glanced to her left at me and smiled politely. And then this paragon actually spoke to me.

"So beautiful, isn't it? Powerful."

She had an accent, possibly British.

"Yeah" was all I could muster. And it was a lie because I was so enchanted by her that I hadn't even read the quote in front of us yet:

> *"The ultimate measure of a man is not where he stands in moments of comfort and convenience, but where he stands at times of challenge and controversy."*

She put her mask back on, took out her phone, and snapped a shot of the quote. Then she turned and walked toward the statue. I played it cool, lingering at the quote panel for a second before totally following her back to the statue.

I stood relatively near her, definitely not social-distanced, and I hoped I was in her peripheral vision. We both stared up at the statue—she in genuine admiration, me cutting my eyes toward her every half-second. She briefly glanced my way.

"It's really wonderful. Such an appropriate celebration of his legacy," she said.

"Yeah. Yeah," I muttered. *Why couldn't I think of any actual words?*

"I love how they decided to render him."

"Me too," I lied, for the second time in less than three minutes.

She stared at MLK for another long moment as my mind floundered for something clever to say. In an instant, she would move on. It was now or never. But what could I say? And then I blurted, "Notice his gaze, how he's looking across the water?"

She looked over her shoulder at the water and then back to the statue. "Yeah?"

"He's purposefully looking *away* from Thomas Jefferson, you know, since Jefferson owned slaves."

"Ohhhh. Really? I didn't know that. About the way he's looking, I mean."

"Yeah, pretty interesting." I'd never tried this hard before. I suddenly felt like a middle-school dork—clueless and desperate for her attention.

45

"Fascinating. Well, thanks for the insight."

"Oh, sure. Sure." Why was I saying words twice? Because I'm an *idiot*.

As my mush brain grasped for some other way to spur conversation, she gracefully turned on her heel and walked away. I know it sounds rather creepy and stalkerish of me, but I followed her. I reasoned the setting made it quasi-okay—after all, we were both tourists in a monument park, and therefore, it wouldn't be unheard of for us to happen to show up at the same monuments. At least that's what I told myself. Like I said, I'm an idiot.

She ambled along the rim of the Tidal Basin for a few minutes until reaching the Franklin D. Roosevelt Memorial, which was a short detour off the main path. I followed her into the Memorial enclave, keeping a very respectful, non-leering distance. I noticed that she read every quote and gave every section of the memorial its due.

On the video, Bob had told me to skip the FDR memorial because "it's absolutely ridiculous that the most elaborate presidential memorial in Washington is dedicated to the closest thing we've ever had to a dictator."

Bob's take made it my favorite monument. To me, FDR was a badass—no president has ever used government to help more people.

I continued apace, well behind the woman as we continued the long walk around the Tidal Basin toward (I assumed) the Jefferson Memorial. On the way, I finally hit upon a genius way to engage her—I would ask her to be my reading witness. It was perfect. I knew I had something Jefferson-related to read aloud, so if she indeed stopped there, I'd go out on a limb and ask her.

My heart skipped multiple beats when the woman ascended the stairs ahead of me that led into the Jefferson rotunda. I followed her up the steps and joined the onlookers gazing up at a towering Jefferson. The woman was already taking in the quotes chiseled into the walls. I followed suit, keeping an eye on her, and looking for an opportunity to talk to her again.

When she began a slow, up-close inspection of the Jefferson statue, I decided to make my move. I pulled the folded-up pages from the back pocket of my jeans. I approached and stood near her, trying to appear interested in the statue like she was. Our eyes met for the briefest second and I thought I detected her smile through her mask. I glanced at the top page in my left hand. It was the Declaration of Independence, or at least most of it. My pulse raced.

Finally, I forced out, "Excuse me, uh, hi." Not a smooth start.

She looked at me with warm, friendly, dark brown eyes.

"It's me again," I said, with a nervous, stupid giggle. "Sorry to bother you. I was wondering if you could help me out with something real quick. Uhhh…this sounds dumb, but I was wondering if you could listen to me read this out loud. It's this dumb assignment I have to do for…well, it's a long story," I stammered. "But basically, I have to have a witness listen to me read various historical stuff aloud and sign and date the page."

"Umm…sure. What exactly are we reading?" she asked with an accent straight out of any number of my mom's period Brit TV shows.

"Oh, uh…" I glanced at my papers again because apparently the powerful allure of this person rendered me incompetent. I would seriously have to pull it together if I was going to impress her. That didn't seem likely. "It's the Declaration of Independence."

"Oh, I love the Declaration of Independence. And I'm *British*."

She giggled, and it was pretty great.

"So this won't be awkward at all then," I joked. Yes—maybe I could pull this off after all.

"No, no," she laughed.

I glanced around at the smattering of visitors.

"Uh, let's see, maybe let's go out here?" I didn't want my performance echoing through the mostly quiet rotunda.

"Sure," she replied gamely.

We walked past the giant columns and down the steps to an open space with a terrific view of the Washington Monument across the gently rippling Tidal Basin.

"Okay," I said.

"Ready?" she asked.

"Sure, yeah, this is a totally normal thing to do on a Wednesday afternoon."

She giggled again, and I was all about it.

"'*The unanimous Declaration of the thirteen United States of America*,'" I began. As I read, I found myself wanting to do a good rendition since she'd said she loves the Declaration.

"'*We hold these truths to be self-evident*,'" I continued, "'*that all men are created equal, that they are endowed by their Creator with certain unalienable Rights, that among these are Life, Liberty, and the pursuit of Happiness. That to secure these rights, Governments are instituted among Men, deriving their just powers from the consent of the governed*.'"

I went on for a couple minutes. Honestly, it wasn't a bad performance for having never read this much of it before. Actually, I would later learn that these were just excerpts—Bob didn't require me to read the long list of grievances against King George.

"'*And for the support of this Declaration*,'" I concluded, "'*with a firm reliance on the protection of Divine Providence, we mutually pledge to each other our Lives, our Fortunes, and our sacred Honor*.'"

The woman generously clapped for my performance and even said, "Bravo!" before adding, "Imagine what might have been if our countries hadn't divorced."

"Right?" I replied. "The ultimate broken home."

I pulled a pen from my pocket and offered it to her with the page.

"Where do I sign?" she asked.

"Oh, just anywhere. And the date too if you don't mind."

She paused momentarily with no hard surface to write on.

"Sorry, guess I need a clipboard or something," I said.

She problem solved by pressing the sheet of paper against the back of her smartphone.

"I'm Tom by the way."

"I'm Amelia. Nice to meet you, Tom."

"Nice to meet *you*. Thanks so much for doing this."

She finished signing her name and handed me the paper and pen. I glanced at her neat signature, which read: *Amelia Curtis*.

"Sure, no problem. So, what kind of assignment has you reading historical documents out loud to total strangers?"

I froze for a second, before deciding truth was the best option. "Well...basically, my long-lost grandfather offered to give me an inheritance *if* I go on this cross-country road trip to a bunch of historical sites. He's like this very conservative Republican, and I'm very much *not* that. So, to earn my inheritance, he's making me do this big tour to learn to appreciate America or something, I guess."

"Hmm, okay. That is *not* remotely close to the kind of answer I was expecting. I didn't think an inheritance was something you earned."

"Yeah, that's what *I* thought too. But, uh, this is kind of a complicated situation."

"I see. So, you've got some more readings to do today then?" She gestured toward the pages in my hand.

"Yeah, I'm supposed to hit the World War II Memorial and Lincoln."

"Ah, well, I'm going that way next. Would you like me to listen to your other readings?"

And that was how I met Amelia. The natural ease of our conversation astonished me on the long walk around the Tidal Basin toward the World War II Memorial. There was an unusual comfort to it, like we were already friends. I learned this was her first time visiting America, apparently a lifelong dream of hers. She moved to the States in January to start graduate school at Wheaton College (I'd never heard of it) in Illinois. She's earning some kind of Christian ministry degree, which I thought was an unexpected choice for a modern young British woman. She'd barely got settled when the pandemic hit and wrecked her semester with online classes and all that. Just a few weeks ago, she bought what she deemed a "very old" used car and was road-tripping to some historic sites on the East Coast. She said that "God willing," she'll continue studying at Wheaton in the fall. Then she casually mentioned that she's basically a missionary to the US. I looked at her, confused. My mask concealed the smirk on my face. I couldn't tell if she was serious—a *missionary*?

"What, you're here to convert America or something?"

"Well, God does the conversion part, but yes."

I found her sincerity intriguing and also slightly questioned her sanity.

"I believe in America," she said. "I *love* America. I believe in its unique capacity to spread the gospel all over the world. But...it's somewhat floundering at the moment, and it needs Christ."

"And you're the one who's gonna bring him to us?"

"Well, I want to do my part. I want to be part of a new Jesus People movement. It's the only thing that will save America from itself. Many people seem to have written off the whole Western world, but I'm not ready to give up on it yet."

I didn't know how to respond, so I settled on, "I guess I didn't know being a missionary was still a thing."

"It most certainly is."

"Isn't it kinda colonial, you know, imperialist? Trying to convert people to your religion never seems to end well."

"Well, my grandfather taught me to be wary of saying 'never.' And I respectfully disagree with you. You'll find that true converts to Christianity do so willingly, joyfully, because they're led by the Holy Spirit, and they experience a remarkably changed life. They're receiving a wonderful gift. But certainly, there has been far too much damage done down the centuries in the name of Christ. And *that* is disgusting."

Fortunately, we reached the oval-shaped World War II Memorial Plaza before she could start trying to convert *me*. I picked a spot on the Pacific theater end of the plaza, on the edge of the central fountain, to read Bob's chosen excerpts from, as I relayed to Amelia, a General Eisenhower address to Congress on June 18, 1945. I began reading:

"*I have seen the American proved on battlegrounds of Africa and Europe over which Armies have been fighting for more than two thousand years of recorded history. None of those battlefields has seen a more worthy soldier than the trained American.*'"

I glanced up from the page at Amelia who raised her eyebrows and nodded, urging me on.

"*Willingly, he has suffered hardships: without a whimper he has made heavy sacrifices, he has endured much, but he has never faltered.*'"

Since Amelia was an eager and engaged audience, I resisted the urge to roll my eyes at the patriotic hyperbole. Her seeming lack of cynicism helped me get through the obvious propaganda.

"'You have read many reports of his individual exploits, but not one tenth of them ever has been or ever will be told. Any one of them is sufficient to fill a true American with emotion—with an intense pride in his countrymen.'"

I read on and Amelia's eyes seemed to be smiling by the time I reached the final line.

"'Though we dream of return to our loved ones, we are ready, as we have always been, to do our duty to our country, no matter what it may be.'"

Again, Amelia applauded generously, inviting gawks from a few bystanders.

"Beautiful, Tom," she encouraged, as if I'd come up with the words myself.

We slowly meandered through the plaza. Amelia found beauty in the Memorial's simplicity and thought it powerful and inspiring. I appreciated the commitment to defeat fascism, but I also found it a tragic tribute to the slaughter of America's lower classes who always have to do the fighting in the wars of white men. I didn't mention that to Amelia though, since she seemed to be so moved by the Memorial.

As we walked alongside the famous reflecting pool toward the Lincoln Memorial, Amelia exclaimed that this is the pool where Jenny and Forrest wade through the water to each other and hug in the epic scene from *Forrest Gump*. Turns out it's Amelia's favorite movie.

I thought the universe must be mocking me.

"It's also my mom's favorite movie," I said. "I think she saw herself in the Jenny character or whatever, because my mom ran away from home too. She saw *Forrest Gump* when it came out, just before I was born, and she loved it so much she named me Forrest."

Amelia looked at me with skeptical amusement in her eyes. "Really?"

"Forrest Tom Brock is my full name. 'Tom' was for Tom Hanks."

"That is *awesome!*"

"Ehhh, it wasn't so great in elementary school. It really sucked actually. I got so sick of all the 'Run, Forrest, run!' jokes. So, by fourth grade, I started telling my teachers I went by Tom. And I told my mom I wanted to be called Tom. And I've been Tom ever since."

"Very sensible. Totally understandable. Forrest is still an awesome name, though."

I shrugged. It was nice of her to say, but I never found my name the least bit charming.

We reached the iconic steps leading up to the Lincoln Memorial, perched like a Greek temple atop a small plateau. After a serious cardio workout of stair-climbing, we crested the summit, past giant white columns and into the memorial where the white marble Lincoln loomed in silence from his throne. Etched in the wall above the president were the words:

> *"In this temple as in the hearts of the people for whom he saved the Union the memory of Abraham Lincoln is enshrined forever."*

Against my will, the relative quiet of the "temple," the clean, potent prose, and the fact that Lincoln was murdered by a white supremacist combined to give me mild goosebumps. But knowing that's exactly the kind of reaction Bob was probably hoping to provoke in me was a powerful antidote to the feels.

I followed Amelia around as she soaked in the soaring Lincoln rhetoric that adorned the walls on both ends of the temple. Out front, she knew to look for the special step marking the spot where Martin Luther King, Jr. delivered his "I Have a Dream" speech. She insisted I should do my Lincoln reading on the MLK step. Her enthusiasm was very convincing, though the central location made me self-conscious since other sightseers were buzzing around us.

I pulled out my printed page and was surprised at Bob's choice for this location—a letter from President Lincoln to a Mrs. Bixby on November 21, 1864. According to Bob's note at the top of the page, she was the mother of five sons who died in battle fighting for the Union.

"*Dear Madam,*" I read aloud, "*I have been shown in the files of the War Department a statement of the Adjutant general of Massachusetts that you are the mother of five sons who have died gloriously on the field of battle. I feel how weak and fruitless must be any words of mine which should attempt to beguile you from the grief of a loss so overwhelming, but I cannot refrain from tendering to you the consolation that may be found in the thanks of the Republic that they died to save. I pray that the heavenly Father may assuage the anguish of your bereavement, and leave you only the cherished memory of the loved and lost, and the solemn pride that must be yours to have laid so costly a sacrifice upon the altar of freedom.*"

This time, Amelia didn't applaud. Instead, she wiped away tears. She took the page from me and, as she signed and dated it, said, "Thank you, Tom. I've never read that letter before, and it's quite stirring."

"No, thank *you*. This was such a huge favor."

I was panic-stricken that we would suddenly have to part ways. Before she could say goodbye, I squeezed in, "Can I thank you with ice cream or a soda or something? Whatever we can find in this godforsaken pandemic?"

"Well, that's unnecessary, but very kind of you."

My hopes dimmed during her brief pause, but then swelled again when she added, "But sure, why not? Ice cream sounds lovely."

We strolled toward the Washington Monument, chatting effortlessly as before. She asked more about my inheritance road trip. I explained about Bob's ancient RV and the box of videotapes telling me where I'm supposed to go. She found it all humorous and very cool. I stopped short, though, of mentioning the massive inheritance amount at stake.

I told her about my struggle to finish grad school and being stuck on finishing my play. She asked how I got into writing plays and I told her about Mrs. Briner, my hip high school drama teacher who encouraged me to write a one-act play when I was a junior. And then how the class actually performed it, and the rapturous audience reaction got me hooked on being a playwright.

We found an ice cream truck along 14th Street, where I bought us each a two-scoop waffle cone. She had cookies and cream; I had chocolate chip. We sat on a park bench and took off our masks. I enjoyed seeing her full smile again. Amelia told me more about London, and how she was raised by her single mother and lived down the street from her grandparents. Her grandfather was pastor of a small evangelical church, and she obviously thought the world of him. She had an American father whom she had never met. I told her we had that in common—I've never met my dad either. She said her father had been an Air Force man stationed in England and had a brief relationship with her mother, which resulted in Amelia. But he'd returned to the US, never to be heard from again. She joked about being technically half American without any of the benefits of dual citizenship. She also credited her lifelong fascination with the US to her father being American.

"I'm trying to get up the courage to find him sometime before I leave the States."

"Does he know you're here?"

"Oh, no. He knows nothing about me, as far as I know."

"Any clue where he lives?"

"Yes—San Diego, I think."

"Ah, San Diego. Beautiful. I miss going to the beach." I don't know why I said that—it's not like I went to the beach that often, even pre-COVID.

"I miss people. And church."

"I miss going to the movies." I really meant that one.

"Yes! And football matches with my grandfather. We've been going to Fulham since I could walk."

Our conversation wound around to her East Coast road trip. She lamented having to attempt it during all the COVID shutdowns, which meant most museums were off-limits. I asked where she was going next, and she said probably Gettysburg.

"If my car survives," she said. "It's really a garbage car. I think I got scammed by the used-car guy."

She asked where I was going next, and I admitted I didn't know. I'd have to return to the VHS tapes to find out. Fortunately, she didn't quiz me on Gettysburg because I knew nothing about it except that it was somehow related to the Civil War.

I went out on a limb and asked her if she wouldn't mind looking up "RV parks near DC" on her phone for me. I explained how my iPhone was in quarantine at Bob's.

"Your grandfather sounds like … an interesting man," she said.

"If by 'interesting' you mean 'dick,' then yes."

I immediately regretted my humor attempt because she didn't laugh. Here we were about to part ways, likely forever, and I was leaving her with the impression that I was the dick for talking about Bob that way. Fortunately, she overlooked my foible and pulled up RV parks for me.

We finished our ice cream, and I was fresh out of options for further hanging out with her. I offered to give her my phone number—my new burner phone number that is. She thanked me, plugged my number into her phone, and used the action as her exit cue. She stood from the bench first, and I followed suit.

"I guess I'll be off then. It was so great to meet you and hang out. And thank you very much for the ice cream."

"No, thank you. Really, you were a lifesaver."

"So, good luck on the rest of your inheritance quest."

"Thanks. Good luck with your car and grad school and everything."

We said bye and walked in opposite directions, she toward 14th Street and presumably wherever she parked her lemon and I toward the RV. I paused and turned to watch her walk away for a moment. My magical late afternoon with Amelia Curtis was really over. I felt sad. Then the weight of the task at hand pressed my mind again and anxiety kicked in. I would have to call Bob for the contractual follow-up conversation. Then I'd have to find the RV park. There would be stressful traffic and that analog map to deal with. All I wanted to do was hang out with this captivating soul I'd just met.

That night, I finally crashed on the RV couch and tackled my final task of the long day: calling Bob. It had only been a little over twenty-four hours since I'd left Bob's house, but it felt like a week.

"So what'd you learn today?" Bob began.

"Don't wear jeans in DC this time of year," I replied.

Bob actually laughed, briefly, which sort of startled me.

"Did you read the Declaration of Independence?" he asked.

"I did."

"And?"

"I mean, it's eloquent, I guess. Just a little hard to get past the twisted irony of 'all men are created equal' when so many of these guys owned slaves."

"Well, you're missing the bigger picture. The Declaration is America's mission statement. Why does government exist?"

I froze, not expecting a pop quiz.

"Hello?" he said.

"What, you're asking me?"

"Yeah, why do Americans believe government exists according to the Declaration?"

"I don't know…to maintain the wealthy status quo."

"*Wrong.* Second paragraph: governments are instituted to *secure our rights.* So, you have a big problem with America's founding documents because some, not all, of the men who worked on them were slave owners?"

"Yes. You don't think that's a glaring problem?"

"I think there's complexity to it that you have to take into account."

"Geez, you find complexity in slavery?"

"Can you just try listening for a minute? You're wallowing in some serious history snobbery if you think that you would've grown up as a white guy in Thomas Jefferson's world and been as woke as you think you are now."

I shook my head in utter mental exhaustion when he uttered the word "woke."

"We're all products of our own times and places," he continued. "That doesn't mean we're incapable of changing our views for the better. But it's mighty arrogant to consider yourself morally superior to Washington or Jefferson just because you're more enlightened on slavery. Look, I don't like that these guys owned slaves. Of course not. But I also don't think it means we should throw out all the good things they established and therefore do communism instead. That's dumb logic."

"Well, it makes me uncomfortable to have all these massive monuments worshipping these white racists."

"You think we need to knock down the Washington Monument then? Yank down Jefferson and turn the rotunda into a safe space?"

"Maybe."

"Then you'll just have a nation with no leaders, no heroes, no role models."

"I think you'd still have some. They'd just be more reflective of America. You know, less white, less racist."

"Oh boy. You've got a lot to learn."

I made a sarcastic snort of a sound that Bob probably heard through the phone.

"The flak that Washington and Jefferson get now compared to, say, FDR and MLK is insane," Bob continued. "I mean, it sounds like you have your own hierarchy of sins and how they should cancel people and their accomplishments. You know, I don't want to believe the scandalous stuff about MLK, but it's apparently true. He slept around on his wife all the time. So did FDR. And Eleanor Roosevelt was a lesbian who lived years at a time away from FDR with her female partners."

"Good for her," I interjected.

"FDR and Eleanor clearly had a marriage of convenience."

"It was a different time," I offered.

"Do you hear yourself? Look, there are either standards of morality that apply universally for all time, or there is no moral code whatsoever and we have a free-for-all. The chaos you see in America now is what you get with the free-for-all."

"Yeah, that great moral code *owned* a race of people and erased Native Americans from their own land. Some moral code."

"I'm not condoning those things. But it was the Judeo-Christian moral code that actually challenged those things. How did the abolitionist movement begin?"

I was getting tired of Bob's questions. "I don't know."

"Christians. It started in northern churches."

"From abolition to MAGA, how far the mighty have fallen."

"Okay," he chuckled, "that's enough for tonight. You get some rest."

I was surprised he didn't counterpunch my last jab, but it was just as well because I was starving and needed to sleep.

As I set the phone on the console beside the TV/VCR, I thought of Amelia and smiled. There was something oddly calming about being around her.

SIX

The following morning, over my bowl of Life cereal, I got my next marching orders from video Bob. I almost choked on a mouthful when he said I was to head to Gettysburg—that was where Amelia had said she was going next. I mostly came to my senses and dismissed the pipe dream of ever seeing her again. *Mostly.*

Later, as I approached Gettysburg, it was hard to imagine such a mellow landscape as the site of what Bob said was the largest-ever battle in the Western Hemisphere.

I turned off Highway 134 onto a slender side road that made it feel like I was sneaking in a back way into Gettysburg National Military Park. Dense, leafy woods skirted the road's edges, making it feel even more like I was wandering into forbidden territory.

I happened on a small parking lot with spaces for maybe three vehicles. Two of them were empty, so I helped myself and took up both spots with the RV. From there I was on foot to my destination: the rear slope of a rocky hill dubbed Little Round Top.

Bob desired that I ascend this particular ridge to appreciate the heroic exploits of the 20th Maine Regiment. He explained that this unit was commanded by Colonel Joshua Chamberlain, an unassuming college professor who'd volunteered to fight for the Union. Bob spoke reverently of how the regiment saved the

Union Army on day two of the Battle of Gettysburg and how their courageous struggle on this wooded hill in Pennsylvania was a pivotal moment in ultimately preserving the nation. I hiked the short distance up a paved pathway to the 20th Maine Regiment Monument, a four-sided gray marker that was set into the top of a massive boulder.

I looked down the slope, panning my vision across the rugged terrain, thick with trees and all manner of green undergrowth, trying to imagine (as Bob instructed me to) the terror of Rebel soldiers charging up at me. Bob said Colonel Chamberlain's men defended the farthest left end of the Union line, ordered to hold their position at all costs. The 20th Maine staved off wave after wave of Rebel attacks and were almost out of ammo. So, when the Rebels mounted yet another stubborn assault, Chamberlain ordered his men to fix bayonets and they performed a sweeping run down the slope that finally routed the Rebels and allowed the Union to keep the vital high ground. Bob said Colonel Chamberlain received the Medal of Honor for his actions at Little Round Top.

That brand of heroism felt otherworldly. I've never been brave.

After painstakingly backing the RV out of the spaces near the 20th Maine Regiment Monument, I exited the way I entered the park, crossing my fingers I wouldn't meet another car. That method proved useless because I met *two* cars, but they each scooted off the road to let me pass. If I had met another RV, we would've been screwed.

My next stop was the Gettysburg National Cemetery. It was beautiful in summertime, if you can say that about a place full of graves. It contained a variety of impressively large, full trees. Honestly, if Bob hadn't mentioned the trees, I probably wouldn't have noticed them.

Bob had me visit the cemetery to read the Gettysburg Address, which Lincoln delivered there when the site was dedicated in November 1863. Bob called this address "America's second founding," which I thought sounded hyperbolic. I hadn't read the whole thing since probably second grade, when I think we recited it for some school assembly. Turns out Lincoln was kind of a boss writer.

Perhaps Bob forgot about this, or maybe he just wanted to harass me, but there were signs posted in the cemetery encouraging "silence and respect," so I wasn't sure how I was going to pull off my public reading. I milled around for a while, searching for someone to recruit. I hung around the Lincoln Address Memorial for a few minutes until I finally asked a middle-aged dude who appeared to be with his wife. They were Pete and Tammy Garcia from Ohio—very chatty and eager to help. With that last name and his complexion, I assumed Pete to be Mexican American. And I guess it surprised me that he seemed to care about American history, considering the way his people have been treated. He said they were on a tour of major Civil War sites since so many things were closed for COVID. Fortunately, they didn't pry when I claimed this was for a graduate school project.

I read quickly, quietly, and through my mask, so the Garcias probably couldn't make out the speech very well. Through all the readings so far, I'd remained emotionally detached. It was simply a job to get through. But the last portion of the Gettysburg Address caught in my throat for the briefest moment:

"*[T]hat we here highly resolve that these dead shall not have died in vain, that this nation, under God, shall have a new birth of freedom and that government of the people, by the people, for the people, shall not perish from the earth.*'"

There was something about reading aloud "*that these dead shall not have died in vain,*" surrounded by thousands of white gravestones in that quiet place, that made me feel a twinge of something. And just as quickly, I dismissed it as Bob's contrived manipulation—feeling something in this circumstance was *exactly* what he wanted to elicit from me. I resolved not to succumb to his patriotic proselytizing.

By the time I made it back to the RV, it was early afternoon, and I felt seriously accomplished for knocking out the Gettysburg leg so fast. I decided to roll with my momentum and launched the next chapter of Bob's low-grade VHS monologuing. My next stop: Independence Hall in Philadelphia. Looked like three hours away, maybe less, according to my subpar atlas reading. I dared to dream I might just be able to knock out Philly in the same day.

I was navigating my way out of Gettysburg and had just taken a sizable swig of Yoohoo when my phone rang. The sudden blast of noise scared the living hell out of me, almost causing me to fumble the bottle. I answered the phone and was astonished, then delighted, to hear Amelia's British-accented voice.

"Hi, is this Tom Brock?"

"Yes, it is."

"Hello, this is Amelia Curtis."

"Yeah, I recognized your voice. The accent kinda gave it away."

I heard a mild laugh, what sounded like a major gust of wind, and possibly passing traffic.

"So, sorry to bother you," she continued. "I've just run into a bit of a problem."

"Oh, what's up?" I asked, hoping I sounded casual yet very supportive.

"Well, I was just wondering what you do in America when your car breaks down in the middle of nowhere."

"Oh, man. That sucks. Uhh…" I desperately needed to be a brilliant problem-solver, but my mind was blank. "So, it won't start, or…?" As if I'd know *anything* about her car issue, no matter how she responded.

"It starts, it just won't go. Forwards or backwards."

"Oh. That's not good." *Very helpful, Sherlock.*

"No. And there appears to be some smoke or steam or something puffing out the front."

"Oh, crap. Okay. Well…so…I would probably try to look up a towing service." *That* was the best I could come up with? I was such a disappointment to myself.

"Okay."

"Where are you?"

"I think I'm about ten or fifteen minutes outside Gettysburg."

My heart sang at my incredibly good fortune.

"You're kidding. I'm just leaving Gettysburg."

"Really?"

"Hold on, I can probably find you in just a few minutes."

We figured out she was on a Highway 15, and I immediately set about finding her. I was suddenly on a heroic mission, a knight in the literally shining armor of Bob's colossal Airstream.

Amelia was leaning against the back of her dingy gray sedan on the shoulder of a straight, remote stretch of the divided highway. I could see the smoke still rising from beneath the hood as she'd described. I eased the RV to a halt behind her car and waved. She waved back and smiled.

I bounded out of the RV and made a decent show of pretending to examine her car. I had no clue what I was looking for, but she didn't need to know that. She had already spoken with a towing service who said it would probably be an hour before they could get there.

I invited her inside the RV to cool off while we waited. She insisted I didn't need to wait on her—she didn't want to delay my travel. I insisted I didn't mind at all.

I showed her the box of Bob's VHS tapes, and she suggested we watch a bit. I demurred but quickly caved. I rewound the tape that was already in the machine to the part I'd just watched about Independence Hall.

"Your grandfather's so cute!" she assessed. I thought that was a stretch.

Bob rambled on about the creation of the Constitution, and what a miracle it was that it was ever written, much less ratified; how Benjamin Franklin, out of all the Founding Fathers, was the one who, after several contentious days of the convention, insisted that they open their sessions in prayer; how George Washington expertly presided over the gathering; how the Constitution is brilliant in its government restraints; how the Bill of Rights is essential to safeguarding precious freedoms; and how the US Constitution is the longest-running self-governing document in the world. I shook my head slightly. Why were conservatives always flexing their patriotism like that? We get it, the Constitution has had a long run.

Since I'd already seen this part, I mostly watched Amelia's reaction to Bob's lecture. Unfortunately, she seemed to dig it. She occasionally exclaimed, or nodded, or raised her eyebrows.

"He's wonderful," she said when that section of the video wrapped up. "You're blessed to have such a knowledgeable grandfather."

"Yeah" was all I could muster. I almost admitted that I'd only met him once in my life—two days ago. But I withheld that part, I guess to prop up her innocent illusion that Bob was "wonderful."

"So, you're heading to Philadelphia, then?" she asked.

"Yeah."

"So was I."

The tow truck arrived and loaded Amelia's car for the short trip back to Gettysburg. I insisted on driving her to the mechanic's shop. She resisted once again, and we did the whole polite tap-dance thing until she was finally convinced that I really did not mind driving her.

The mechanic wouldn't be able to assess her car until the next morning. So, I offered to help her find a hotel for the night, but she said I'd already done far too much. She just didn't get it—hanging out with her was *all* I cared about at the moment. Fate gave me the gift of a second afternoon of interaction with Amelia, and I was determined not to blow it.

We found Amelia a room at a Hampton Inn on the outer rim of Gettysburg. I desperately wanted to invite her to dinner but didn't want to press my luck. I quickly strategized that I would offer to pick her up for breakfast in the morning before giving her a lift to the mechanic. She said that sounded great. I thought so too.

I found a decent RV park east of Gettysburg and was eager to chill for the night until I remembered I had to do the requisite post-mortem with Bob. I reluctantly called him and after at least ten rings, he *finally* answered. Bob asked me some questions about Gettysburg and reemphasized his reverence for Lincoln's Gettysburg Address. I was mostly zoned out until I realized he had some-how pivoted to bitching about a news story regarding New York City's birth certificates that now apparently include an "X" gender option. Bob wasn't onboard with that.

"I saw this *New York Times* story a while back with a headline that said, 'The Hardest Part of Having a Nonbinary Kid Is Other People.' Are you kidding me? '*Nonbinary*?'" he exclaimed. "Lefties are always harping on science. Well, that's not how science works.

If your child can't figure out what sex he or she is, that might be on you as the parent."

I was momentarily stuck on the revelation that Bob actually read anything from the *New York Times*. Not even *I* read the *New York Times*. I wanted to; I just couldn't afford a subscription.

"That is child abuse, plain and simple," he continued. "Not to mention a slap in God's face. He clearly created *male* and *female*. The arrogance it takes to say, 'Sorry, God, you screwed up and gave me the wrong parts.'"

"I guess I don't see how it's such a big deal for a person to choose what gender they are."

"You're joking. You really believe that?"

He didn't give me a chance to answer.

"See, this postmodern garbage is what the Left has always dreamed of. This free-for-all, anything-goes, you-do-you culture. All this chaos is the end result of people thumbing their noses at God. All this crap started fifty years ago, and the long leftist takeover is finally complete. They've got the colleges, the media, the government agencies. It's all anti-American, anti-God, and anti-freedom."

"So, you're really pining for America's glory days?" I interjected. "When things were a lot whiter, more anti-black, and anti-women? When everyone 'knew their place'?"

He chuckled.

"I hear that stuff in the media all the time, but it's extra crazy to hear it in real life. Look, the Left, the Democratic Party, is totally divorced from reality. They think they're making progress by giving people make-believe gender options. That's not progress— that's *implosion*. The only things that can salvage America now are the Declaration of Independence, the Constitution, the Bill of Rights, and a big ol' helping of God. When's the last time you heard anyone on your side mention one of those? Huh?"

He left a brief pause for me to answer, but I didn't bother.

"The Left *never* mentions those," he continued, his voice now at an excited pitch. "They want to cater to roughly half the nation and pretend the other half doesn't exist or try to cancel it altogether. And lefties don't know how to talk about faith. They certainly don't know how to talk to *people* of faith. They're committed to winning votes and power by offering benefits to different groups of people. When the only benefits that will save us long-term are in the First Amendment—freedom of speech, religion, press, assembly, and the right to petition the government."

I briefly considered interrupting his rant to tell him no one's stopping his side from doing those things. But I just let him finish.

"Those guaranteed freedoms make Americans the freest people in the world," he pled as if wrapping up his case before a jury. "The Founders added the Bill of Rights before they would accept the Constitution. The First Amendment is for everyone, you know. It's not a Left or Right thing. It's an *American* thing—*the* quintessential American thing."

Now that he'd concluded his anti-Left TED Talk, I didn't have the energy to give him the pushback he deserved. So we hung up, but not before he told me to "drive safe," which sounded out of place after the ear-scorching he'd just put me through.

The next morning, I picked up Amelia at her hotel and we made our way to a local diner. She was denied the full greasy-spoon experience she had hoped for as they were doing carryout only due to COVID. At least we had a place to sit at the table inside the RV.

Over breakfast, we quickly slid back into easy conversation. I asked how she ended up at Wheaton College. She explained that she was sort of living out a dream her grandfather had when he was younger. She said it started when he "accepted Christ" in 1954 because of Billy Graham.

"Poppy—that's my grandfather—went with a friend to a Chelsea match at Stamford Bridge, which was odd because Poppy was only ever a Fulham supporter. But this friend invited him, so there he was at Stamford Bridge, and this American evangelist he's never heard of called Billy Graham comes out at halftime and speaks to the crowd and invites them to accept Christ. And Poppy was really grabbed by this man's message. So he went to Billy Graham's crusade in London the next night and he accepted Christ. And as he learned more about Billy Graham over the years, he found out he was a Wheaton graduate. So, he used to tell me when I was younger that if I ever had the chance, I should go to America—to *Illinois*"—she attempted *Illinois* in an American accent and giggled at her attempt—"to study at Wheaton College, where the great Billy Graham studied."

I didn't want her to know the extent of my ignorance about Billy Graham. I sort of knew he was a famous preacher, and that was it.

"So, that's how Poppy became a pastor. He says otherwise, he probably would've been an accountant or banker or something incredibly boring like that."

Few things sounded more boring to me than being a pastor, but I kept that one to myself too.

We got around to talking more about our moms and growing up with essentially nonexistent dads. Amelia said her mom is a devoted Christian now but went through a real "prodigal" phase before Amelia was born. I assumed "prodigal" was a British term for degenerate or something. Her mom and Amelia's father had a whirlwind romance, her mom got pregnant, and he wanted to pay for an abortion. Her mom briefly considered it, but Amelia said God "got the better of her" and she decided to keep the baby.

She said her mom and this American guy moved in together and convinced themselves for a while that they were in love. But the pregnancy was hard, and the first few months were miserable. They fought all the time until one day, a couple months before Amelia was born, her father abandoned them. He was transferred to another country. He sent her mom a note renouncing all parental rights—he didn't want Amelia—and he never contacted them again.

She asked about my dad.

"Your guess is as good as mine," I replied, explaining how my mom has always had a boyfriend in progress. "I mean, she went through some drought periods when I was growing up, and I usually liked those times better than the times random guys were hanging around. The truth is, my mom doesn't know who my dad is because she was seeing a couple dudes at the same time and, well, I've never pried for more details. I don't wanna know. Eventually, when I was a teenager, she told me she was basically too wasted at the time to know exactly who knocked her up. So, I really don't think she knows. I probably couldn't look him up even if I wanted to."

"That's *awful*," said Amelia. "That's worse than *my* nonexistent father story," she said with a joking tone, which I assumed was to mask the pathetic reality of our lame fathers.

"I know," I said with a wry grin.

I went on to tell her about when my mom and I lived in a commune in Oregon for a couple years when I was six. And how she changed jobs a lot so we moved a lot, all over Oregon and Washington. By the time I graduated high school I had been to something like fifteen different schools. We were basically poor all the time when I was growing up, with Mom buying generic food brands and barely keeping our car duct-taped together. Meanwhile, Mom had this uber-rich father back in Virginia. I finally told Amelia that my grandfather, Bob, owned the Liberty's chain of convenience stores.

"Oh, I stopped at one of those yesterday! You know, back when my car worked," she grinned, with mock lament in her eyes.

I half expected her to ask why Bob hadn't shared the wealth with his poor daughter and grandson. But maybe she was too polite to dig like that.

Talking about Mom reminded me I *still* needed to call her. I actually had to count how many days it had been since I'd flown to Virginia because it was all a blur. It didn't seem possible that I'd only been gone three days.

Our pancakes and coffee were long gone, but we were in no danger of running out of things to talk about. I wasn't used to people in my life listening to me as well as Amelia did, and I dug it.

Her phone rang, disrupting our conversational groove. She answered cheerfully, and it was quickly apparent from the back and forth that it was the mechanic with a dire prognosis. Her car's transmission was shot. To replace it would cost almost as much as she'd paid for the lemon.

"I guess I'll just cut my losses and scrap it," she said, thinking out loud. "I suppose I'll just fly back to Chicago and figure out what to do with the rest of my summer from there."

I was blindsided with a brilliant idea.

"I can give you a ride to the Philadelphia airport. I mean, I have to go to Philadelphia anyway."

"That's so kind, but I'll figure something out. You've already been far too generous."

"No, really, it's no big deal at all. I'd be glad to. What, are you going to Uber your way to Philadelphia? That'll cost a fortune."

While she demurred some more, I tried to sweeten the deal. "And I mean, it's still early so, you might as well just tag along with me to Independence Hall since you're into all this American history stuff."

Her eyes seemed to light up a bit at that prospect.

"I don't know... maybe. Would you mind, really?"

"Are you kidding? I'd love it!" I really hoped the "I'd love it" wasn't laying it on too thick. Being smitten did not do positive things for my brain-mouth coordination.

"Well, okay then. Let's do it," she said.

I did feel slightly bad for her car misfortune, but mostly, I thanked my lucky stars that her transmission expired in such a timely fashion. Now, if the transmission in Bob's giant tuna can RV would only continue hanging in there.

We stopped by the mechanic so Amelia could gather her personal effects from the car. The shop would take care of sending it to the junkyard, and she would receive a pittance for the scrap. Amelia didn't seem too torn up about it, since she'd owned the car less than a month. Once she'd cleared the interior, she closed the driver's side door and paused for a brief salute.

"Goodbye, Joe Wilson," she said in mock solemnity, "We'll always have Indiana, I suppose. And part of Ohio. And Kentucky. And West Virginia. And regular Virginia. I'll always be grateful for that."

As we walked to the RV, I asked, "Joe Wilson?"

"I've always named cars. And he looked like a Joe to me. And Wilson seemed a proper American name. So, it was Joe Wilson."

"Gotcha," I said, amused.

"You mean you haven't named your RV yet?"

"Not yet."

"I'll help you, then."

"Thanks."

SEVEN

I knew it was too good to be true that someone like Amelia would be romantically unattached. Of course she had a serious boy-friend-turned-fiancé. But...there was still an unexpected glimmer of hope. The three-hour trek to Philadelphia was plenty of time for Amelia to relay the story of her recent *broken* engagement.

She brought it up by explaining she'd bought the dilapidated Joe Wilson with money that had been earmarked for her honeymoon. She was engaged to a guy her age (twenty-four, she said), a longtime family friend who is a professional "footballer."

"He plays for a third-division side, so he's not like a superstar or anything yet. But he's got potential," she said.

They got engaged the previous October. Their plan was that she would attend Wheaton in January, and they'd get married over the summer, during his offseason. But barely three months into her first semester, and just after the pandemic took over the world, he confessed to cheating on her.

I stole a glance at her eyes, which glistened with tears from this still relatively fresh, deep wound, and it made me feel a small lump in my throat.

"I broke off the engagement, obviously. Instead of going home and getting married during the summer, I'm now hanging out in America, going on a failed road trip, during a pandemic, and hanging out in some guy's 1960s RV." She tried to joke her way back from the tears.

"Actually, I believe this is a 1979 model according to Bob. So, a *lot* newer than you're giving it credit for."

"Oh. Wow." She grinned. "My apologies."

She was quiet for a while after unloading the burden of her broken engagement. Her sadness made me feel a sudden urge to comfort and protect her. At the same time, my own woeful inadequacy engulfed me. She was obviously a woman of rare character and soul—what could I possibly offer her?

She snapped me out of my self-bullying session with, "You're a good listener, Tom. I appreciate that."

Her compliment caught me off guard. And it pretty much made my day.

Parking an RV in downtown Philadelphia is something no one should ever try. And I wouldn't have attempted such terror myself if I hadn't been trying to appear brave for Amelia. I was getting marginally better at making turns, but each one still felt like cheating death, and I may have scraped a sign or some other unidentified object or two in the process. I never would've found my way without Amelia's phone locating a parking lot that claimed to accommodate RVs (thank God it turned out to be true). Technically, I wasn't cheating on Bob's contract with the smartphone help since it wasn't *my* phone. Bob would probably say I was violating the spirit of the contract rule. But what Bob didn't know wouldn't hurt him.

We ended up in a lot near the Delaware River, which was a toasty twenty-minute walk to Independence Hall. Of course, since Bob sent me on this odyssey in the middle of an epic pandemic, Independence Hall was closed to tours. So was the Liberty Bell.

Not that I would ever admit it to Bob, but it was kind of interesting to see Independence Hall, even if I didn't share his reverence for the luminaries who toiled there. Amelia, on the other hand, would've been Bob's class pet, because she seemed in awe of our historical surroundings, just as she had been in DC.

"Imagine the legends that gathered in there," she said earnestly as we approached the red-bricked Independence Hall. "George Washington. Benjamin Franklin. John Adams. Thomas Jefferson, James Madison." She shook her head. "It's absolutely brilliant."

I glanced at her to confirm she wasn't being sarcastic. I didn't really think she was, but I felt sarcastic hearing her gush like that about the dudes on our money.

We found an unoccupied shady spot in the courtyard just across Chestnut Street from Independence Hall. But as we stepped into the shade, I realized I'd left the required reading in the RV.

"No problem. Hold on..." Amelia sprang into action, pulling her phone from the back pocket of her shorts. "I think I remember what they were."

I'd seen the video twice and I couldn't remember. Man, I sucked.

"I know it was the Preamble to the Constitution," she continued, tapping her phone screen, presumably looking it up. "And the Bill of Rights. And then, wasn't it Benjamin Franklin? Ah, yes, Benjamin Franklin's address in favor of the Constitution."

"Great. Sounds riveting," I said, smirking.

"Undoubtedly, it *was* for those who were there. Your grandfather said Franklin was something like eighty-one years old when he wrote this speech."

I didn't have a comeback for that—I was too entranced by her insane cuteness in seriously trying to keep me on track to complete the task.

She handed me her phone and I read aloud the preamble of the Constitution:

"*We the People of the United States, in Order to form a more perfect Union, establish Justice, insure domestic Tranquility, provide for the common defence, promote the general Welfare, and secure the Blessings of Liberty to ourselves and our Posterity, do ordain and establish this Constitution for the United States of America.*"

"Lovely," said Amelia. "The Bill of Rights should be in the next tab there."

I proceeded to read the Bill of Rights, which fortunately, was much shorter than I anticipated. Bob would be appalled if he knew I'd never read them in their entirety before.

When I finished the Bill of Rights, Amelia smiled and said, "And that's why you're the freest people on earth."

"Are we?" I retorted, only half-joking.

Then it was on to Benjamin Franklin's post–Constitutional Convention curtain call. It didn't take very long for me to figure out why Bob included this speech in my assignment. I think it was this part at the beginning:

"*For having lived long, I have experienced many Instances of being obliged, by better Information or fuller Consideration, to change Opinions even on important Subjects, which I once thought right, but found to be otherwise. It is therefore that the older I grow the more apt I am to doubt my own Judgment, and to pay more Respect to the Judgment of others.*"

When I finished Franklin's address, Amelia applauded like she always did. She was an easy audience.

"Franklin kinda sounds like the Dumbledore of America," I quipped.

Amelia laughed, which was music to my ears. "Yes, I suppose he was, in a way."

I was devastated that my time with Amelia had expired once again.

Amelia had an endearing innocence about her. She was obviously very intelligent, but she seemed to be joyfully uncynical. Depressingly, I didn't know how *not* to be cynical. Anyway, I just liked spending time with her. She seemed to like life. And the British accent helped.

On our long walk back to the RV, I hatched a desperate, last-ditch ploy to continue spending time with her. I mentally rehearsed my pitch so that by the time we arrived at the RV, I was ready to go for it. We climbed inside and I cranked the engine to get the AC flowing. Amelia settled into the front passenger seat. I grabbed two Pepsi cans from the fridge and offered her one.

"Yes, please!" she said, removing her mask and dabbing her forehead.

I climbed into the driver's seat, cracked open my Pepsi, and took a sip. My stomach was in knots, but it was now or never for my pitch. I went for broke with the blurting approach: "So, here's kind of a crazy idea. Instead of flying back to Chicago, why don't you just come with me? To wherever it is I have to go next."

My proposal caught her mid-drink. She swallowed hard, crinkled her brow a bit, and gave me an empathetic smile.

"That's an extremely kind offer, Tom. But I can't."

"Why not?" I ventured, trying my best to sound casual instead of desperate. "I mean, you were going to drive yourself around the country in your clunker anyway, right? Why not do it in my bigger clunker?"

She chuckled, which provided me the briefest hope.

"It's very sweet of you to offer, really. But you're a single guy. We barely know each other... it's rather strange, isn't it? I can't."

I was mildly wounded that she thought we barely knew each other, when I thought we were already fast friends.

"I know, I know, maybe it sounds a little weird. But we've already spent most of two days together and I think we make a great travel team. And look, if you're worried about any, you know, hashtag-MeToo stuff, I get it. But there's absolutely nothing to worry about with me. If anything, my radar is *overly* tuned to MeToo stuff, probably thanks to my mom drilling it into me my whole life. So, nothing to worry about. No ulterior motive here. I am strictly focused on the task at hand. I just think you're really cool and it would be fun to have you tag along."

I was almost entirely truthful, except for the *ulterior motive* part—I did already have a massive crush on her. Clearly, I had made it more difficult for her to say no. And yet...

"I appreciate your honesty, and I'm flattered. But I just don't think it's wise."

I had thought she would say no, so I'd already prepared a deal-sweetener. I took a contemplative swig of my Pepsi before continuing the negotiation.

"So, how 'bout if you'll finish this trip with me, I'll buy you a new car."

She raised her eyebrows at me very suspiciously, then laughed off my suggestion. "What? No. That's absurd. You can't do something like that."

"Why not? I'm gonna be rich."

"Well, assuming you finish the entire trip, right? And I don't recall you saying you would be 'rich,' exactly."

"Well, we had just met. I didn't want you to think I was totally nuts. So, full disclosure—if I jump through all of Bob's hoops, I will inherit twenty-five million dollars."

Her eyes widened in alarm, and I assumed, disbelief.

"No. You can't be serious."

"One hundred percent."

"Because you realize this sounds like the beginning of a Nigerian prince email or something."

"Yes, I realize that."

I reached into the console between the seats for my copy of Bob's signed contract. I pulled it out of the manila folder and showed her the page with the inheritance amount. I handed her the contract, and she looked the whole thing over, occasionally shaking her head.

"That's incredible," she finally said.

"I know. I told you, my grandfather owns the Liberty's store chain. You can look it up. He's super wealthy."

She did look up Bob on her phone, right away, and shook her head after confirmation.

"Of course, you could still be a con man. Anyone could google Robert Brock and work up a phony contract..."

"That hurts. I can really appreciate your skepticism, but ouch."

"Sorry, I don't mean to offend. I don't really believe you're a con artist, it's just...rather *peculiar*."

"I know. It is." I leaned over the console and lifted one of the VHS tapes from the box. "But how would a con man get the real Robert Brock to make a boxful of old-timey videos like this?"

I grinned at her and she slowly grinned back.

"I suppose you're right. You'd have to *steal* them."

I shook my head at her. "I can't win."

She glanced at the box of tapes. "That's a very convoluted treasure map."

"I know! That's why I need a navigator."

"But don't you have other friends to go with you?"

"I mean, maybe. But no one has a clear schedule. Plus, they're in California."

"I still don't think it's a good idea."

"You don't want a brand-new car?"

"I don't think it's wisest to, you know, make promises—"

"That I can't keep?"

"Well, yes."

"But I *will* keep it. Buying a car will actually be chump change if I get this inheritance."

She closed her eyes tightly and hung her head for a quiet moment before saying, "I'm sorry, but I can't accept."

"Okay...what if I buy you a new car *and* pay for the rest of your graduate school?"

She cocked her head sideways and winced at me, kind of like my mom does when I've let her down. "Tom...that's *insane*."

"No, it's not. I'm serious. I'll buy you whatever new car you want, and I'll pay the rest of your tuition. Think of it as a scholarship—the Forrest T. Brock Great American Road Trip Scholarship."

She grinned at my attempt, and it finally seemed like her wheels were slightly turning.

"The car. A scholarship. Look, I don't want to annoy you at all. But this is a very real offer."

"It's too generous," she protested.

"It's really not."

"What if I said yes?"

"I...I would be super pumped. And surprised."

"So, you're guaranteeing me a brand-new car and full graduate school tuition? Because it is *not* cheap, you know."

"I'm painfully aware, yes. No matter what it costs, full tuition and a car, I promise. And you can even have the bedroom." I held up finger quotation marks for "bedroom."

"And we can get all of that in writing?"

"Definitely."

"And I'm free to leave at any point on the journey?"

I wasn't expecting that wrinkle, so I had to do a quick recalculation. But my brain was a little fuzzy because I was growing giddy with the feeling that she was about to agree to my brilliant plan.

"Of course. How 'bout we say if you bail before the trip is officially complete, you forfeit the tuition part, but you still get a new car."

"Counteroffer," she said, "if I leave early, no car, but I still get the tuition."

"Done. So, it's a deal?"

"Well, after we get it in writing."

"Right. Let's do it!"

She glanced around the RV interior and wrinkled her nose.

"And part of the deal must include a full exfoliation, fumigation, and sterilization of this entire space. No offense, but it could use a serious going-over."

"No offense taken. I actually agree."

Amelia extended her hand, and we shook on it. And yes, my heart skipped multiple beats touching her hand for the first time.

The rest of the afternoon and early evening were jam-packed. First, we sat across from each other at the pull-out table and hammered out a contract. Amelia wrote it out in her lovely penmanship on lined sheets of paper from what I surmised was her travel journal. Obviously, she didn't owe me anything, but she insisted on splitting all food and RV park fees with me. We also agreed, without knowing anything about our upcoming destinations, it was fair that she stay on for a minimum of the next three destinations before she could exercise her "bail at any point" option. When we finished drafting our agreement, she drew two separate lines for each of us to sign. After the signing was complete, we shook hands again and giggled like teenagers.

"I must be a nutter for doing this," she said. "You better not end up murdering me."

I thought that was a rather dark turn. "Jesus," I said, "Somebody's watched too much *Dateline.*"

Her face fell a bit. "Oh, and if you could refrain from using Jesus's name in vain. I can't condone that. He is the Son of God, King of Kings, Lord of Lords. He is the way, the truth, and the life. The only hope for humanity. He is only worthy of praise, so…"

"Got it. My bad. I'm very sorry. Won't happen again."

I mentally flogged myself for stepping into that one. I'd never heard someone get so defensive about a simple Jesus utterance before.

Once the contract business was done, we found a store for cleaning supplies and additional food since I wasn't going to subject my new favorite friend to my Yoohoo and frozen burritos. Then we gave the RV interior the full rubber-glove treatment. Amelia was the definition of thorough in the cleaning and I struggled to equal her effort. She even bought a small, rechargeable hand vacuum, which was genius.

Late that evening, after settling in an RV park south of Philadelphia, Amelia curled up on the couch in her "room" with a book—*To Kill a Mockingbird.* I almost admitted to her that I'd never read it but stopped myself—no point in letting her know how pathetically unliterary I actually am.

I went outside to finally call Mom out of Amelia's earshot in case things got testy. It wasn't that Mom and I had a bad relationship necessarily. It's just that Mom is alternately needy and erratic, loving and standoffish. I do love her. But she can also be a real pain. If I caught her in the right mood, we could be totally in sync, laughing and sharing everything. If she's in the wrong mood, it's misery.

Fortunately, I caught Mom in a rather mellow mood. She had not been worried about not hearing from me for several days, which made me kick myself because that meant I probably could've gotten away with not calling for at least another week. I ripped it off like a Band-Aid and told her I was on a spontaneous road trip with a friend, hoping she wouldn't ask what friend.

"What friend?" she asked immediately.

I gave her the briefest, vaguest rundown possible, just striving for a passing grade. But of course, because moms have the most insanely irritating sixth sense, she had to ask if said friend was "a guy or gal?" And when I replied "gal," she said, "Oooooooh," in that annoying, sing-song way moms do when you come home telling her there's a girl you want to ask to prom. She had to know where we met, so I told her "a park," which was technically true. I told her that Amelia and I were strictly friends, nothing to see here, nothing to infer here, move it along. Fortunately, mellow-Mom left it at that for the time being.

Of course, before I could hang up, she had to ask why I was calling from a different number. So, I told her my phone was getting repaired. Yes, I lied to my mom when I'd sworn to her multiple times in adolescence never to do so, but this truly was for her own protection. She would lose her mind if she knew what I was really up to. I would somehow have to break this Bob business to her gently and gradually—like maybe over the next couple decades.

Speaking of Bob, I still owed him a post–Independence Hall call. First, I smoked a cigarette to help me chill a bit before dealing with him. I know smoking's a dumb habit. It's something I picked up when I was a student at Reed, trying to seem cool. (I don't think it had the desired effect.)

Bob loved him some US Constitution, especially the Bill of Rights. Clearly, one of his primary beefs with America was "big government" growing way outside what he sees as the boundaries set by the Constitution.

"If there was a Mount Rushmore of executive overreach, it would have Woodrow Wilson, FDR, LBJ, and Obama on it," he said. "They are most responsible for the progressive, anti-American bullcrap that we may never be able to shovel our way out of now. They made the presidency way larger than it was designed to be. The president was originally supposed to have *limited* responsibilities, you know, defend the nation if attacked, check Congress if it violates the Constitution, enforce the laws, be an administrator—that's it. None of this setting policy or having an agenda—that's Congress's job."

I spontaneously determined that I was going to have to push back and call Bob's BS when I detected it.

"Wait, hold on," I started. "If you're such a Constitutional-limits-on-the-president-guy, how the hell do you excuse Trump? You really think he knows shit about the Constitution?"

"Well, now we're in this situation where we have to use the presidency as a last line of defense against the insane Left. Look, I certainly don't love the guy, but I respect him because he respects people like me."

"He *uses* people like you. He's a greasy, D-list, reality-TV huckster."

"Your side can't handle Trump because he's rough around the edges. But he's not a politician. And that's his biggest virtue to a lot of folks. He didn't go to president school. But he was the only one who saw flyover Americans. Hillary called us 'deplorables.' He asked for our vote. Where's the Democrat policy appealing to people like me? It doesn't exist anymore. Trump sees the Left destroying this nation we love and he's willing to fight back."

"But he lies, like literally every day. And the Right is completely okay with it. And he bullies and dehumanizes people all the time. And props up conspiracies. He's just totally corrupt. And, God, his stupid Tweets."

"Y'all get so worked up over his tweets. Look, Trump's always been at least eighty-five percent bluster. When you understand that about him, you know which stuff to take seriously. What matters is what he *does*. He's advanced some conservative policies and appointed conservative judges. Yeah, he's unpolished. He's kind of a junkyard dog. But he's *our* junkyard dog for a change. The Left's not used to a fighter. The media did the same crap to George W. for eight years, but he was just too polite to stand up for himself. Trump gives 'em that goofy Cheshire Cat grin, flips 'em the bird, and the Left and the media lose their minds. And it's glorious. They can't stand it that one of his dumb tweets gets more eyeballs than a hundred of their idiotic hit pieces combined."

"You don't see the hypocrisy? I mean, he was asking a foreign power to investigate his political opponent. How's that not just as bad as Watergate?"

"Yeah, I love how you lefties worshipped Robert Mueller. I saw it on the news—there were even candles and pillows for sale with Saint Bob on them. And then, oops, tens of millions of dollars and two years of investigation didn't turn up squat. 'Oops, our bad, Trump *didn't* collude with the Russians after all.' Or what about that clown Michael Avenatti? Remember when he was going to run for president? How'd that turn out?"

"What about Paul Manafort? Roger Stone? Steve Bannon? All in various stages of prison last time I checked."

"Yeah, well, Trump's not the best at hiring help."

"You people excuse and justify anything and everything with this guy while he puts the country through hell."

"You mean the hell of a booming economy and low unemployment?"

"Sure, for the top percent."

"Son, your brain's fried from a few too many Bernie rallies. Do you get how our economy works?"

"I know enough to know it's a genius system for the rich, like you."

"I wasn't born rich. Far from it. And the system never gave me anything. I earned my wealth the old-school way—hard work."

"Yeah, hard work. If that's such a magic bullet, why does the top one percent in America make something like eighty times more than the bottom half of Americans? Does that one percent work eighty times harder than everyone else? You know the US is the most unequal society of all developed nations, right? We're more like China and Russia in that way than Western Europe."

"Man, you've got your Bernie Bro talking points memorized, don't you? The Bernies and AOCs of your party think they're Robin Hood. They're gonna steal from the evil rich through taxes and redistribute this evil wealth to the poor masses. Make things 'more fair and equal.' But it's never gonna be fair enough. Someone will always have a grievance. Charity is good for temporary help, for filling gaps. But you can't take away the incentive of work and working your way up. Humans need that incentive to thrive."

"You call this cutthroat, capitalist free-for-all *thriving*?"

"Let me show you how it works. In my business, entry-level employees start at eighteen dollars an hour. I started doing that before Bernie ever heard of such a thing. I don't do that because I'm forced to, at least not yet. I do it because it's a great incentive. It makes Liberty's a desirable place to work. It makes most people want to do a good job, because it's competitive and they know if they do a poor job mopping the floor, there's a line of folks who'd jump at the chance to try to do a better job than them. And it's incentive to try to work their way up to more responsibilities in the company. Because they figure, 'If they're paying me eighteen dollars an hour to mop floors, imagine what they pay to be a supervisor or a store manager or work in marketing.' But those entry-level jobs are service jobs. You can't pay a cashier the same as a store manager, 'cause then the incentive is all screwed up. But your socialist pals want a 'living wage' for a fast-food drive-thru worker to support a family. No, that's a stepping-stone job! We used to understand this in America. When I was your age, if you didn't like your career flipping burgers, you did something to move up and out. Incentive. It wasn't easy, of course. But if you didn't have money for college, you scrimped and saved until you could afford a couple classes. Then you saved up to take a couple more. Now people stay in those service jobs they hate and expect to make a manager's salary. I've had tons of examples of employees who have worked their way up from those minimum-wage positions."

I didn't know exactly how to counter a guy running a multi-million-dollar company. His incentive thing made some sense I guess, but I still couldn't wrap my brain around America having such unprecedented, obscene wealth, yet over 10 percent of its people living below the poverty line. Bob's "incentive" factor didn't explain the whole story.

Back inside the RV, I tried to discreetly return my cigarette pack and lighter to the front pocket of my duffle. I don't really know why I tried to hide my smoking from Amelia. I guess I just didn't want her to know I had such a bad habit, even if it was an irregular one.

EIGHT

Bob's next requirement was that I visit the newest Liberty's store in America, near Atlanta, Georgia. I thought that was lame enough, but much lamer was his requirement that I drive the entire length of the Blue Ridge Parkway on the way to Georgia. Glancing at my atlas, the Parkway looked like a haphazard twisting mess starting somewhere in Virginia and ending somewhere in the wilderness of North Carolina. My rough estimate was that it would take approximately five years to complete the Parkway in Bob's mailbox-on-wheels.

Amelia's outlook was considerably rosier. She pulled up the Blue Ridge Parkway on her phone and exclaimed that it looked like an amazing drive. I begrudgingly loved her positivity. But it wasn't enough to override my annoyance at such a long detour.

As we watched Bob's video, he slipped into a nostalgic mood onscreen. He sunk back into his leather couch and his posture and face relaxed. He even took off his glasses and managed some mild smiles as he recounted how he met my grandmother. I'd never heard any of it before.

He said that after high school, he was drafted to go to Vietnam. When he made it back home a few years later, his parents wanted him to use the GI Bill to go to college, so he went to Hampton University for a couple years. He didn't know what to major in, so he defaulted to history only because he "kind of liked it" in high school. He said he briefly considered becoming a history teacher, but he never really liked kids all that much. That may have been the least surprising revelation in the whole box of VHS tapes.

During the summer before his junior year of college, he was working for a company cleaning carpets in office buildings in Norfolk when he saw Betty, my grandmother, for the first time. She was out for lunch with a few other women from her office job. He followed her to the same lunch counter where he had a "surge of boldness" and asked her out in front of her colleagues.

"I don't know why she said yes," he wondered with a grin, slight chuckle, and shrug of his shoulders. "Even back then, I wasn't much to look at." He brushed his hand over his predominantly bald head. "Had more hair, though."

Just a few days after that first meeting, he took her to a seafood place for dinner. Afterward, they walked along the Norfolk harbor, and he held her hand.

"Three weeks later, we were engaged. A month after that, we got married."

They drove to Asheville, North Carolina, via the Blue Ridge Parkway for their honeymoon at the Grove Park Inn. He could only afford to stay there two nights. But he loved the fact that, at the time, seven US presidents, including Calvin Coolidge and Herbert Hoover, had stayed at the inn.

After their honeymoon, Bob and Betty were driving back on the Parkway when they stopped at an old coffee shop attached to a gas station—"Bluffs Coffee Shop and Service Station. A place you could sit down and eat," Bob said. He was so inspired by the concept that on the long drive back to Hampton Roads, Virginia, he hatched a wild plan to drop out of college, which was boring him anyway. He planned to get a small business loan to start his own gas station/retail/café business. And that's exactly what he did.

"As a young guy, I thought I was sorta clever coming up with the name 'Liberty's' 'cause of the history tie-in, and my young bride was too sweet to let on that it was anything less than genius."

It was Betty who then designed Liberty's logo of a cartoon eagle wearing one of those triangular Revolutionary War hats, with a bayonet musket over his shoulder.

In the early 1990s, once Liberty's was a well-established business and Bob was in his mid-forties, he took night classes at Hampton to finally finish his history degree.

"I didn't need a degree by then, of course. But I just needed to tie up that loose end," he said, looking directly into the camera, "It's *very* important to finish things you start."

"Your grandfather seems like such a delightful man," Amelia offered when the video was over.

I tried not to wince but only partially succeeded.

"How long ago did your grandmother pass away?"

"I think I was a year old, maybe? I'm not sure. I never knew her, though."

After a minute of Amelia and I both frozen in a haze of late-night silence, I said, "I wonder how different everything would've been if she hadn't died."

We grew drowsy in the stillness, so Amelia proceeded to her bed in the back. She said "goodnight" and closed the accordion partition separating her "bedroom" from the galley.

I pulled out the bottom half of the couch between the galley and driver's seat, converting it into the flat surface "bed" mode. Thank God I remembered to buy a pillow when we were at the store earlier—it was heaven compared to my rolled-up clothes.

When I woke up around 7:30 a.m., Amelia wasn't there. The partition to her room was open, but I didn't hear her in the bathroom.

I had a momentary jab of panic that she'd changed her mind about doing the trip with me and fled in the night. I peeked around the window shade opposite my bed and was relieved to find her sitting at a picnic table next to the RV, reading. I opened the door, and she looked up.

"Good morning," she exclaimed, with more enthusiasm than I was used to from anyone, ever, in my life.

I raised my hand in bleary-eyed reply.

She stood from the picnic table, gathering her book and what looked like a notebook. "I'm glad you're up. I'm dying for a coffee, but I didn't want to wake you."

"Oh, yeah, about that…the coffee maker seems to be busted."

"Oh," she said, unperturbed as she stepped up into the RV behind me. "Tea it is, then."

I'd never had tea for breakfast. It wasn't half bad.

On the road later that morning, Amelia insisted that the RV needed a name. I suggested "Boaty McBoatface," thinking she might find the nod to something from her culture clever and amusing. She did not. But she gave it a courtesy grin before suggesting "Betsy—for Betsy Ross."

"Who's that?" I asked, even though of course I was going to go with whatever she came up with.

She couldn't believe I didn't have a clue who Betsy Ross was. I told her to get used to the disappointment. Amelia said, according to legend, Betsy Ross helped design and make the first US flag. I found it difficult to pretend I cared. But I tried to cut Amelia some slack—she was in her honeymoon phase as a first-time visitor to America.

Amelia navigated us southwest, through a sliver of Delaware, back into Maryland, skirting Washington DC, and into Virginia's rolling green hills. All these wide-open landscapes were rather alien and daunting. They were also beautiful.

Midafternoon, near the north entrance to the Blue Ridge Parkway, Amelia declared it teatime. Who was I to deprive this lovely lady of her cultural trappings? I pulled off the highway at the first convenient parking lot, where we stretched our legs outside with Amelia's tea and my snack contribution: Double Stuf Oreos. She said the Oreos weren't really teatime accurate, but she just rolled with it.

While it was annoying that taking the Blue Ridge Parkway added a whole day to the journey, it turned out to be stunning. Admittedly, I'm not a well-traveled guy, but I'd never seen anything like these views: massive hills covered with broccoli-like trees in every iteration of green, as far as I could see in any direction.

Shortly after entering North Carolina, we came across the old Bluffs Coffee Shop and Service Station that had been Bob's inspiration for Liberty's. I pulled off the Parkway to check it out, but it looked abandoned. There were no longer any gas pumps. The place was shut down, probably for COVID. It also looked like it was under renovation. Stopping there wasn't a Bob requirement, so I figured I was owed bonus points for that one.

Somewhere in the South Carolina hinterland, I tried to get Amelia to reveal her politics. She laughed politely before deflecting.

"I like what I read once that the Reagans used to say—'politics ends at six o'clock.'"

"I don't know what that's supposed to mean, but of course, of all the presidents, you'd quote Reagan."

"What's wrong with quoting Reagan?"

"I mean, I think he's like the godfather of the American Right. But other than that..."

"Well, I like Ronald Reagan. I haven't quite figured out all the nuances of your 'Left' and 'Right' here yet. I can say I've never been assaulted with politics more than when I moved to the States though. You guys need a national Xanax or something."

I grinned. "You'd get along with Bob. He loves him some Reagan."

"I've always been sort of enamored with US presidents. I read a bunch of books about them when I was younger. I used to daydream that my movie-star-handsome American dad would end up being president, and I'd get to go visit him and have my own bedroom in the White House. I went to sleep many nights when I was young, dreaming of that silly scenario. And then I saw that movie, *The American President,* which just fueled the daydreams of being that daughter in the White House, living my charmed life in the spotlight. For school, I even wrote a story about how my dad was the president of the United States and we lived together at 1600 Pennsylvania Avenue. Isn't that ridiculous?"

"No," I replied, grinning. "So, you've studied our presidents, but you're not into American politics?"

"Just a curious observer I suppose."

"That's very diplomatic of you."

"Well, I am just a foreign visitor, so it's not really my place to have a say. How did you get so into politics then?"

"That's easy—*The West Wing.* I grew up watching it with my mom. She was a huge fan. We never missed an episode. Although, looking back, I don't really know why she was so into it because she was never super political. Besides snide comments now and then about something she'd read or hear. I don't even know if she voted. I think watching *The West Wing* was her middle finger to her dad because he was so anti-Clinton when she left home. Or, maybe she just liked Rob Lowe. Mom used to say, 'America overpromises and underdelivers.' So, I guess that was the foundation of my political philosophy. I don't know, I guess she liked *The West Wing* because it was the fantasy version of American politics. But as a kid, I *believed* the fantasy and wanted to see it fulfilled. And it would be if not for all the damn obstructionist Republicans."

She smiled but didn't follow up on my comment. So, I stopped trying to pry political feelings out of her, at least for a while.

There was one positive thing to be said for this particular Liberty's store—the parking lot was enormous and even had multiple spaces reserved for RVs.

On the flip side, the store was crawling with people. And even from the parking lot I could tell there were widely varying degrees of masking. It was pretty terrifying. No wonder we were having a raging pandemic.

I didn't really want to go inside the store and expose myself to the COVID petri dish, but I had to check in with Gene Stewart, the manager, who was supposed to show me around. It was weird that Liberty's was the thing that had made Bob uber-wealthy, yet I'd never been to one of his stores before.

Amelia accompanied me inside the store. My grandmother Betty's logo of the grinning eagle in the Revolutionary triangle hat was plastered everywhere—on the signage inside and outside the store, on T-shirts, caps, mugs, keychains, beach towels, and every other conceivable clothing item and trinket. The inside of the store was kind of a cross between a 7-Eleven and Target. It was at least ten times larger than any convenience store I'd ever seen. There were all the usual drink machines and coffee and every possible bad-for-you snack on Michelle Obama's do-not-resuscitate list. And all of that was completely separate from the sit-down restaurant in the back, which looked like a cross between an In-N-Out Burger and Chili's.

This Liberty's was doing brisk business in spite of COVID. I felt uncomfortable with so many people racing around me. I hadn't been around so many people jammed together indoors since 2019. Two dudes ambled past me with nasty, hacking coughs. One wore a mask; the other didn't. People are the worst. My skin crawled with COVID fear.

Also, I spotted at least three people wearing MAGA hats, which didn't help my unease.

Manager Gene's Liberty's tour took forever—at least two hours—as he overexplained every aspect of the store's operation. I did not need to know the fine details of their industry-leading spacious and pristine restrooms, nor how Bob himself approved every recipe for their proprietary snacks. Yet, Gene provided all those details and much, much more.

Meanwhile, Amelia treated it like a behind-the-scenes tour of Disneyland. She even bought herself a baseball cap with the Liberty's eagle logo on the front. And every time Manager Gene asked whether we had any questions, Amelia actually asked a question. Later, she told me she was just asking questions to be polite since I wasn't asking any. "For future reference," I said, "don't feel obligated to do that."

On the way to our RV park for the night, I griped about how the Liberty's stop was just part of Bob's Republican-old-man way of getting me to learn the value of a dollar, sweat equity, the great American work ethic, and all that patriotic capitalist bullshit.

Amelia listened to me patiently, without saying anything. When I was done ranting, we rode quietly for a minute. Then she said, "You don't really believe that about work, do you?"

"Maybe a little hyperbole sprinkled in, but yeah, mostly. Why?"

"Because work is good. It's good *for* us. It's a gift."

"You're serious? Who sold you that? I thought Great Britain was a lot more socialist than *that*."

"It's not an economics thing. I mean, it *is*, but it's more than that. It's part of how God designed us. We're made to do work."

"If you say so." The Liberty's tour had put me in a mood. "I've never really thought about it, I guess."

"Have you ever had a job that you enjoyed?" she asked.

Crickets. I shrugged, hoping she wouldn't dig for more. "I don't guess."

"Have you ever *had* a job?"

I hesitated far too long before saying, "Yeah, I guess not really outside of school."

"You mean you've never had a proper job?"

I shook my head, then added, "Not a paid position, I guess."

Fortunately, we arrived at the RV park, with all the check-in/site hookup distractions that it entailed, so she didn't have an immediate chance to drill deeper into why I was such a jobless waste of a human being.

Later, Amelia went for a walk while I got my Bob call over with. "Did you forget about COVID?" I asked. "Because I was stuck inside for like three hours with a horde of maskless morons. I could literally die."

"Do you have some kind of preexisting condition?"

"Yeah, the condition of wanting to survive," I replied.

"You're not gonna die of COVID," he said with exasperation, "And they're not morons. We call them *customers*."

Bob went down a rabbit hole on their industry-leading customer service standards at Liberty's. I did not care. I rolled my eyes and sank into the couch.

"We're very diverse," he continued, "but we only hire US citizens. We're leading by example. If every employer in America did that, we wouldn't have this mass influx of immigrants sucking the system dry."

"Good thing you've got your Trump wall going in then, huh?"

"Well, that's just a Band-Aid on a fire hydrant."

"Very expensive Band-Aid. By the way, it's so interesting that Trump people say they're for limited government, but they want the government to pay for a massive wall to keep out the undesirables. I don't get it."

"Well, you're young. You may get it yet."

"I get this part—American whiteness is getting uncomfortably diluted, so it's time to turn off the tap, right?"

"You actually believe all that oppression stuff as the root cause of everything, don't you? Man, that must be a debilitating way to live. Here's the thing—I believe in law and order. You cannot operate a free, peaceful, orderly society if you're bending the rules all the time. I resent the immigrant who cuts in line. Let's say you've got two immigrants: One who applies for citizenship, studies for the test, checks all the legal boxes. And the other who sneaks across the border; lives under the radar; uses public facilities, roads, schools, parks, police, and fire departments; but never pays a dime in taxes. Now, you lefties are all about fairness and justice. Which one's fairer? The one going through the legal process or the one who cheats and jumps the line? Even kindergartners understand what cutting in line is: it's not fair."

"It's not fair to put the border-crossers in cages," I countered.

"Obama built those cages," he retorted. "Look, I want people to thrive. I do. Lefties don't believe that about conservatives, but it's true. I want immigrants who get in here *legally* to thrive—and by extension, America to thrive. But we're not thriving. And a big reason for that is our massive victim culture. If you want to come here, great. But you gotta dig in and be willing to do the work. The US is not a charity, although the Left is working hard to turn it into one. Several years back, I was working with this church thing that helps immigrants. I assumed these were people fresh off the boat, you know, probably in dire straits if they're showing up at a church to get free stuff. But then I start talking to this guy who was from Eritrea. You know where that is?"

"No," I replied with a rather impatient sigh.

"I didn't know either. It's in Africa. Anyway, I ask this guy how long he's been in America and he says, 'Nine years.' Now, I don't mean to be callous, but *nine years*? I'm sorry, that's more than enough time for a man to start to get on his feet. I mean, nine months I'd understand. But what the heck are you doing snatching up church charity when you've already been here nine years? You're not really a refugee anymore after nine years."

His arrogance really agitated me. I felt my neck and shoulders tightening.

"That's real easy for you to say from your ivory tower of white privilege. Your huge house with miles of ivory-colored fence around your billion acres of empty land. It's obscene for you to have all that and complain about someone just trying to get on their feet."

"Yeah, and I worked hard for every darn cent. None of this was handed to me."

"But you had a huge head start. And the contest was rigged."

"Your Marxist college teach you that? See, this is why America is slowly swirling down the toilet. Because your generation doesn't understand jack about how and why this is the greatest nation on God's green earth. And why it *might* be worth preserving."

"Here we go," I said with as much sarcasm as I could muster in my voice.

"Yep, here we *do* go. You're gonna hear this—how your *white* ancestors succeeded in *spite of* the white privilege they didn't have. My grandparents were German. They ran a successful dairy farm in Bavaria. World War I breaks out and the German government commandeers their dairy farm for the war effort. So, my granddad decides they're moving to America, where the government doesn't just take things from you. I remember, he used to say that he told my grandmother, 'Europe has gone insane. America has some sense left. Let's go there before they run out too.' So, 1914, they immigrated. Settled in Columbus, Ohio. Their last name was Uhlenbrock. But there was a lot of anti-German feeling in America at the time, so they shortened their family name to *Brock*. He and my grandmother worked in a factory six days a week. Lived in a one-bedroom slum apartment. They ate one meal a day to save every penny they could. Took every odd job after hours and on weekends. It took years, but they finally saved enough to move out of the slum and into a boarding house. They learned English. They *assimilated*. They *wanted* to become American. They were *proud* of that. They worked their way up at the factory—he became a manager, she found a secretary job at another firm. After a while, they could afford to rent a house. Then my dad was born. A few more years and they saved enough to buy a house. My dad served in the Navy in World War II. After the war, he settled in Norfolk and built ships for his career. So *that's* where I came from. If I had any kind of head start, it was only from the back-breaking work of my German grandparents, who started from *zero*, and my shipbuilder dad and schoolteacher mom who started from *almost* zero. And our immigrant family's story is not unique by the way."

"So, you begrudge immigrants the same opportunity you had. You talk about this great promise of America, but you just want it for *your* kind."

"That's your takeaway? I actually feel sorry for you, son."

It roiled me to hear him call me "son" and I almost said so, but I glimpsed Amelia out the window, returning from her walk, and I decided to try to escape the conversation.

"Seriously, if I get COVID I'm suing."

"You're not gonna get COVID. But if you do, I've got plenty of Ivermectin. I'll ship you some."

"Oh my God."

He was still laughing when we hung up.

NINE

I woke up and glanced out the window to see Amelia sitting on a bench next to our pad, looking serene and beautiful in the earliest morning light. She had a book open in her lap and her eyes were closed—maybe she was praying? I stepped out of the RV into the already humid Georgia air and sat beside her on the bench. She opened her eyes and smiled at me.

"Good morning, Tom."

I barely lifted my chin in reply.

"Did you sleep well?"

"Not really," I said, rubbing my neck.

I glanced at the book in her lap. "Some light morning reading?"

She grinned. "Not that kind of light, but it is quite illuminating. The book of Ephesians."

The Bible, I presumed. Instead of leaving it alone, I impulsively asked, "So, why Christianity? Out of the buffet of world religions, it seems to be the one that's gone bad."

"I'd have to disagree with you about that. It's always thriving somewhere. It's not like shopping for jeans or something and picking the one that fits me best. I really believe Christianity's the only true one."

"Isn't that exclusivity thing, no offense, kind of arrogant? I mean, assuming there's a God, which I don't necessarily assume, it makes more sense to me that all these faith traditions around the world are just different ways of getting to the same higher power or whatever."

"I understand that perspective. I just believe Christianity ultimately gives the best explanation for the way the world is and the greatest hope for what it will be."

I glanced away from her to cough briefly. *Better not be the first hint of Liberty's-induced COVID,* I thought.

"Then why are Christians such jerks? I mean, besides you."

"You've known a lot of Christians, have you?"

I only answered with a slight shrug. As I thought about it, I wasn't sure I knew any Christians personally, other than Amelia.

"I suppose you don't hear much from the ones quietly and faithfully following Jesus, actually loving and serving people like him," she said. "You hear the noisy fringe who are maybe more interested in winning, being right, and promoting themselves than they are with following Jesus. I *am* ashamed of the noisemakers."

Later that morning, when we were back on the road, she turned the tables and asked, "So, where are you on the spectrum of belief in God?"

"Uhhh... I don't really know. I'm not convinced," I said. "But I guess I assume that if there is a God, life is probably a kind of scale system, and you hope in the end that the good side of your scale outweighs the bad."

"You think it can, for anyone? The good outweighing the bad over a lifetime?"

"Yeah, I think so."

"I don't. I know mine wouldn't."

I glanced at her with raised eyebrows. "I find that hard to believe."

"You shouldn't. I went through quite the prodigal phase of my own."

There was that presumably British word again—*prodigal*.

"I sowed all my wild oats and then some while I was at university. I drank everything. Smoked *everything*. I slept around a lot. I used men. I let men use me. It was all totally empty and dehumanizing in the end. I hit complete rock bottom, as they say."

I was stuck on the revelation that she'd "slept around." I couldn't help wondering if that meant my own chance of scoring with Amelia wasn't as far out of the realm of possibility as I thought. I quickly snapped out of that futile reverie when a minivan zoomed past us with a Trump 2020 bumper sticker that said "Make Faith Great Again."

"I find it kind of a waste to spend time on questions of God when there's real world work to be done, so much injustice to fight," I said.

"How do you even know what justice is apart from some kind of higher power standard?" she asked. "Who says what is actually moral?"

I stared at the road ahead while I blanked on an answer. If I said basic morality was innate, she'd probably attribute it to God. Finally, I offered, "Humanity's lived experience."

"That's quite subjective, though. Sounds rather frightening. And constantly in flux."

After we'd been on the road several hours, Bob called. He had heard from Manager Gene about my friend Amelia and wanted to know (in an accusatory tone) if she was traveling with me. I considered lying for a split second before confirming that I indeed had a friend traveling with me.

"Your girlfriend?" asked Bob.

"Not exactly," I said, keeping it cryptic. Amelia gave me a curious look.

"Could you be more specific?"

"It's a female friend, but, uh … we're not romantically involved."

"Well, you're supposed to be doing this trip on your own."

"But there's nothing in the contract against it, so …" I held my breath that I was right about that (I was far from certain).

I heard some paper rustling noise on the phone.

Finally, Bob said, "I wish I'd thought to prohibit that. I mean, this violates the spirit of our agreement, but …"

"But it's not specifically in writing, so …"

"Well, how long is she going to be along for the ride?"

I lied: "I don't know."

"Shoot. Well … I don't like this one bit. But … I guess I can't technically disallow it."

"Okay then," I said.

When we'd hung up, Amelia looked at me with an expectant smile.

"Grandpa Bob's not thrilled that I have a traveling companion," I said.

"I'm certain Poppy would *not* approve of my road-tripping with you either."

"Are you gonna tell him?"

"Yes. Eventually," she laughed.

When we stopped at a roadside rest area for teatime, I decided I should probably tell Amelia the truth about my nonexistent relationship with Bob.

"If you've detected any weirdness about my relationship with my grandfather, uh … it's because there really is no relationship."

She looked at me quizzically. "What exactly does that mean?"

"It means I had never met Bob in person until about a week ago."

She looked a bit alarmed at this revelation.

"See, my mom and her father—Bob—hate each other. With a rare passion. They're completely estranged. They haven't spoken to each other my whole life, as far as I know."

Amelia studied me patiently as I took a deep breath, then a sip of my tea.

"The way I understand it, when my mom was home from college one summer, she was struggling, depressed, a lot of stuff going on. And she was drunk one night. That was a regular thing with her. She called her older sister, Christine, asking if she could come pick her up from a party because she was too wasted. Apparently, Christine bailed Mom out a lot like that back then. So, Christine goes to pick her up, and on the way home, they were in a horrible wreck—a driver crossed into their lane, hit them head-on. Christine was killed."

"Oh…that is just…"

"I know. Christine was apparently the responsible daughter. Straitlaced, never in trouble kind of thing. At least that's what Mom says. She says Christine was her dad's favorite."

"There were just the two siblings?"

"Yeah. So, Mom recovered in the hospital, wracked with guilt, of course. She's always felt responsible for Christine's death. I know it's haunted her my whole life. Bob must've blamed her too, because so much more tension developed between them. After the accident, she drank even more, trying to cope. Finally, one night, I guess all the tension and emotion just exploded, and they had this huge screaming fight. And Bob told her that the wrong daughter survived the crash."

Amelia squinted and slowly shook her head in disbelief.

"And that's when Mom walked out and turned her back on him forever. She swore she would never go back home. She'd never speak to him again. If he wished she were dead, she would, you know, make herself dead to him."

Amelia leaned back in her chair with a glum expression.

"Tom, I'm *so* sorry."

"So, then my mom roamed around out west. She was a college dropout. Got pregnant. Had me."

"What about your grandmother? Did she and your mom have a relationship?"

"That's the other shitty part. My grandmother died just a couple years after the accident. Mom always said it was probably from a broken heart because she'd basically lost both daughters. Mom always assumed that Bob probably blamed her for my grandmother's death too. My mom is stubborn as hell. So much resentment there. I mean, I guess it wasn't fair to my grandmother that Mom ran away from home, but that's the way it was."

"Wow. Your life would have been completely different, if…"

"I know. It's crazy to think about. I might not even exist."

"Now you think your grandfather is trying to make up for lost time or something by sending you on this journey?"

"Maybe? I guess. I don't know."

We polished off our tea, lost in our own thoughts about my stupid family drama.

TEN

Using her phone, I took a photo of Amelia standing in front of the *Welcome to Florida* sign. She was thrilled to be racking up visits to so many new states. Admittedly, having her along for the ride did help shift my perspective somewhat on the novelty of this peculiar road trip. These were completely new states to me too—places that seemed sort of familiar and rather foreign at the same time. I was so focused on getting this trip over with, getting that money, getting rid of the massive debt weight pinning me down, that I would've plowed past something as mundane as the *Welcome to Florida* sign if it wasn't for Amelia.

Per Bob's video, our Florida destination was somewhere near Cape Canaveral. We were to go to the home of Rosa Felix Young, whom Bob endorsed as "a remarkable, resilient woman." Apparently, she worked at Liberty's a long time ago, but that was all Bob divulged about her background because he wanted me to hear her story from her. He also hoped the timing of this leg might coincide with an actual rocket launch at the Cape. He went on a tangent about how mind-blowing an accomplishment it was for the United States to go from having virtually no space program to landing on the moon in less than a decade.

He tossed out some numbers too—how four hundred thousand Americans worked on the Apollo program and how the whole thing cost $25 billion in 1960s dollars. He said the common phrase today about how the entire command module had less computing power than the average smartphone is misleading because: "The more remarkable thing is that, at a time when computers used to fill entire rooms, they invented a powerful computer, something like seventy pounds, that fit inside the spacecraft. It took a team of three-hundred-something people to invent all the software for it too. That team was led by a woman, by the way."

Naturally, he had to toss in a generational barb about how young people today don't appreciate the marvels of space flight. I was pretty ho-hum about space stuff, honestly. I wasn't that kid with planets on my bedroom walls and spaceships dangling from the ceiling. Outer space to me mostly represented utter darkness, extreme isolation, terrifying danger, and highly probable death. Mom showed me *Apollo 13* when I was in second grade, and I had nightmares for a week about being stranded alone in space.

Bob did not provide a phone number for Rosa Felix Young, just an address. So, we awkwardly showed up at this stranger's house and rang the doorbell well after 8 p.m. The house was an incredible, two-story Spanish colonial. It was a mansion by my standards. The whole neighborhood had similar houses. The houses were all on a canal too, and each house seemed to have a boat in the back.

Rosa answered the door. She was a wiry woman, with some gray streaks in her wavy black hair that flowed past her shoulders. She was barefoot, wearing jean shorts and a red tank top. She squinted skeptically at us when she opened the door. But as soon as I introduced myself, her face brightened into an insider-knowledge kind of smile.

"Oh, yesssss," she said. "You're Mr. Bob Brock's *socialist* grandson. Yes, I've been expecting you," she added with a slightly mischievous twinkle in her eyes. She spoke with a non-American accent that somehow made me trust her, despite her semi-irritating "socialist" jab.

I forgot to introduce Amelia because, well, I'm a dummy in social situations sometimes. So, Amelia politely introduced herself. I braced for Rosa to question Amelia's presence, but she just accepted Amelia's "friend of Tom" explanation and left it at that.

Rosa was cordial, but matter of fact. "There is a rocket launch at the Cape scheduled for tomorrow. But you will have to arrive here early. Eight a.m. sharp. Because my boat will leave at 8:10 a.m. *very* sharp. Have you ever watched a rocket launch from a boat?"

As Amelia and I simultaneously answered, "No," we glanced at each other as if we needed to confirm that neither of us had ever been within a thousand miles of a rocket launch before.

"Okay, okay, well then, you will be in for a super treat."

With that, she bid us good night. And I was mega-pissed about having to wait until the morning to check this Rosa stop off the list.

We barely made it by 8 a.m. Getting Betsy Ross anywhere with relative speed was essentially impossible. As soon as Rosa greeted us at her front door again, she was ready to go. She wore white capri pants, a long-sleeve T-shirt with a US flag on the front, and a wide-brimmed visor. At the dock behind her house, she introduced us briefly to her husband, Walker, who was doing something to ready their large boat for departure.

I hate to admit it, but I assumed Walker would be our boat driver. He was not. Rosa drove. (Chalk up my bias to American systemic sexism, I guess.) In fact, once we boarded the boat with Rosa, Walker stayed on the dock to unhook the vessel, then we motored away without him. Rosa explained that Walker was working from home, "Like everyone else in America right now." She said he worked in finance. "It's very boring and over my head." She laughed.

Rosa deftly navigated us through the canal and soon to the open ocean. I'd never seen the Atlantic before, well, besides the Atlantic-connected Chesapeake Bay at Bob's house if that counts. It was unnerving to be out on the choppy, endless water, especially after Rosa ramped up the speed. But she seemed in confident, almost casual, control of the craft, chattering loudly to us as the powerful, warm, salty wind whipped through us. She spotted something ahead of the boat and pointed.

"Dolphins!" she yelled.

Rosa made a sharp right turn (toward the "starboard" side, as she pointed out) and slowed the boat. She pointed to the "port" side, and Amelia and I rushed over to the boat's railing. A pod of dolphins rocketed past us. The dolphins' effortless glide through the infinite blue was one of the most incredible things I'd ever seen. Amelia's elated reaction wasn't bad either.

"Spotting dolphins—it's a great omen of good luck," said Rosa.

"Really?" I asked.

"No," said Rosa with a teasing grin, "not really."

I enjoyed our ocean excursion so much that I almost forgot what we were doing in Florida. After maybe ten minutes of general joyriding, Rosa slowed the vessel and cut to the chase.

"Bob wanted us to meet so I can tell you my story about escaping communism," she began.

"That sounds like him," I quipped.

"He is apparently concerned about your, what's the word? *Enthusiasm* for socialism."

I smirked as I replied, "Yeah, well, I think his concern is overblown. I mean, I think he equates my socialism with communism."

"To-*may*-to, to-*mah*-to," she enunciated carefully.

She apparently had feelings about socialism.

"Here's the thing, Tom, with all due respect, of course," she continued, "socialism, you see, is the ultimate bug zapper. Have you ever seen those cage lantern things with the bright light? The light is very attractive to the bugs, and it lures them in. The light is mesmerizing, but it ends up with a deadly shock. Socialism is the gateway drug to communism."

I took issue with her people-as-bugs metaphor, but I kept quiet (for once) to be polite. Not that I could have gotten a word in anyway. She told us how she was born and raised in Cuba, under Fidel Castro's "brutal thumb," with "the kind of deprivation you can't imagine." I braced for the familiar song and verse about the bare shelves of communism, which to me implies that the chief black eye of communism is that it has the audacity to offer consumers perhaps one brand of toothpaste instead of twenty—oh, the horror! I did not share that observation out loud either.

"All the time, we were in short supply of food and other basic necessities. But the real deprivation was the deprivation of *life*. Communism deprived me of my grandfather and my brother. My grandfather worked at an underground anti-communist newspaper, and when he was caught, Che Guevara had him executed. They shot him for speaking out for freedom. So, every time I see someone wearing one of those insanely stupid Che Guevara shirts, it makes me want to vomit. They are celebrating evil that they have no clue about. Che Guevara was a mass murderer. So was Fidel Castro. They murdered over ten thousand Cubans for daring to speak out against their evil."

Rosa continued telling us her life story. How she wanted to be a doctor, but because of the association with her grandfather, there was only opportunity for her to be a nurse in Cuba. She dreamed of escaping for years.

The ocean was mesmerizing. I was listening to Rosa but kept searching the water for more dolphins as she talked.

"Did you know Fidel Castro canceled Christmas for like thirty years?"

Amelia and I shook our heads.

"I mean, a person can't really cancel Christmas. But he tried. He thought he canceled it. Who does that?" asked Rosa incredulously. "I already knew Castro was an evil man, but then he also dared to say Jesus Christ was a communist."

I looked at Amelia, gauging her reaction since she was our party's resident Jesus-expert. She listened intently to Rosa. She was a much better listener than me.

"He was serious about that. Castro truly believed Jesus was communist. In that same speech, he said Che Guevara would have become a saint if he was Catholic. I don't know when murdering people became one of the qualifications to be a saint, but Castro was serious about that too. I remember Castro said those things because it was in 2000, around the same time that my brother was killed by the regime."

Rosa stared silently at the water ahead, seemingly searching for the right words in the depth.

"My brother, Luis—he was older than me. He was only thirty-five. He was a leader in this pro-freedom, pro-reform group that was starting to grow a lot. He was already in prison a bunch of times because of leading this group. Finally, the government got too paranoid about this group. Luis was traveling to a meeting in a small town in southern Cuba and he disappeared. We never saw him again. People from that town later told our family that they saw Luis forced into a car. But Luis always took care of his family. So, many months before he disappeared, he gave me this note with an address—no names, no phone number, just one address—and said if anything ever happened to him, we should go to that address and some people will help us escape Cuba. So, I went to that address, alone at night, and found out what to do. I got my parents and Luis's wife and we escaped to Florida on a boat at night. It was terrifying and dangerous. But God protected us to get here."

Rosa said she spent most of the next decade working her way through medical school in South Carolina. She worked shifts at Liberty's for the first few years, which is how Bob became acquainted with her. She met Walker, her American husband, during her residency. Eventually, she realized her dream of becoming a pediatrician. A version of the American dream, I guess—the kind of immigrant success story Bob could get behind.

Eventually, Rosa navigated us into an area she said was the Mosquito Lagoon (which sounded oh-so-inviting). I couldn't believe how many people were gathered onshore, on piers, and in the backyards of houses. No social distancing in sight. It was like Florida had never heard of the pandemic.

After settling on her desired viewing spot, Rosa sat and offered us bottles of water from a cooler, which we gladly accepted.

"Anyways, my message to you is simple, Tom," said Rosa. "I get scared for my new country that I love when I see the young people flowing toward that false light of socialism. Because it reminds me of the young Cubans who did the same thing with Castro."

Rosa spoke with absolute conviction and her personal experience lent her credibility. But I couldn't resist the urge to get a word in for *my* conviction, mainly because I felt misunderstood.

"Rosa, one thing I just wanted to clear up is that I think what a lot of people, like Bob, do is mischaracterize the democratic socialism that I'm for. I'm not for brutal dictatorship. I'm for Scandinavian-style socialism. You know, quality government services, free healthcare. Those countries always top the list of happiest nations in the world. They're *not* communist."

Amelia interjected, which surprised me. Maybe she felt she had an ally in Rosa, or maybe she felt the need to defend her fellow Europeans. "Yes, but I might add that Scandinavian countries would not define themselves as socialist at all."

I didn't have time to react before Rosa took over again. "I think maybe your heart is in the right place that you actually want to help people. I hope you can discover that this political way you want to help only has a track record of more and more control over the lives of people. It always starts with hope and promise to help—to rescue oppressed people. But it ends up with prison bars. That is just the nature of it."

I decided there was no convincing Rosa that there was any merit to socialism. But then the thought hit me that if I had experienced what Rosa and her family endured, I'd probably refuse to find any merit in socialism too. I wasn't eager to share that mini-revelation with Bob, though, because he would probably chalk it up as a win.

Rosa tuned her boat's radio to NASA's control room broadcast. The rocket on the pad was a SpaceX satellite vehicle. The anticipation and final countdown were more nerve-racking than I expected. My old anxieties about space exploration came flooding back.

Rosa had two sets of binoculars for Amelia and I to use. There was a sudden, volcanic-sized spew of white-gray smoke that reminded me of a metastasizing kernel of popcorn. A moment later, out from behind the colossal smoke monster surged the white tip of the rocket and then the sun-like glow of the flickering fire propelling it. The sound was startlingly powerful, like a steady rumble of thunder infused with the crackle of static electricity. Rosa clapped and whooped.

I watched the rocket climb the sky, its flame trail at least as long as the rocket itself, until it became an imperceptible dot in my binoculars. I felt like I had witnessed a sort of miracle, and it was strange to pause and think that humans built a contraption that could actually escape earth.

Amelia lowered her binoculars, her face beaming with delight. "Oh Tom, didn't you have something you're supposed to read while we're here?"

"Damn, I forgot the paper again," I replied. "I remember something about *Apollo 8*."

Amelia pulled out her phone to research.

"The Christmas Eve message?" suggested Rosa. "It was broadcast all over the world."

"Yes, that's it!" said Amelia. She pulled up the transcript and handed me the phone.

"Okay, let's hear it," urged Rosa as she took a drink of her water.

"'December 24, 1968,'" I began. "'*We are now approaching lunar sunrise, and for all the people back on Earth, the crew of* Apollo 8 *has a message that we would like to send to you. In the beginning, God created the Heaven and the Earth. And the Earth was without form and void and darkness was upon the face of the deep. And the spirit of God moved upon the face of the waters and God said, let there be light. And there was light. And God saw the light, that it was good and God divided the light from the darkness. And God called the light day, and the darkness he called night. And the evening and the morning were the first day.*'"

I had no idea what this was, but from the look of reverence on Rosa's face, and the way Amelia's eyes were closed, I figured it was something biblical.

"'*And from the crew of* Apollo 8,'" I finished reading, "'*we close with good night, good luck, a Merry Christmas and God bless all of you—all of you on the good Earth.*'"

Rosa applauded as I handed the phone back to Amelia.

"My father told me that even Radio Havana carried that broadcast. He said he never understood why the Cuban government allowed it, but it happened. Some Cubans said it was an accident. But my father always thought it was God's special way of saying, 'I'm still here. I see you. And there is hope for you.'"

"Oh, I love that!" said Amelia.

I cringed inside at their reactions. I briefly wondered where my strong instinctual cynicism came from but abandoned that inquiry just as quickly because I was afraid of the answer.

Later, back onshore, we said our goodbyes to Rosa. I really liked Rosa, even if she was hostile toward my brand of socialism (and probably voted for Trump). Her maturity, wisdom, and resilience seemed out of my league. At the same time, she seemed like a person I could be neighbors with.

Rosa shook Amelia's hand, then mine.

"I hope you find your way, Tom," said Rosa, as if I was lost or something.

I kind of resented her insinuation, but I said, "Thank you," anyway.

ELEVEN

We didn't know where we were headed next, but rather than linger outside Rosa's house in the RV, we drove until we came across a Publix grocery store parking lot with room enough to accommodate Betsy Ross for a while.

It was early afternoon, but since I usually did my follow-up calls to Bob at night, I decided to switch it up and try him right away. Maybe I would catch him in a better mood.

I caught him in a different mood alright, but not what I'd hoped for.

"Did you see the rocket launch?" Bob answered the phone without saying hello.

"I did," I replied, stepping out of the RV. Amelia followed me out, motioning that she was heading inside the store.

"And?"

"It was incredible."

He laughed with what seemed like genuine delight. "Well, I wish I could've been there to see that. Heckuva lot better view than I'm staring at right now."

"What do you mean?"

"I'm back at the hospital today. My chemo is starting back up."

I was momentarily tongue-tied because he'd never mentioned anything about cancer. When I was at his house, he seemed a bit creaky maybe, but mostly fine. I leaned my back against Betsy.

"What, uh...'starting back up'?"

"I had a tumor a couple years back. They seemed to have pretty well zapped it, but now it's back, and it's getting big apparently. So I'm on chemo again for a while."

"Sorry to hear that." And I *was* sorry, although I didn't know what else to say about it.

"Me too. So, what'd you think of Rosa?" he asked, quickly changing the subject.

"She's, uh...she's an interesting person."

He laughed harder than I thought my observation merited, which then brought out my sarcasm. "She totally converted me," I continued. "I denounced socialism. I'm all-in on conservatism now."

There was a brief pause on the line before Bob asked, "Really?"

"No."

"Somehow, I think you're a bigger smartass than your mom was."

I didn't appreciate that—as if he really knew Mom.

"So how's Florida?" he asked. "Is it the coronavirus hellscape that the media claims it is?"

People milling about the grocery store parking lot were a total mix of masked and unmasked. If that parking lot was all you knew about the state of the world, you'd never know there was a pandemic wreaking global havoc.

"I mean, I don't really feel safe down here. It's like they're pretending COVID's not a thing."

"Good for them. You gotta live life. What is it with your generation and needing safe spaces, and words are violence, and all that? It's nuts. I even saw something recently called 'eco-anxiety.' Young people who are deathly afraid of climate change disaster claim to have this now. Psychologists are diagnosing it."

"You can make fun of it all you want, but it's a real thing."

"What, eco-anxiety or climate change?"

"Both."

119

"Come on, you're one of these climate change nuts too? Well, I guess you couldn't much help it growing up on the Left coast."

"And you're one of these climate change denier nuts?"

"Oh, I don't deny the climate might be changing some. Just like it *always* has since the dawn of time. I just deny this notion that we've got to dismantle every aspect of our way of life, including reliable energy, to save the planet. This overhyped climate crap is mostly driven by Far-Left globalists who are all about control."

"Or maybe they're smart people who actually follow the science and just want to save your ass from getting fried. It's people like you who have caused our government to drag its feet, so now, we're way behind a very real existential threat."

"You honestly believe all that AOC garbage that 'this is our World War II,' and if we don't get a Green New Deal, we're all gonna die in five years?"

His defiant ignorance was about to make me explode.

"She's not making up the facts! There's like a million species threatened with extinction because of humans. CO2 levels at their highest point for three million years. Something like a quarter million deaths per year from climate change. Record high temperatures from greenhouse gas emissions. More extreme storms. Droughts. Wildfires. Have you ever witnessed a California wildfire? Because I have. These are all very real things. Why would you deny it?" I picked up steam and talked even faster. "And Trump is burying government reports on climate change. He dropped us from the Paris Agreement. Rewards all the greenhouse-gas-producing industries. So, yeah, eco-anxiety is most definitely a thing. I don't know why anyone would even think about having kids now. It's cruelty."

After a condescending chuckle, he said, "Okay, simmer down there, Captain Greenpeace. I get it, you're a passionate climate guy."

"And for the record, it kinda sucks that you've got me driving across America in this carbon-spewing coffin. It takes like fifty barrels of oil a day to run this thing. It's shaving a year off the planet by itself."

He chuckled *again. Was he actually enjoying this?* "Climate change hysteria is just a money-making racket. Green is just the new gold rush," he said.

I was fuming after our phone call. I paced outside while I had a cigarette, trying to chill out somewhat. As I paced, I saw Amelia emerge from the grocery store, with a plastic bag in hand. I watched her curiously as she approached a young man (he looked like a teenager) who was apparently the store's shopping cart wrangler. The kid had an obvious and terrible limp, his arms and legs clearly deformed. He was struggling to get a long train of carts unstuck from their parking lot stall. Amelia walked over to him, talked for a moment, then proceeded to help him untangle the carts and get the train headed in the right direction. After her help, the kid kept smiling and nodding at her, evidently thanking her. Then he wobbled away with his awful limp, nudging the cart train toward the store.

I put out my cigarette, marveling at her kindness. Dozens of people had raced past that kid in the parking lot without noticing him. I would've been one of them. Maybe he didn't actually need Amelia's help, but she offered anyway. She *saw* him.

I reluctantly cued up the next video installment of Bob's propaganda. Onscreen, Bob sat on the outdoor couch on his back patio, his right foot perched on his left knee.

"Booker T. Washington is one of my favorite Americans of all-time," he said.

Poor Booker T., I thought. I knew virtually nothing about him, but Bob declaring his fanboy love for Booker automatically made me not want to like him.

Bob rambled an extra-long time to the camera. He said most Americans don't know enough about Booker T. Washington, even though he was a civil rights leader on par with Martin Luther King, Jr. (I was even more skeptical after a claim like that). Bob talked about Booker T. being born into slavery, his hardships in West Virginia after the Civil War, working as a child in a coal mine, and barely scraping by just to get a shot at attending the Hampton Institute in Virginia. Bob found inspiration in the lifelong friendship between Booker T. and Hampton's president, Samuel C. Armstrong—a former Union general. Armstrong recommended Booker T. as the man to head up the new Tuskegee Institute in Alabama and helped him with fundraising efforts. According to Bob, Tuskegee grew from thirty to four hundred students in just seven years.

"All these talking heads in the media who think America is irredeemably racist clearly don't know about the friendship between Booker T. Washington and Samuel Armstrong," said Bob.

He claimed that Booker T. Washington and W. E. B. DuBois were contrasting examples of modern American paths—Booker T.'s approach being the "glass-half-full path," according to Bob.

"He wasn't willfully ignorant of America's racist streak. He lived right in the middle of it! He had multiple death threats—sometimes he even had to travel with bodyguards—but he chose to plow ahead, without giving up on America. Know what happened to DuBois?" he asked into the camera. "He got so bitter and angry at America, at the very free market system that gave him all his material success in life, that he died in a third-world country in Africa. He sold out to communism. The Soviet Union even gave him an award. And guess what? There are no national parks in America with DuBois's name on them."

"I don't think an old white guy from Virginia is in any position to project the experiences of Washington and DuBois onto 2020 America," I retorted at the screen. "America is just as racist today as when those guys were alive."

I glanced at Amelia for moral support, but she just kept watching the TV as Bob finally announced that we were headed to the Tuskegee Institute National Historic Site in Alabama.

When the video session finally ended, I shook my head incredulously. Amelia finished the last bite of her sandwich then exclaimed, "Wow, he sounds so inspirational!"

"Who, Bob?"

"Well, Bob too, I suppose, but I mean Booker T. Washington."

"You are..." I grinned and looked at the floor while my mind scanned for the right word. "...remarkably *polite*."

"You don't find his story inspirational?"

"I think Bob is a historical cherry picker. He can't handle the whole racist, oppressive, horror-show reality of American history, so he carefully selects the things that support *his* American exceptionalism worldview. Sounds like Booker T. was probably an acceptable black guy to Bob, one who knew how to mind his p's and q's and play by the white man's rules. Bob would've been one of the guys just writing a check, patting Booker on the head, and sending him back down to Dixieland."

She took a drink from her water bottle and glanced out the window for a moment.

"That's quite cynical of you, Tom. You know..." she paused again and pressed her lips tightly together, like she was hesitant to finish her thought. Finally, she said, "There *is* the possibility that Bob is telling you the truth, and that he is simply trying to offer you a different perspective. We could all use a bit of that, no?"

"What you're on Bob's side here?"

"I'm not on a *side*. I'm an impartial, curious observer of America. And by the way, I've observed that if Bob is an historical 'cherry picker' as you say, well, you might be one too. Except you seem to pick all the cherries that support *your* worldview that America is the evil empire."

"You don't have to search hard for those."

"I'm not sure America is so disproportionately bad. I think it might just be an accurate reflection of humanity. You know, deeply flawed *and* full of potential at the same time."

I never enjoyed the feeling of getting put in my place. And she did it so *kindly*—which was somehow better *and* worse.

We stopped at a gas station in the Florida panhandle for another expensive refueling. As much as I loved being around Amelia, I wasn't in the mood for teatime. I was still fired up over Bob harassing me about climate change. But Amelia made an excellent cup of tea, and she'd purchased a package of some kind of chocolate "biscuits" (as she adoringly called them), which I'd never had before. So, I joined her at the table and vented my beef with Bob's flippancy about our global climate emergency.

Amelia calmly sipped her tea and took small bites of her biscuit as she patiently listened to my rant. I soon realized I couldn't tell whether Amelia agreed with my climate stance, and I desperately craved her validation. Surely an enlightened, young, intelligent European like her would share my conviction on this issue.

"You know this requires drastic, worldwide coordination, on a World War II–like level, right? And that's not even to turn the tide of climate change, that's just the bare minimum required to *survive* it."

I grew uncomfortable in her quiet pensiveness.

"I don't know," she offered, as ordinarily as if I'd asked her what she felt like having for dinner.

"What do you mean you don't know?"

"Well, I can see you're quite passionate about the climate, and I can appreciate that, but I honestly don't know, because it's not my area of expertise."

I set down my mug and leaned back in my chair, a little stunned.

"This is an all-hands-on-deck emergency. You don't have to be an expert to see that."

"Here's what I *do* know: that this world is wasting away, and perhaps climate change, global warming—I think it's probably part of the groaning of creation that scripture talks about. It's part of creation longing to be set right by the return of Jesus."

I didn't know what the hell she was talking about.

"You can read it in Romans, chapter eight. But it's not creation groaning like it's totally dying—it's groaning like birth pains. Yes, perhaps all the climate groaning is the world in the process of ending. But it's an ending to give way to a new, even more amazing, more beautiful, more perfect world. Jesus said, 'Behold, I am making all things new.'"

I wondered how I'd managed to pick up what had to be the one and only genuine Jesus freak from the entire island of Great Britain. Sometimes I wondered if she spent her days back home hanging out on street corners, thumping her Bible, and wearing one of those sandwich boards that says "Repent, the End is near."

"Must be nice to have it all figured out," I said, like a jerk.

"I do *not* have it all figured out."

I felt bad for my snarky comment. She had been nothing but nice to me—why would I demean her with sarcasm like that? Honestly, part of it was my own insecurity. Plus the fact that my mouth had always gotten me in trouble. When I was a kid, I'd mouth off to Mom about something and she'd start scolding me for it. Then, in the middle of letting me have it, she'd catch herself and say she was being too much like her dad. She'd get very quiet, and I'd feel bad for a while about pissing her off. Eventually, I would apologize. Then not long after, I'd shoot off my big mouth again. I couldn't help myself.

"I'm sorry."

"For what?" asked Amelia.

"For my sarcastic comment."

"Oh, forget it. I'm sorry if I made it seem like I think I have all the answers."

I glanced at my red arms because it was rapidly sinking in that I was very sunburned.

"In other news, I am turning into a lobster."

"It appears so," she said. "I really should have recommended sunscreen."

We finished our tea and biscuits and made our way back onto the interstate. We had a long road ahead of us.

TWELVE

Fortunately, we found ourselves on the Tuskegee University campus after hours on a Wednesday evening, so there were few people around. Between COVID and it being summertime, there was barely a student in sight.

I turned left off Booker T. Washington Boulevard and stopped Betsy Ross in a semi-circle drive behind a statue that was on my to-do list. I left the RV running while Amelia and I hopped out to investigate the gray-green monument. A bowtie-wearing Booker T. Washington stood, gazing into the distance, his left hand outstretched, palm up, as if offering something. His right hand removed some kind of cloak from covering the face of a shirtless African American man who seemed to be rising from a crouched position, his left hand clutching a book. I thought it was kind of dynamic, powerful imagery. I didn't know enough about Booker T. to know if I liked him, but I really liked his statue. The words engraved at the base of the statue read:

> "Booker T. Washington 1856–1915. He lifted the veil of ignorance from his people and pointed the way to progress through education and industry."

I hopped back into the RV to turn it off and decided to risk leaving it parked where it was while we meandered through campus until we found Booker T. Washington's beautiful brick house called "The Oaks." There, on the sidewalk, I read the excerpts Bob had selected from Booker T.'s autobiography *Up from Slavery*:

"'I have learned that success is to be measured not so much by the position that one has reached in life as by the obstacles which he has overcome while trying to succeed.'"

I glanced at Amelia and could tell by her eyes she was smiling behind her mask. I continued with the next quote:

"'I have begun everything with the idea that I could succeed, and I never had much patience with the multitudes of people who are always ready to explain why one cannot succeed.'"

Several retorts flooded my mind, not least of which was the thought that that quote could just as easily have come from Bob Brock. But I restrained myself because Amelia actually listened with interest to Bob's selected quotes, and I still wanted her to like me.

I read the final quote:

"'If no other consideration had convinced me of the value of the Christian life, the Christlike work which the Church of all denominations in America has done during the last thirty-five years for the elevation of the black man would have made me a Christian.'"

Amelia closed her eyes and nodded with sincere approval.

She pulled out her phone, and I was close enough to her that I could see her add *Up from Slavery* to a reading list.

I really pissed off Bob by saying it seemed like he was going out of his way to convince me he's not racist by bragging so much about

Booker T. Washington. I could practically hear Bob building up steam over the phone.

"You see, that just shows how much this critical race theory crap has trained your generation to look for racism under every rock. You can't even entertain the possibility that I could honestly admire Booker T. Washington as a genuine American hero apart from some racial motivation."

"It seems a little convenient."

"How's that?"

"Well, your civil rights hero just happens to be a guy who seems to line up with your conservative flexing. You know, another mythical tale of pulling yourself up by your bootstraps."

"You're way too young to be this cynical. You're missing the point—Booker T. Washington *refused* to be a victim. Even though he had *way* more reason to claim victimhood than pretty much anyone alive in America today. And *that* is heroic." The tension suddenly left his voice as he continued. "He believed that America was good—that our founding was fundamentally good. I just wish you could see that too."

"*Was* the founding good? White, male, slaveholding elites, keeping every other color down, slaughtering Native Americans."

"There you go again. You are *enslaved* by this race narrative. It's a brilliant strategy by the Left, I guess. Pulling the race card every time shuts down debate, makes it unwinnable."

"But why do you need to win it?" I asked, feeling clever. "That's your white patriarchy shining through."

"Look, the Bible says God examines man's heart. And that's what I believe. So, color is ultimately irrelevant. I'll be darned if I'm going to be told that everything in my life flows from some kind of white supremacy. Believing in inherent racism is just as evil a lie as believing a person is inherently inferior because of their skin color."

I tried to formulate a sharp rebuttal, but I took too long.

"And by the way, homogeneous people groups all over the world are quite normal. Diversity is *not* a virtue—it's just reality, a fact of life, a pillar of God's creation. These days I guess mostly you see what you want to see in America."

I let his last statement sink in for a moment and was startled that I mostly agreed.

"Yeah, I guess that's pretty much true," I muttered.

"Well, how's the RV holding up?"

Bob's ability to sometimes turn on a dime from contentious to mundane in our phone chats was odd. I was still distracted by wanting to prove to this old-timer how messed up America's racism is and he's moving on to regular stuff.

"Fine, I guess."

"No problems?"

"I don't think so."

"Good. Well, don't forget to check the oil."

"Yeah, of course," I said, even though I had no clue how to check the oil or why that's even a thing.

After my call, I think Amelia could tell it had put me in a mood, so she gave me space. We stopped for the night at an RV park near some lake in Alabama not far from Tuskegee. I went for a walk by myself, but it was hot, even after eight o'clock at night, and the air was suffocating. Southern air was the worst—that's what I'd gleaned from this trip so far, that I'd never want to live in the South. The heat actually made my mood a little worse, so I returned to Betsy Ross and the prospect of a cold beverage. Then I snapped open the fridge and muttered, "Damn it," when I discovered I was out of Yoohoo.

"Wanna play Dutch Blitz?" asked Amelia, looking up from her book on the couch.

I didn't know what that was and had zero desire to find out. But she asked with a sweet smile, and I think her offer was an attempt to draw me out of my funk.

"What's Dutch Blitz?" I asked half-heartedly.

"It's a card game. Come on, I'll teach you."

She moved from the couch to her makeshift bedroom in the back and returned with a box of cards. She sat at the table and began shuffling the cards. I sighed deeply and finally joined her.

Amelia's Dutch Blitz therapy eventually worked. We laughed for over an hour, and the game was pretty okay too. How had I possibly lucked into meeting this unusual woman? I wasn't usually so lucky.

The next morning, I awoke earlier than usual. I glanced out my bedside window and, like clockwork, saw Amelia at a picnic table, her Bible and journal open in front of her. Her eyes were closed and her brow slightly furrowed. I watched her for a moment as she turned her palms skyward and then rested her hands on the table in front of her, palms still facing up. I turned from the window and shook my head. She was different alright.

Pressing play on the VCR, I felt a heavy surge of anxiety about my debts, the credit cards, my dwindling funds to get through this quest. I caught myself, rolled my neck and shoulders a few times, and tried to take some deep breaths. I didn't want Amelia to see me have a panic attack.

Onscreen, Bob deadpanned, "So, next you're heading to Tennessee, to the birthplace of the inventor of the internet—Al Gore."

Bob giggled softly at his own lame joke. I just shook my head and yawned.

The *actual* next task was another example of why I was starting to dread Bob's video installments. I had to drive somewhere in

Tennessee, outside Nashville, to meet another one of Bob's pals. Some guy named Ferguson Hill.

I ripped the tape out of the VCR and was about to toss it on the table in frustration but stopped myself just in time (I couldn't risk breaking the treasure map). Then I slumped onto the couch and fumed.

I was pissed that he wanted me to stop off to visit friends of his. He never mentioned that aspect of the trip when I signed the agreement—only that I had to follow each and every one of his dumb video instructions.

Once we got on the road, moving north through Alabama toward Tennessee, my cloudy mood began to clear up somewhat. I was helped along by Amelia's camaraderie. We whiled away many miles chatting about music. At one point, I suggested we confess our musical guilty pleasures. Without hesitation, she admitted, "Richard Marx." It appalled her that I didn't know who he was, so she played me a couple samples of his hits and I conceded they sounded vaguely familiar.

My guilty pleasure admission was Carly Rae Jepsen and Amelia didn't believe me.

"That's way too peppy even for your *guilty pleasure.*"

"What? I can be *peppy,*" I protested.

"But can you?" she teased.

"The music of my childhood was mostly my mom's music— Nirvana, Alanis Morrisette, Foo Fighters, Eminem—so my pep never had much of a chance to develop."

"Your pep was stunted. How tragic."

We continued down the music rabbit hole until our minds were blown when we landed on a guilty pleasure we had in common: Canadian rocker Bryan Adams. I said I hadn't listened to him since he got canceled. Amelia had no knowledge of his cancelation because she's not on Twitter. She didn't want to know about it, and I couldn't remember the particulars anyway.

We listened to vintage Bryan Adams for the rest of the day's drive, badly belting out the choruses together.

As I drove across the Tennessee state line, for some reason I remembered my thesis project play. I hadn't touched it or even thought about it in the week or so since I left Bob's house. Stress suddenly tensed my body because I hadn't made a shred of progress on the play. I didn't even have any good ideas for advancing Act Two. I was never going to get it done.

I also realized I hadn't thought about suicide since starting the journey. I sort of felt like thanking God, but that felt wonky, because I didn't know God, or even if he is real. And that made me mad at God a little, if he's there, because why would he make himself hard to be known? Still, I felt less suicide-curious than I'd felt in a long time, and I mostly attributed that to hanging out with Amelia.

I glanced over at her, asleep in the early afternoon sun. I grinned, thinking about how we'd settled into a comfortable routine. I wondered if this is what it was like to be married. Without the sleeping together part of the equation, of course. I was still utterly attracted to her, but already respected her enough to be okay with the fact that that was off the table. Sometimes things felt a little flirty between us and my hopes would escalate fleetingly, but mostly we were just easy friends. At least I hoped we were genuine friends by now. I hoped she wasn't simply faking friendship due to the fact that this was ultimately a financial arrangement. It was depressing reminding myself that she was probably only with me because of my promise to pay for graduate school and buy her a new car. The reality is I'm a pretty sucky human—of course it would take a deal like that to get someone to hang out with me so closely for so long. I don't know anyone who would volunteer to do it otherwise.

Also, I'm pretty good at messing up a good thing. For example, after Amelia awoke from her short nap, I guess the boredom of the road was getting to me, so I tried to engage her with my latest argument with Bob. I railed against racist policing in America and how we need reparations payments to start making amends for our systemic injustices. She listened to my mini rants but mostly stared ahead at the droning interstate. I was slightly annoyed by how she seemed so dispassionate about politics in general.

Then, because I'm a moron and can't control my mouth, I remarked, "Wow, you're actually kind of boring, aren't you?"

I instantly regretted saying it when I detected a flash of hurt in her eyes.

She shrugged mildly and replied, "I'm quite comfortable with boring."

"Silence on these issues is complicity."

"Not always. Sometimes, silence is wisdom."

"But you've gotta have opinions on these things. They're important."

"Are you sure you want my opinion?"

"Yes!" I said a little too loudly. "I really do!"

"Okay, well, I think you just want me to agree with you."

"You don't have to agree with me," I protested.

"There's much more to life than politics. That's what I think. Everything's not an outrage. Every single issue in life doesn't require pithy hot takes. It seems being right is extremely important to you. I want to love mercy more than being right."

"You can't just be apolitical during such critical times though."

"I'm not. It's just that politics isn't my religion."

"Fine, okay. But where *do* you stand on the Left–Right spectrum?"

"See? You simply must know whether I'm on *your* side."

"Yeah, basically!"

"But it shouldn't matter so much, should it?"

"I think it should when this much is at stake."

She sighed and stared ahead for a moment, before seeming to cave to my pressure.

"Look...basically I'm for human freedom. And from what I know about it, I'm pro-US Constitution because it has allowed perhaps the best chance on earth for human flourishing and, most importantly, for the spread of Christianity."

I raised my eyebrows. "That's uh...a unique take. You're pro-Constitution even though it was written by racist slave owners who rigged the rules to make sure they stayed rich and in charge?"

"That's what you believe about it?"

"Yeah, because that's what happened," I said forcefully.

"Well, I have done *some* reading on this, and I recall that not all the signers of the Constitution were slave owners. Is there no merit in creating a system that at least led to the demise of slavery?"

"They could've ended it right away, but they didn't."

"'He who is without sin, cast the first stone.'"

I assumed she was quoting someone. "Let me guess—Benjamin Franklin?"

"Jesus Christ, actually."

"I can't believe I'm being lectured on the merits of the US Constitution by a British person."

"What do you mean? You were begging for it! I just don't find it constructive to denigrate and obsess over leaders of the past and their mistakes. We're all in the same boat—'all have sinned and fall short of the glory of God,' according to the New Testament. We ask forgiveness and move on."

"It's that easy, huh?"

"I'm not saying it's easy."

We both watched the road ahead for a minute. A semitrailer truck roared past us in the left lane.

"It's interesting," she continued after the roar of the truck subsided, "I think you and your grandfather are actually a lot alike."

I sort of grunted in protest and shot her an incredulous look.

"No. We're *not*," I said emphatically.

"Yes, you're both caught up in this parallel universe, this social media, hyper-political world that is divorced from the reality of most regular people's daily lives. Most people are primarily occupied with making a living, paying their bills, taking care of their family, and if they have time, catching the football match at the weekend."

"I wish things were that simple."

I felt bad for agitating her because she was so pleasant and kind. She was also naïve.

THIRTEEN

I rang the doorbell, and Ferguson Hill very promptly opened the door.

Bob did not mention that Ferguson Hill was African American. I shuddered at my own inadvertent racism for expecting Ferguson to be a white dude based simply on the fact that we pulled up to a brick mansion in a swank neighborhood in Brentwood, Tennessee. What's wrong with me? I really hoped my assumption was cultural indoctrination and not an inherent part of my whiteness, because that would mean there's still hope for me.

Ferguson was slightly taller than me, with a slight potbelly. He had a mostly gray mustache and goatee. He wore a striped, navy-blue polo tucked into jeans, complete with Allbirds sneakers.

"Good afternoon," he said with a booming voice and gregarious smile.

I introduced myself and Amelia, and he shook hands with us. Apparently, even some African Americans in red states perpetuated the pandemic handshake.

"Ah, yes, yes, welcome!" he said. "Please, come on in."

He held the door open for us as we stepped inside his posh, cavernous living room.

"Y'all feel free to take off your masks. Whatever makes you feel comfortable, of course. I just don't want you to feel like you have to wear them on account of me being a vulnerable old man. Old-*ish* man at least," he laughed—his laughter was booming, too, and contagious.

Amelia removed her mask and stuffed it in her shorts pocket. I hesitated a moment longer than she did. I honestly preferred she be my partner in protesting these maskless suicidal Southerners, but I relented to peer pressure and removed mine too.

"Please, have a seat," Ferguson urged.

We sat on a plush gray sofa while he sank into a nearby wingback armchair.

"So," he said with a grin as he looked me in the eye, "Bob tells me you're an aspiring communist."

"Uhhh…" I started, knocked off guard by the accusation (even though his tone was playful). "That's not exactly how I would describe myself. But I'm not surprised Bob would say that."

Ferguson laughed his loud laugh and leaned forward a bit as he said, "It's okay. I used to be one too…until I saw the light."

He spent a good half hour just asking us questions, without talking about himself. He asked me all about my background, college, and graduate school. He seemed extra inquisitive toward Amelia because she was from Britain. After his interview of us had been going for quite a while, I began to wonder what we were doing there. Ferguson seemed like a nice enough guy, but I wanted to move things along and wasn't sure how. I was grateful for Amelia's genius when she finally asked him, "So, how do you know Bob?"

Before answering, he asked if we wanted some lemonade. We said yes, though I followed Amelia's lead because honestly, I could've skipped it. He invited us to follow him into the kitchen where he made three tall glasses of icy lemonade and then suggested we enjoy it on the veranda. He apologized for the absence of his wife Laura, whom he called his "superior officer—superior in *every* way." He explained Laura has three sisters and they were on their annual girls-only trip to Sedona, Arizona. "They're doing spa stuff, and round-the-clock shopping, and all kinds of mischief. Thank the Lord I'm not there," he added with his signature laugh.

We followed him through a sliding glass door into his giant backyard, landscaped to the hilt and featuring a large, uniquely shaped swimming pool. We sat at a round patio table, shaded by the veranda's awning.

"How do you like my swimming pool? Bet you've never seen a pool shaped like a hamburger!" he guffawed.

I confirmed it was indeed my first.

He went on to explain that his hamburger-shaped pool is an homage to the regional burger restaurant chain that he started in 1990, as "Ferguson's Hamburger House." Later, as they expanded, he shortened it to "Ferguson's."

He explained that, like Bob, he got drafted and served in Vietnam, though he and Bob did not meet each other in the military. Ferguson was a career Army man until he retired in 1988, "Still young enough to get a life," he joked. That's when he started working on his actual life's ambition, starting a business: his Ferguson's burger chain. He first met Bob at an entrepreneurial conference, "in Memphis," he recalled, and the pair became fast friends. He said he was just getting his business off the ground at the time, while Bob was in major expansion mode with Liberty's. Bob mentored him.

"But more than that, we were just buddies. We had the same dumb sense of humor. We commiserated about Vietnam. We just clicked and stayed close friends for thirty years," he said.

Internally I groaned because the visit started to make sense. This was Bob flexing on me that he had a black friend.

"Anyway, three years ago, we sold Ferguson's for a pretty penny, and now we run the Ferguson Foundation. Having the time of my life!"

He took a long sip of his lemonade, squinting with satisfaction. "In America, if you can dream it, you can try to achieve it," he marveled. "The *try* part is key, see, and that's the part young people don't understand as well now. We're not guaranteed the dream, only the *try*. The American birthright is not success. The birthright is the freedom to try."

"You believe everyone has the freedom to *try*?" I asked.

"Yessir, I truly do. With all due respect, the fact that you even ask the question shows the success of the whole progressive mindset that permeates the Left. They've convinced a few generations that you cannot try because you're oppressed sixty different ways to Sunday. Therefore, trust in papa bear government to fight the bad guys who are keeping you down and also care for you, cradle to grave."

I needed to change the subject somehow. I wondered how the hell someone like Ferguson gets brainwashed by Republicanism.

He grinned at me. "I've seen that look before on students' faces. They wonder how a guy like me, with my pedigree, with my *skin color* let's be honest, pulls the switch and starts rumbling down the conservative track."

I shrugged and nodded. My guess was that he was seduced by his money and success, which granted him the golden ticket into the Republican cult. But I didn't say so out loud.

"Well, let me back up a minute. I was young and angry in the early sixties. I rode the buses to Alabama. Did the marches. Did the sit-ins. I got arrested, spent nights in jail down there, the whole thing. I was so impatient for justice. Dr. King's love and nonviolence approach was wearing my patience thin. I wanted to believe in it, but it was a slow, painful strategy. So, I started veering radical. The Black Panthers started to sound pretty good to me, and Malcolm X started appealing to me. And then I got drafted, and I was livid. The audacity of this nation, a nation that was turning water hoses and German shepherds on kids like me, to now want to send me across the globe to fight *their* war of ideology? No sir, no way. I wasn't having it! So, I was on the verge of being a draft dodger, ditching my papers and going down the radical road a hundred percent."

He took another long draw on his lemonade.

"By God's good grace though, I had an older cousin, Charles, rest his soul. He and I were just like brothers, lived under the same roof most of our growing-up years. He'd already been drafted, been through basic. He was Navy. And he was home one night just for a brief visit, and I was going on and on, telling him my plan to ditch the draft, head to Canada, and all this nonsense. And he slapped me across the face to get my attention. Literally slapped me. And Charles was a big guy. It *hurt*! He said if I ran, I'd always regret it, that it'd ruin my life. He said I'd get caught and go to prison, and even if I got away and started running with radicals, that would eventually get me killed. Boy, I was mad. That's not at all what I wanted to hear. That was a long night of arguing. But he convinced me in the end.

"You've never seen an angrier soldier than I was. I *hated* Vietnam with a burning passion, and I hated the Army. But then, very, very slowly, God got a hold of me in that grimy jungle. He started melting down my anger bit by bit so he could make something new out of it. Somehow, by some miracle, I hung in there. I started reading a lot during my downtime. Now that's a dangerous activity, reading. That will start changing your life one way or another," he laughed. "Eventually Charles sent me a book by this professor named Thomas Sowell. I'd never heard of him. Brilliant economics professor who happened to be black. And that was the beginning of the end of my flirting with any radical, anti-American, anti-Constitutional politics. I mean, you crack open your mind to a Thomas

Sowell essay, and you're not pulling the lever for a Democrat ever again. No going back after that!" He laughed heartily.

Amelia laughed too, and I couldn't help but join them, even though I'd never heard of Thomas Sowell.

"Anyway, it's getting hot out here. Y'all want to go see the foundation?"

I wasn't sure we had a choice. Bob hadn't indicated how long we were required to meet with Mr. Hill.

"Come on, I'll show you around. It's fully air-conditioned," Ferguson assured us as he pushed back his chair from the table.

Ferguson drove us in his Cadillac sedan, with me riding shotgun and Amelia in the back seat. He casually talked as he drove, seemingly without a care in the world. I glanced at Amelia periodically and she never stopped smiling, apparently relishing Ferguson's musings.

"You want to understand the difference between our main political philosophies?" he asked rhetorically as we drove under a freeway sign pointing toward Nashville. "Here's what it is in a nutshell. A conservative says, 'If it ain't broke, don't fix it.' A progressive says, 'If it ain't broke, fix it anyway.' And a libertarian says, 'Whether it's broke or not, smoke dope.'"

Ferguson erupted in laughter for the hundredth time that afternoon.

The Ferguson Foundation was an old elementary school that the Hills bought and repurposed. The remodel wasn't exactly luxurious, but it was nice, bright, and clean both inside and out—a solid place to hang out. I was surprised by how many people, mostly young adults, were there. At least they were all wearing masks. I was also pleasantly surprised that Ferguson donned his mask too when we first entered the building.

"We're limiting our inside capacity right now. Trying to follow all the safety protocols, you know. Doing as many activities as we can outside. But this place is a lifeline for a lot of people. It's a real community hub, so shutting down entirely was never an option. But we're getting through, doing the best we can like everyone else on the planet, I guess."

Everyone that passed Ferguson in the hallway or glimpsed him from inside a room greeted him with, "Hey, Mr. Hill," or some variation, but always with "Mr. Hill." Impressively, he knew every person's name. In between greetings, he explained the array of programs at the foundation. Essentially, it was a career development resource center with a focus on entrepreneurship and mentorship. There was a library and computer center, and they hosted regular classes and seminars.

"Truth is, we've all got something to learn all the time," he explained as we walked the halls. "We've just got to have the humility to realize it and then do what we can to bridge that knowledge gap. And that means we're probably going to need some help along the way. We're just trying to offer a little boost here."

Quotes were painted on the walls throughout the building. Some of the quoted individuals seemed an odd fit for a foundation catering to inner-city African Americans, like one from Dwight D. Eisenhower that read: *"A people that values its privileges above its principles soon loses both."*

Ferguson paused in front of the large US flag that faced the main entrance. He slowly looked the flag over and said, "We teach the truth here: America only guarantees opportunity, not success. Equal opportunity, but not equal outcome. That's still going to require elbow grease, and even that might not be enough for the kind of success you dream for yourself."

He shifted his gaze from the flag to Amelia and me.

"People want the outcome without the elbow grease, but that's never how America has worked, and that was never the promise. No clear-minded immigrant ever came here and expected a free ride."

The rapturous look in Amelia's eyes told me she was inspired (as usual). I didn't really know what to think. I'd never met a guy like Ferguson. I'm pretty sure I disagreed with his politics, but he was less bitchy about it than Bob, which made his takes somewhat easier to tolerate. I liked Ferguson, but my cynical side felt he simply got seduced by the white Republican game and wanted a piece of that action himself, so he sold out his own people and got his. Maybe I don't just have a cynical *side*—maybe I'm *wholly* cynical.

On the drive back to Ferguson's house, he told us that Bob was the foundation's top donor every year since they began operation.

"He wouldn't approve me telling you that," he said. "But it's true and I wanted you to know it. Your grandfather is a very generous man."

I didn't know what to say to that. *If he was so generous*, I thought, *why didn't I ever get a birthday card with a fat check?* Instead, I asked Ferguson if he shared Bob's opinion that "diversity is not a virtue."

He chuckled. "Sure I do. I'm the one who gave him that line."

"Really?" I asked incredulously.

"Absolutely. Look, a corporate board room is not automatically improved by meeting some quota of skin tone, sex, or whatever. That's absurd. What does that have to do with competently running an organization? Do you care how racially diverse your favorite basketball team is? No, you care whether that team is good at basketball! Or think about this, a bomb squad gets called to the scene. Is anyone truly going to care about the diversity of that squad? A thinking person wouldn't. Who cares? You just want the squad who can do the best possible job diffusing that ticking bomb! So, no, diversity is not a virtue, because there's nothing inherently moral about skin color. It's when folks start attaching virtue to skin color that we get into all kinds of trouble."

Back in the circular driveway at Ferguson's house, we got out of his car and I asked, "Doesn't it bother you that we're still trapped in the legacy of so much oppression in America?"

"Of course there are consequences of the decision-making of past generations. I imagine we probably disagree on where the bulk of that blame lies."

Ferguson stepped around to our side of his car and stood within arm's length of me, face-to-face, his eyes full of sincerity. Being that close to him, I saw that there were lines on his face and wrinkles around his eyes that I hadn't noticed all afternoon.

"But here's the thing, Tom—you seem like a very earnest young man. Your heart seems to be in the right place. It's good that you're sensitive to racism and the effects of racism. But, if I may be so bold, I've got to say, don't be captured by this lie that you need to do 'the work.' Know what I mean? This white-guilt work that the racial grievance industrial complex is pushing you to do, in order for you to somehow exorcise the demons of racism. Because let me tell you a little secret about 'the work'—it can *never* actually be done. And that's the whole point. That's the con of it. You can *never* pay the full penance to wipe away the stain of ancestral slavery and racism. Only Jesus himself has the power to do that. So you need to release yourself of that burden. You and I have plenty of our own sin to deal with without also trying to atone for the sins of our ancestors. Okay?"

Meeting with Ferguson Hill was a lot. A lot to process, I mean. I was confused how someone from his background, someone who marched in the Civil Rights movement, and spent nights in jail for being black, could like America so much. And not just like it—*love* it. And try to talk other people into loving it too. I didn't know how to deal with that. I felt like Bob knew this would mess with my head. I didn't know how to deal with *that,* either.

FOURTEEN

With little fanfare or explanation from Bob on the videotape, he revealed Pikes Peak, Colorado, as the next destination. Finally heading to a western state fairly excited me. Surely this meant the finish line was almost in sight (although I was only on the third of Bob's five tapes). I had fought the urge so far to skip to the last tape in the box and discover the final stop. But I didn't know how much longer I could resist.

It was early evening when we finally left Ferguson's house. Amelia mentioned trying to find an RV slot for the night because she's smart and wisely plans ahead. I should've listened to her.

Instead, feeling restless and distracted by sifting through all of Ferguson's views in my mind, I shrugged off her suggestion. I was exhausted by the hassle of finding an RV park, checking in, parking Betsy Ross, figuring out the utility hookups, and all the rest. Making millions of dollars was turning out to be a lot of work. So, I said I wanted to just keep driving for a while.

Three hours later, we were in Memphis, on a bridge crossing the mythical Mississippi River. We cruised under a sign welcoming us to Arkansas.

"'Arkansas, the Natural State,'" Amelia said, reading the sign. She pronounced the "Kansas" part of Arkansas, like the pronunciation of Kansas the state. When I corrected her pronunciation to

"Ark-an-*saw*," she wanted to know how that could possibly be correct if we pronounced Kansas the way we do. I didn't know what to tell her. She insisted I must be messing with her. I finally gave up trying to convince her I was serious.

We made a convenience store run where I restocked on Yoohoo and introduced Amelia to Little Debbie Oatmeal Creme Pies. The first bite made her reiterate her love for America.

The Yoohoo and Oatmeal Creme Pies helped power me through Little Rock, but just half an hour of interstate later, my eyes began closing involuntarily. I caught myself the first time and tried to slap myself awake. Amelia had tried to stay awake with me, but sometime before Little Rock, she passed out in the front passenger seat. The third time my eyes closed, I veered onto the shoulder and the rumble strip noise finally jarred me awake again. I recovered the steering in time to keep us on the road but realized driving any longer was pointless.

Without waking Amelia, I took the next possible exit and meandered until I found a Walmart parking lot where I fell fast asleep, still buckled in behind the wheel.

When I finally woke up, it was still dark, and I didn't know what planet I was on. My watch helped slowly clear some confusion—it was 5:35 a.m., and I'd been out for four hours (I think).

Amelia entered the RV with her usual cheerful "good morning," which further threw me off since the sun wasn't up. She said she'd been wandering inside the Walmart a while, reading her book and generally trying not to wake me.

After securing the largest-size coffee on offer at McDonald's inside the Walmart, I eventually got my bearings and returned to the road. Several hours later, we left Arkansas behind and entered

Oklahoma territory. By then, I was wide awake, and the interstate was flat and dull, so I called Bob and put him on speaker as I drove.

"How was Ferguson?"

It was a loaded question, like basically all of Bob's questions. Maybe I was feeling extra cheeky (as Amelia would say), but I told him I thought he and Ferguson were "systemic racism deniers."

Amelia looked at me wide-eyed and I grinned cockily at her.

"Look, you can be polite to a certain point," he said. "But eventually you've got to stand up for yourself when people say, 'You're racist but you just don't know it.' I am *not* racist, and I take serious offense to anyone suggesting otherwise. Slavery is not a uniquely white or American sin. It's a universally human sin. There were more white European slaves shipped to North Africa than black slaves shipped to North America. Saudi Arabia had slavery into the 1960s. Look, America paid for our sin of slavery. We paid in blood. You don't understand the utter destruction of the Civil War. *That* was paying for the sin of slavery. Lincoln thought that too, and that's what he talked about in his second inaugural address."

Bob's voice was suddenly garbled by a long patch of poor reception. The only words I could make out were "Christian nation." I didn't ask him to repeat anything—"Christian nation" was more than enough for me to pounce on. So I said, "What kind of Christian nation obliterates Native Americans? Owns slaves? Drops atomic bombs? Invades Iraq to stop imaginary WMDs?"

"Well, you're forgetting a few things, like *ending* slavery. Defeating the Nazis. Uh…rebuilding Europe and Japan *and* keeping them from starving. Winning the Cold War. Bringing Saddam Hussein and his sons to justice."

I ignored his comeback and jumped straight to, "And how the hell do Christians explain Donald Trump? I mean, *they* put him in the White House."

"Trump has a lot of flaws. Like all of us. But there has never been any politician who's defended American Christians more than Trump. That's why so many Christians support him. That, plus the fact that they didn't have an alternative. What were we supposed to do, vote for Hillary? I'm not saying I necessarily like Trump—he annoys the heck out of me all the time—but I respect him for being a fighter."

"Come on. From day one, he played you all like ..." I swallowed the word I really wanted to use (for Amelia's sake, I suppose), "like *effing* fools. Evangelicals are total hypocrites, and that's why they go for Trump. Either that or they're more ignorant and stupid than I thought. See, that's why people like me can't stand religion. Because Christians worship a leader who's the exact opposite of what they claim to believe. *Of course* my generation doesn't go to church anymore, because churches are full of frauds."

"Frauds just because they support Trump?" he asked.

"The Catholic Church gave Hitler a pass. Now the American church is giving Trump a pass. That's a big part of why my generation hates religion."

"No, that's just an excuse not to have to explore the truth for yourselves. You're too busy taking selfies for any self-reflection. But if you did for two seconds, you'd find your souls every bit as dark and hypocritical as you accuse Christians of having. The problem is your generation is brainwashed to think that you're super righteous because you were taught to follow your heart. It's probably the worst thing we could've taught you."

"You know, it's hilarious getting all these lectures from you of all people. Your faith panned out really well when it counted—you know, like ruining your relationship with your daughter and completely alienating her."

The line went quiet, and I hoped that I'd cut him deep.

"See, that's a real misunderstanding of Christianity by the Left—that it's the religion's fault when people screw up." His voice grew quieter and more deliberate. "A major life failure does not implode the truth of Christianity. It just reveals our desperate need for it. It's not a failure on God's part. It's failure on *my* part."

I was pretty much stunned to hear him admit he failed. Amelia turned toward me, and I took my eyes off the road for a moment to look at her. I shrugged my shoulders slightly.

Finally, I heard other voices on Bob's end, and he said he had to get to a meeting.

A moment after we ended the call, Amelia said, "'The heart is deceitful above all things and beyond cure. Who can understand it?'"

"I should know this. Shakespeare?"

"The book of Jeremiah. In the Bible."

I glanced at her, confused.

"That's why your grandfather said that about following our heart being the worst thing we could've been taught."

"Maybe let's just call him *Bob*. We may technically be related, but…you know…he's just Bob to me."

"As you wish."

Amelia let another minute or so of central Oklahoma landscape roll by before she voiced what else was on her mind.

"I'm an evangelical, you know."

Our eyes met.

"Uh, yeah, I guess I knew that." But I didn't know what she was getting at. I didn't really even know what an evangelical was either, besides a brand of hardcore Christian, but I didn't admit it to her.

"You told Bob evangelicals are ignorant and stupid. And hypocrites."

"I wouldn't put you in the same category as the Trump worshippers. I mean, you didn't vote for him."

It occurred to me that we'd been on the road together for a week and this was the first time she appeared miffed at me. I thought that was an impressive streak, on *her* part I mean. I usually annoyed people a lot faster.

About an hour north of Wichita, we hit I-70 to take us the rest of the way across Kansas. No offense to Kansas, but compared to the rolling hills and greenery of the southeast, Kansas was the flattest, most monotonous landscape I'd ever seen. In Kansas's defense, maybe I didn't notice subtle shifts in the landscape or any noteworthy scenery because Amelia and I basically argued our way across the state. We weren't *fighting*-arguing, more like passionate debating. Perhaps she was still edgy from the way I talked about evangelicals to Bob. It all started shortly past Wichita as I replayed my latest chat with Bob in my mind and expressed to her my annoyance at the notion that America is somehow a Christian nation.

"There's no such thing as a Christian nation," she said. "Christian-influenced maybe. But a government can't be the church, and whenever they've tried, it's terrible."

"Thank you!" I interjected, trying to celebrate some common ground.

"But I don't think that's what people like your grandfather—I mean, *Bob*—mean or really want when they talk about a Christian nation."

"How do you know?"

"Well, I know normal Christians don't sit around in their churches plotting how to create a theocracy. But they do want to see Christian values reflected in government policy. Or at least not have their values ostracized."

"Okay, how can you tell who the 'normal' Christians are then?"

"They're the ones much more concerned with building Jesus's kingdom than an American kingdom."

"Why does it seem like Christians always want to force their beliefs on everyone else?"

"Well, honestly, so does your side." Before I could object, she added, "But if Christians give you that impression, then we're doing it wrong. What I've noticed about Americans in general though, on both sides, is that your *true* religion is partisan politics. The most devout Democrats and Republicans are like different denominations of the same religion. It seems that's the case even for way too many Christians. But true power is in prayer, not politics."

"Okay. Preach it!"

"You're mocking me."

"No, no. It's my lame way of agreeing with you. Christians should tend to their own church business and leave government to the experts."

She chuckled in a way I thought was atypically condescending coming from her.

"Expertise in government seems to be in very short supply, no matter what nation you're talking about." she said.

I almost sparred with her on that point but decided to let it slide. "I get the feeling with Christians that they think they have a monopoly on truth."

"We're certainly not supposed to be prats about it, and far too many of us are. I think the ones who really get it, who really adhere to the faith, like my grandfather, are not prats about it. But Jesus does say he is the way, the truth, and the life. That's quite arrogant if he's anything other than precisely the way, the truth, and the life."

"Yeah, well, those are totalitarian claims that always lead to oppression. I mean, the idea of proselytizing is pretty intolerant."

"But everyone proselytizes *something*. Your blog, for example. That's definitely proselytizing your views."

"You've read my blog?"

"I've perused some of it."

I raised my eyebrows and grinned in appreciation of her patronage.

"Have you ever read the Stoics?" I asked. "Seneca was a contemporary of Jesus and he had a lot of the same wisdom, but Jesus gets all the press."

"If Seneca didn't claim to be the Son of God and rise from the dead, then the press is going to go to Jesus. Because that's controversial. We don't get to be neutral about Jesus. His exclusive claims demand a response. He says you're either for me or against me."

"What's wrong with just great-role-model-teacher-Jesus? Without all the magical stuff?"

"It's not magical stuff," she said sharply.

"Okay, sorry." I lifted my hands briefly off the steering wheel in mock surrender.

"The little I know about Stoicism, it doesn't really seem like it would be very compatible with a diehard socialist."

"Well, I guess I'm still figuring things out," I admitted.

Another carbon-copy gas station and the same fast-food places glided past on both sides of the flat, straight, never-ending interstate. Kansas was like a treadmill.

"If the resurrection of Jesus *really* happened, then Christianity *does* have a monopoly on ultimate truth," she remarked. "If he rose from the dead, we have to lose every single argument we think we have with him."

"Oh, that's not unnerving at all," I noted sarcastically.

"It shouldn't be unnerving because that ultimate truth is free for everyone."

"How do you know so much?" I teased, to take some of the edge off my discomfort with her Jesus talk.

"I don't."

"I can't really get onboard with a god who sends people to hell."

"So, it can only be a god that fits your ideas and values?"

"I don't know. Theology is hard," I joked.

She finally grinned and said, "As it should be."

"I guess I tend to go with the psychological understanding of religion. You know, that Christianity and other belief systems were just primitive man's attempt to cope with the scary, dangerous world. Christianity's just another mythology. Great men throughout time are seen by their followers as gods, and cults grow out of that. Thus, the cult of Donald Trump. Although he's missing the *great man* part of that equation."

"Have you ever read any of the New Testament?"

"I mean, some. A little, maybe. Not much, really." That was a *very* generous assessment.

"You should revisit it. I don't think you'll find it very mythological."

"I guess I'm mostly agnostic. I just don't really think about it much. Live for today, you know? I can't really get behind the hocus-pocus of Christianity."

"Again with the magic," she interjected, sounding more irritated than typical for her. "It's *not* magic. The eyewitness testimony in the New Testament is compelling."

"Do you ever doubt that the Bible is true?" I don't know why I felt the need to rock her religious boat.

"I have before, yes. But not so much now."

"Do you ever think that might just be denial? That you're afraid to doubt it because if it was ever discredited, it would blow up your entire worldview?"

"I suppose it would definitely do that. But people have been striving to discredit it for a couple thousand years and it hasn't been disproven yet."

"I believe in science," I said. "I'm not necessarily opposed to belief in God. But I wonder what the point is of all the evil in the world. Why does evil even exist? If you say it wasn't created, that it just came from man, then why would God allow men to come up with evil knowing how much destruction it would cause? I guess if there is a God out there, the diversity of religions makes most sense to me. It makes sense that different cultures and times would have their own ways of relating to this same, ultimate God force, whatever it is."

"I don't understand much about the world, or evil either. But if we recognize evil, then there must be an opposing good, right? I believe Jesus is actually God in the flesh as he says he is, and that's validated by the resurrection. At one point, some of Jesus's followers were starting to abandon him, and he asks his disciples whether they're going to leave too. Peter says to him, '*Lord, to whom would we go? You have the words that give eternal life.*' So, ultimately, that's me too. Where else would I go?"

She was good at sounding convincing. It had to be the accent. The British accent automatically made everything that came out of her mouth at least 75 percent smarter sounding than it might otherwise. Plus, she was so damn cute.

At dusk, we finally ended our crawl across the Kansas prairie and stopped outside a town called Wallace. The RV park was completely different than any previous one on our trip. It was basically an open grass field—which was fitting since that's basically what the state of Kansas is—but it had full hookups. And Betsy Ross's shower felt nice, in spite of the claustrophobia, which I was only slowly getting used to.

Our food stores were running low, so dinner was canned vegetable-beef soup. The air was a bit cooler and drier on the Kansas plain compared to the Southern sauna we'd been melting in for days, so we ate outside. Amelia sat on Betsy's steps and I stood, pacing now and then as I ate my soup.

Dinner and the quiet sunset seemed to cheer up Amelia. I was still concerned about offending her earlier with my evangelical bashing. I stole several glances at her as the fading sunlight accentuated her face with a dash of golden glow. The wind blew her hair across her eyes, and she tucked the stray strands behind her right ear.

Amelia and I had settled into a rare sort of rhythm, despite how different we were. I suddenly realized that as much as I craved earning the inheritance, part of me didn't actually want the trip to end. Because I liked spending all my time with Amelia. Butterflies suddenly pinged the pit of my stomach.

Then, because I'm an expert at screwing up a perfectly good vibe, I opened my big mouth and asked her if she'd ever consider dating a guy like me.

"A guy *like* you, or *you*?" she asked with her heart-melting smile.

"I, uh…" I stuttered like a fool. "Yeah, okay, I meant me."

"Well," she looked at the ground with a hint of sheepishness on her face and tapped at an imaginary something in the grass with her right sneaker. "I like you in the friendliest-friend sort of way. Which seems most appropriate for our current arrangement, doesn't it?"

"I guess so," I replied. "I'm sorry. It's easy for a guy to get curious… about my chances in the, you know, *special* friend realm."

"Uh, well. Ummm, how should I put this? I'd say you could be in the realm of possibility, except…"

She glanced up at me and I raised my eyebrows in the most eager anticipation (but mostly fixated on her "except").

"Well," she continued, "my faith doesn't allow me to be un-equally yoked."

My eyebrows fell, and I'm sure a dumb expression overtook my face.

"I'm not talking about yoking, whatever that is. I mean just going out for a drink or something," I said.

She laughed, briefly covering her mouth with her left hand. She squinted and looked at me sympathetically. "I'm sorry, I don't want to hurt your feelings, Tom. But since you asked, the truth is, I couldn't go out with you because you're not a Christian."

"Ouch. Truth, man. Sometimes it *suuuuucks.*"

"I know."

I wasn't quite ready to slam that door shut. So, after we both stared at the setting sun for a few minutes, I sat down in the grass facing her, my hands behind me, propping me up.

"What about the, you know, that crazy stretch you told me about when you were in college? Were those guys Christians?"

"Most definitely *not.*"

"So…"

"So, I'd argue I wasn't really a Christian then either. Unfortunately."

She stood, scooping up my empty soup bowl and spoon from the grass beside me. She set my bowl inside hers as if she was re-turning inside the RV, but then she paused, cradling the bowls, and watched the disappearing sun. I finally stood and joined her.

"I don't know how anyone can watch a sunset like this and not be at least curious about God," she said.

Growing up, Mom often told me I didn't know when to let go of a subject. She was probably right about that. Later that night, as we lay in our respective beds in the dark, I breached the silence: "So, even if I was basically perfect, like a male Mary Poppins, but I wasn't a Christian, you still wouldn't consider giving me a chance?"

She didn't answer, which made me fear she'd already fallen asleep. But then I heard her let out a short sigh.

"I mean, yes, that's the commitment."

"I can respect that," I fudged, just so I wouldn't alienate her any further.

"Thanks."

"You almost seem kinda relaxed about me not being a Christian. Aren't you concerned about the fate of my soul?" Then I tagged on some snark. "Aren't you worried about my hell-bound status?"

"Of course I am. But I can't coerce you to become a believer, can I? That's the work of the Holy Spirit. Besides, you said you're against proselytizing. But I am praying for you."

"Really? You pray for me?"

"Yes, I really do."

Huh, I thought. And then I said, "Thanks, I guess."

"You're welcome. Good night, Tom."

I grinned in the darkness.

"Good night."

FIFTEEN

We drove under a sign on a twisting, tree-lined road that read "Pikes Peak Highway." Less than a mile later, we reached a tollgate plaza. I didn't know there would be a toll or a gate. The toll was thirty dollars, which sucked. But that was the least of our problems, because the female park ranger sternly informed us that Betsy Ross could not proceed if she was more than twenty-four feet long. I had no clue about any of Betsy's dimensions. Amelia dug around and found the decrepit Airstream manual. She confirmed our disqualification—Betsy was twenty-eight feet.

After considerable (and stressful) maneuvering, with tollgate rangers holding up traffic in both directions, I finally managed to turn us around and headed back the way we came.

"Shit, what are we going to do?" I moaned.

Alarm overtook me that this could be the technicality that got Bob out of having to pay me $25 million. All because I couldn't find a way up Pike's damn Peak.

Amelia calmly said, "Pull in here."

I glanced ahead in the direction of her vague gesture. I glimpsed a sign on the right that said "North Pole."

"What, here?" I asked, in an annoyed tone, as the turn approached uncomfortably fast.

"Yes, right here!"

"Oh my God!" I exclaimed as I turned way too hard and fast. It felt like we started tipping over a bit, but it was probably just my panicked mind playing tricks.

We roared beneath a rooftop entryway that had a Santa Claus and multiple reindeer on top. It was apparently some sort of chintzy North Pole–themed amusement park. But I didn't care, because it had a giant, almost completely empty parking lot, which was an oasis to me.

"You gotta give me more warning!"

"I was just trying to help," she said quietly.

Only a handful of vehicles dotted the lot. I slowed us to a stop in a sea of vacant parking spaces.

"What now?" I wondered aloud.

I hung my head in defeat and fatigue. Having to get to the top of Pikes Peak suddenly felt like a cruel challenge.

"I don't know. We'll figure it out."

I let my forehead sink forward until it rested on the steering wheel. Maybe I had been way overconfident that I could complete Bob's maniacal road trip maze.

Suddenly, Amelia jettisoned herself from her chair and disappeared outside without saying anything. I lifted my head to inquire after her, but then gave up. Maybe she just needed some mountain air. Then I saw her out the right-side window as she donned her mask and approached a dude playing with his brown Labrador next to a black Jeep (which also presumably belonged to him). In no time, she was chatting up this blond, bushy bearded guy who appeared from my vantage point to be around our age. He was decked out like an experienced hiker: cargo shorts and long-sleeve quarter zip with hiking boots and wraparound shades.

A moment later, Amelia was petting the dog. I thought about joining them, but my introversion kicked in and instead I stepped over to the couch and collapsed on it, face down. I felt a headache coming on. I might have fallen asleep but just as I felt drowsy, the door swung open.

"Great news!" she announced, "I found us a ride up the mountain."

I grabbed my mask and reluctantly followed Amelia to the dude's Jeep where she introduced me to Jake and his dog, Blazer.

"How's it going, bro?" asked Jake, stepping toward me and leaning in with his elbow extended for the now-requisite elbow tap.

I bumped elbows with him even though it's a really dumb, pointless gesture.

Amelia and I sat in the Jeep's junky, ripped back seat, with Blazer lovingly buckled into the front passenger seat.

And then Jake treated us to the single most harrowing ride of my life.

The road up Pikes Peak was scary enough on its own, but with Jake's wicked speed factored in, the ride was petrifying. Sure, there were pristine pines, fantastic switchback sections of road, and truly astonishing vistas punctuated by deep-blue water, but those were mere glimpses for me because we climbed so high, so fast, I could barely look out the window. At any moment, I feared that Jake's driving was going to propel us over one of the terrifying ledges to our deaths.

Jake talked as fast as he drove, too, which contributed to my woozy feeling. He wasted zero time loudly informing us that he was a "hardcore libertarian." I didn't know there were "core" variations of libertarianism.

He punctuated every other word with "bro!" for emphasis, even if it didn't fit the context. Blazer just sat up front, cool as a cucumber, with his tongue flopping about, seemingly agreeing with his owner's libertarian insights.

"The Founding Fathers weren't conservatives *or* progressives, you know?" asked Jake rhetorically. "Bro, they were libertarians!

They had to be. They were all about the liberty, man! And they were tough sons o' guns too. They were stubborn and driven to succeed. You know a lot of the Founders lost their dads at an early age? That'll make you put on your big boy pants fast. But they weren't victims about it like all the pansies nowadays. Victims didn't build America, that's for sure!"

As I feared for my life rounding the umpteenth blind curve, I wondered if Jake subjected every "bro" he met to his historical lectures. Blazer stared out the window to his right as if he'd heard all of this before, oblivious to our repeated brushes with death.

"Like, when did we become such a nation of whiners? We don't know our history anymore because college is all about safeguarding your feelings and raising hell about it when you get offended. It's all about microaggressions, race, sexual identity, and all that stuff—as if *that's* the most important thing about a person. Identity politics goes completely against the principle of equality from the Declaration of Independence. I mean, all we're supposed to get out of American history now is oppressors and victims. It makes me crazy! Like, *bro*, none of this is constructive!"

I didn't feel like arguing with Jake too much, since my life was in his hands. We rounded another curve way too fast, and my stomach did a couple flips. I glanced at Amelia. She couldn't see me rolling my eyes behind my sunglasses. Perhaps she sensed my annoyance though because she finally chimed in with, "So, you're a history enthusiast then?"

"*Enthusiast*—yeah, I like that. Great word! Oh yeah, I'm a total enthusiast. If I'm not working or hitting a trail somewhere, I'm probably reading history."

"What do you do for work?" Amelia asked.

"Construction contractor. Mostly interior remodels. Yeah, man, I love it! It's an art form."

I tried to imagine this surfer/stoner–sounding bro picking out tile for backsplashes and couldn't quite picture it. Regrettably, he didn't take Amelia's change-of-subject bait.

"We gotta know our history, bro. It's important. Like, did you hear that Ocasio-Cortez Congress lady? When she called the detention centers on the border 'concentration camps?'"

He glanced in the rearview mirror at us as if he expected an answer. I just wanted him to watch the road.

"I'm like, dude, this is an opportunity for us to realize how important it is to learn from history, 'cuz you can be upset about immigration and whatever, but bro—these are *not* concentration camps. That's an insult to all the people who have suffered and died in *actual* concentration camps. Like, did you know last year the San Francisco School Board spent like six hundred thousand dollars to paint over this amazing mural of George Washington at a high school? I mean, *George Washington*? You know, we only named our capital city after him. But sure, let's cancel him 'cause he's too dangerous for high school kids to know about. Bro, *what*?"

I thought I should give Bob's number to Jake. They'd be fast pals.

"Never mind, *by the way*, that the mural was painted by a communist during the Depression," Jake continued. "And dude painted Washington owning slaves because he was trying to make a complex depiction. As you should! I'm not saying edit out the bad stuff, but, like, we don't teach kids about complexity and nuance today. Now it's all about using history just to whine about the 'underrepresented' and the 'marginalized' and whatever, but I'm like, bro, why can't we all just be Americans? Why can't that be good enough? Leave each other alone, you know? Relearn some liberty around here." He laughed at himself. "You guys been up Pikes Peak before?"

"No," we answered simultaneously.

"It's a little gnarly if you're afraid of heights."

I just closed my eyes and swore silently.

Eventually, we made it to the top—shockingly alive. There was a construction mess with excavators in motion, something about redoing the visitor center. It melted my brain to think about how they got heavy machinery to the top of Pikes Peak. We thanked Jake for the ride. Amelia did a better job thanking him than I did. I was just happy to be in one piece (and relieved to be out from under Jake's liberty rants).

The summit was relatively flatter than I thought it'd be, with an unusual field of brown boulders and sharp rocks below the visitor center. I saw some sort of woodland creature darting in and out of the crevices of the boulders, which made me less inclined to explore. I had to keep up with Amelia, however, who bounded toward the nearest drop-off to take in the view. She removed her sunglasses for a moment, and I wish I had a photo of her awed smile. We had an unobstructed, jaw-dropping view. I'd never seen anything like it. It felt as if we were at the top of America. An endless sea of mountains, valleys, hills, and lakes in every direction—all painted in every shade of green and brown against the deep-blue crystal sky.

Amelia sat on a giant rock slab, soaking in the view. I sat next to her and unfolded my required reading page.

I had to read aloud all four verses of "America the Beautiful." In his video, Bob explained that an English professor named Katharine Lee Bates first started composing the poem in 1893 at the summit of Pikes Peak. I never knew "America the Beautiful" had more than one verse. I didn't know it was written by a woman either (in an America where she couldn't vote at the time).

"I think she was a leftie," Bob noted. "But she seemed to love America, so she gets a pass."

Gazing out over the "spacious skies" and "purple mountain majesties" that Bates wrote about, I understood the rapturous inspiration for her poetry, even if I didn't share her patriotic feels.

When I finished reading the verses, Amelia grinned at me. She didn't say anything like she usually did following my read-alouds. Maybe she just wanted to let the words linger and swirl in the chilled mountain wind. I glanced at the page again, settling on the words at the end of the second verse that pricked something in me when I first read them:

> *America! America!*
>
> *God mend thine every flaw,*
>
> *Confirm thy soul in self-control,*
>
> *Thy liberty in law!*

Maybe it spoke to the justice streak in me—my longing to see every flaw mended. Maybe I didn't believe there was a God who could or even wanted to mend the flaws, otherwise he would have. I felt tears in my eyes and a slight burn in my nose. Perhaps it was my worsening headache, or the altitude, or the stress of this insane trip that triggered my sudden mistiness. Or maybe it was Katharine Lee Bates's words, resonating down the ages with my own dream for an America I could actually believe in. I could never admit to Bob that I want to like America. I guess I just can't ultimately like it because it has been, and continues to be, so bad that it's beyond redemption. Kinda like me. Maybe there was still legitimate hope that the ship could be righted in Katharine Lee Bates's time. But it seemed like a pipe dream. I mean, Donald freakin' Trump was president.

"May I?" asked Amelia, extending her hand toward the page. I handed it to her. As she read the words to herself, I stood and massaged my throbbing temples. The cold wind felt good on my face.

We posed beneath the Pikes Peak "SUMMIT" sign, which listed the elevation at 14,115 feet. A middle-aged woman behind us in line took our photo with Amelia's phone.

Next, we went inside the nearby Summit House, which was a mistake because of the shoulder-to-shoulder crowd. No wonder America had thousands of people per day dying of COVID.

I hoped eating something would help my head feel better. We bought some of the supposedly "World-Famous" donuts on offer. They were totally so-so. And I still had a horrible headache afterward.

When Jake deposited us at the top of the mountain, we had not worked out how we would get back *down* the mountain. So, I was relieved to discover a free shuttle ride for part of the return trip. The fierce winds and the rattling frame of the small bus didn't make our descent any less scary, but at least it didn't cost anything. We debarked at the Glen Cove Inn, a sort of waystation about halfway down the mountain. On my way out of the restroom, there was Jake tossing a tennis ball to Blazer. I couldn't duck his view.

"Dude!" he called my way. "How was the peak?"

"It was cool," I blandly replied.

Then Amelia spotted Jake, she made a beeline for Blazer, and it turned into another whole thing.

Jake explained that he and Blazer were on mandatory brake time-out. Every vehicle has to have its brake temperature checked by the rangers just before Glen Cove Inn. Jake said if the brakes are deemed too hot, you must wait half an hour until they cool before you can continue the descent. It was hardly a shock that Jake got flagged for excessive brake heat.

Naturally, Jake offered to give us a lift back to Betsy Ross, which we had to accept for lack of any other option. That meant more of his unsolicited "America-used-to-be-resilient-and-now-we're-weenies" chatter. He seemed like a pretty smart and earnest guy, but he clearly had no ability to read the room.

As Jake rolled us to a stop next to Betsy, he had some parting words that we didn't ask for.

"We live in challenging times, man, 'cause we've got it so *easy* compared to our ancestors. Let me leave you with this quote from a wise bro—C. S. Lewis. He said, 'None can give to another what he does not possess himself. A man whose mind was formed in a period of cynicism and disillusion cannot teach hope or fortitude.'"

"Wow, thanks for that, Jake," Amelia said charitably.

"You're so welcome. May you both find much hope and fortitude, so you can share it with others."

He twisted around in his seat to give us farewell elbow taps. Amelia gave Blazer one more head rub before we got out of the Jeep and watched Jake—the hardcore libertarian guru of Pikes Peak—peel away into the unknown.

By the time we finally found an RV park with a vacancy, I felt miserable. Raging headache. Nausea. I told Amelia I was afraid I contracted COVID from the atrociously crowded Summit House. She assured me that COVID doesn't work that fast.

I collapsed on the couch, and Amelia did some googling on her phone. She determined I was probably experiencing altitude sickness. And then I started barfing. The next twelve hours or so dragged by in a miserable haze. Amelia seemed to be there the whole time, keeping watch like some battlefield nurse. She found ibuprofen for me and kept a cool, damp bandanna on my forehead. If she was repulsed by my illness, she never showed it. If I were her, and this wasn't altitude sickness, I would've been afraid to be around my germs. But she showed no reluctance to take care of me.

Sometime in the middle of the night, I had a fitful stretch of sleep. In the darkness, there was just enough light creeping around the window shades that I could make out Amelia curled up in the passenger seat, asleep. I was enamored with her kindness, generosity, and all-around vitality. I didn't know what to do with these feelings, except fall further in love with this oddly wonderful woman. It was a helpless, hopeless feeling to realize I had no similar qualities that might induce her to love me back.

In that perplexing, fever-dream fashion, these thoughts meandered back to my illness, which in turn made the short leap to thoughts of death. What if this was the end for me? I'd led a very shallow, narcissistic life with absolutely nothing to show for myself. I thought again of my unfinished play. I could maybe grind out some drivel, but it doesn't mean they'd give me a passing grade. Maybe I could make something of myself with this inheritance money. If it was even real. In my feverish state, I began to doubt the whole erratic journey. What if Bob was just some bitter kook out for revenge on the daughter who understandably spurned him? What if he was actually out of his mind and has no money?

I suddenly felt paranoid that I was the victim of a horrific con. I took several slow, deep breaths to try to stave off a panic attack. Then the fever-dream thoughts took another strange turn as I recalled Jake and his rants. And Bob's point of view on everything. And Ferguson Hill's curious love for a country that has no justice for his race. The startling, alien part of this thought-barrage was that for the first time in the whole journey, I actually wondered if there might be a hint of truth in their worldview. I didn't truly believe it. I didn't *want* to believe it. But there it was—a tiny green shoot poking through a crack in the pavement of my brain, alone and very out of place, but there nonetheless. I hated to admit it with every fiber of my being, but what if there were fissures in my ideology? I had never doubted my worldview for a second. Never doubted my side. But nothing I believed had ever been challenged before. In college, and especially grad school, no one questioned my worldview. There was no reason to. It was sacrosanct.

The thought that Bob and these alternate perspectives could have even partial merit made me shudder. A wave of chills coursed through my body. Surely it was just the altitude sickness.

Then I silently begged God to heal me. I don't know why I prayed. I guess I was desperate.

SIXTEEN

By the next afternoon, I felt so much better, I actually didn't mind that much having to call Bob.

But then I called Bob.

In my euphoria over being headache-free, I said something to Bob about the antiquated patriotism of "America the Beautiful" and how the system hasn't exactly panned out in the century-plus since Bates composed her mountaintop verses.

Bob seized the opportunity to accuse my generation of being attracted to socialism because we didn't grow up with true knowledge of the Soviet Union and the countries behind the Iron Curtain and all that.

"Of course I don't want a Soviet dictatorship," I argued. "But I do want to end poverty and racism and increase opportunity for people on the edges of society. If you want to call that socialism, then I'm proud to be a socialist."

"Of course, the only way you envision any of that utopia happening is if the government does it. Serious question—has anyone ever taught you anything about the free market system?"

"Yes," I said matter-of-factly (though that was mostly a stretch).

"Well, they did a darn poor job then. Otherwise, you'd understand that the free market system is still the best bet for lifting people out of poverty. Hands down. No question. Even Barack Obama admitted it one time—he must've not been feeling well."

"If it works so great, why are millions of people still left out—including your own daughter, by the way—and why are so many people still getting rich through exploitation? The so-called free market is totally abused by the powerful upper class and corporations, and they get all the social advantages of their rich network. Great system for members like you."

"You need to branch out from Bernie's stump speech. The world will always have crooks, no matter what the economic system is. Your generation never sacrificed a darn thing for anyone other than yourselves—much less your country. Yet you want to take advantage of all your nation's blessings while you plot and work to undermine the very system that lets you enjoy all your lattes and Marxist book clubs. Honestly, it's disgusting."

I let out a brief, exasperated laugh.

"No. No. Your precious capitalist system undermined itself. It's not because we never knew the Soviet Union. It's because of 2008 and the Great Recession that we grew up with. We watched government bail out the banks whose royal screw-ups caused the crisis in the first place. The system has to be upended because it's completely corrupt, and it lied to my generation. It told us we could have this American dream that our parents had if we just got a college degree. But then the carpet was yanked out from under us. And we didn't get those promised opportunities."

Bob laughed back at me.

"Your own side herded you into college. That's how they pump out their socialist converts. They promise all kinds of security in exchange for your freedom."

I managed to lower my voice slightly and tried to take the wind out of his sails. "Why does your free market have to be at odds with a good social safety net? If America's crazy excess wealth can be used to ease the burdens of the poor, you know, a minimum income, shelter, food, health care, and some protection against injury and climate change—why wouldn't we want to provide that? Don't we have a moral imperative to provide those things? Europe does that stuff."

Bob tried to cut in, but I didn't let him. I paced outside, and Amelia walked past me on her way into the RV just as I said to Bob, "Europeans are happier than Americans on every index."

"Not the Brits," she commented wryly, though I don't think Bob overheard her.

"It's because they have some financial pressure relieved," I continued. "Imagine people here having to scrape and claw to make ends meet their whole life. Always just one medical disaster away from being totally wiped out. And yet we have an obscene number of millionaires. That's messed up."

"Would you really prefer an even *more* imbalanced society, with ten percent of super-wealthy people doing all the work to support the other ninety percent who squeak by on whatever the government gives them? That's a recipe for total meltdown. Thanks to LBJ, we've already got half a century's worth of evidence to prove that taking away people's incentive to work doesn't end well."

"Really? You're gonna blame welfare? Is that like one of the boxes you have to check to register as a Republican?"

"Look, the free market system doesn't just make people ultimately better off—it helps develop virtues. Thrift. Being industrious. Delayed gratification—do you even know what that is?"

"Yeah, it's the name of this whole wild goose chase you sent me on. *Painfully* delayed gratification."

"Son, if you think this is painful…" He chuckled, while I cringed hearing him call me "son" again.

"Capitalism doesn't make everyone better off," I snapped. "The rising-tide-lifts-all-boats-thing is total bullshit. It leaves far more people behind, thanks to those at the very top. And I'm familiar with your whole Protestant work ethic thing, because it's a white supremacist trope."

"Wow, your mouth sure reminds me of your mom's sometimes. Not everything in life boils down to race or sex. It's gonna be really hard for you to undo years of brainwashing with that stuff. But for God's sake, for your own good, you better try. You know, it's clear to me that one of your biggest problems is a total lack of perspective. You're jealous of the rich because you think they all got there unfairly, and because at the same time it seems unreachable to you. Or at least it *did*, before this trip. But let me tell you—envy is destructive. It'll tear you apart. It's no way to live. At the same time, I think you feel guilty because you have it so good. You have no idea what to do with that when the world is still so cruel and unfair."

I tried to come up with some biting retort, but I was pissed that he somehow called out my guilt without truly knowing me. I told myself it's probably because he struggles with guilt himself.

Something that might knock him off his high horse suddenly struck me. I stopped pacing.

"Bob," I said, pausing for a moment as I chose my words. "You want me to become a Republican convert as, like, some qualifier for this inheritance. You just want me to become like you. And you need to know that that is *never* going to happen."

"Believe it or not, I have little to no expectation that you're gonna become a Republican, but I'd settle for you being inspired enough to pause and think about your own beliefs, to really think critically about everything you've bought into. I get the impression you've never had to do that. See, I *have* done that. I understand the left-wing position inside and out, and it does *not* promote human flourishing. Oh, they market themselves as if they do— that they're for the little man, all the oppressed minorities and all that. But most of the time, their actions actually *prevent* human flourishing. To constantly tear down the free market economy. To take away incentive to work. Tearing down law and order. When anything goes with sexuality. Abortion on demand. Destroying the family. Demeaning religion. Promoting racial strife. Increasing centralized power. No exaggeration—that's literally what your side of the aisle's all about, Tom. And my sincere hope is that you'll eventually stop and truly evaluate those things. Because government is *not* your family. It's not even your friend. The Left says, 'Oh, it *can* be, if we just have enough money and the right experts in charge.' Nope. Never works that way. It can't. Don't get me wrong, government is necessary to have decent, civilized society. But government must be kept on a *very* short leash. That's what the Constitution is supposed to do. And the only reason that leash hasn't snapped yet is because there are still a bunch of old farts like me trying to protect what's left of it."

"Oh God, you people are always wrapping yourselves in the flag and Constitution, as if it gives you some kind of moral superiority. That effort has really worked out, huh? Your generation had your chance. It didn't work, and now the world's moving on. So, if you're not okay with some of this inheritance money finding its way to the Democratic Socialists of America, or the Biden campaign, or Black Lives Matter, then you better just call off the deal."

My stomach dropped a little when I let the "call off the deal" part tumble out of my moronic mouth. Maybe I shouldn't have given him such an out.

"You haven't earned the money yet," he added with a brief, disconcertingly calm laugh. "But if you do, a deal is a deal. We signed it. I'd never go back on that. Your word is worth way more than any inheritance."

I was just about to hang up when he added, "By the way, your mom wasn't left out of the system, as you put it. She chose to leave. Everything she did ... well," he stopped himself for some reason.

"What?" I demanded impatiently.

"Just remember, life is all about choices. My door was always open."

I wanted to yell a hundred different things back at him. Did he have any clue about some of the total shit apartments and crumbling rental houses we endured over the years? The stained, smelly carpet and grimy, peeling linoleum? The carousel of crap cars with broken handles and missing hubcaps? All while he was a multimillionaire. How dare he blame her.

I somehow restrained myself and simply replied, "She did not feel welcome."

"That's her version."

I wanted to argue. I'd always believed Mom's version. And yet, as I got older, and we were struggling through the latest car repair bill or our millionth Hamburger Helper dinner (without the hamburger), I sometimes wondered why she didn't just give up and ask her dad for help. If she had, would I have grown up visiting his house in Virginia? Would Bob have taken me fishing? Would we have played catch? Would he have taught me to shoot his guns? Would I have been his little Republican apprentice?

But I never asked her about it or suggested she reach out to her dad, because I knew she would never do it anyway. She had a prodigious stubborn streak—and now I understood where she got it.

Later that afternoon, we headed north through Denver and then hung a left to start a long westward trek toward our next destination: Promontory Summit, Utah. We had been riding in silence at least an hour, when Amelia suddenly announced, "Today was supposed to be my wedding day."

I looked over at her, surprised.

"Sunday, June seventh," she said wistfully.

"Man, I'm sorry. That totally sucks."

"Yeah. Well…anyway. I suppose I just felt like announcing that."

"So I'd feel sorry for you?"

"Right. Precisely," she laughed.

"Well, I do."

"Thank you for your support."

That evening, the mountain gods showed us favor with an RV park along the swiftly flowing Eagle River. As the sun started slinking behind the peaks, we strolled along the water's edge.

"I could do this forever," Amelia said contentedly.

I was thinking the same thing, but was too self-conscious, or something, to admit it out loud. The low roar of the water rippling over the rocks was an idyllic, addictive sound.

"I wonder if this is what heaven will be like?" she continued. "Endless diamond days, filled to overflowing with peace and gratitude for God's presence."

"With Yoohoo and Oatmeal Creme Pies," I added.

"Of course," she said with a laugh.

I spotted a smooth, flat stone, plucked it from our path, and tried to skip it on the river surface. It didn't skip but sliced into the water with little splash.

"We *could* do this forever, you know?" I suggested. "Assuming I finish this trip and cash in."

It was risky saying the "we" part, but the atmosphere felt right to go for it. I ventured a glance at Amelia, and she grinned, though I read it as her sympathetic look, which to me said she appreciated my earnestness but was totally unconvinced.

"Unfortunately, I don't think that would be a fulfilling way to live."

"You might be surprised," I countered.

"So, what *are* you going to do with all your wealth?"

"I don't know," I admitted honestly. "It still doesn't seem real. But if it *is* real, it's a little overwhelming to think about. On one hand, I find the whole thing repulsive because it goes completely against my entire philosophy. I don't think anyone should be allowed to be as rich as Bob. But do I think that mainly because I never thought there was a chance in hell I'd ever be rich? I don't know. I'm still against the idea on principle. But at the same time, I desperately need the money. And I kinda hate how much I crave it now that it seems within reach, you know?"

"I understand."

"So, you got any Bible guru money wisdom for me?"

"I don't know. Perhaps you might be a wee bit too hard on money. I don't think it's evil in and of itself. It's the *love* of money that is the root of all evil."

"Oh, so *that's* what's wrong with Bob," I joked.

She seemed on the verge of a courtesy giggle, but she took a drink from her water bottle instead.

"I think you know my default is the way of Jesus. And Jesus's ethic is that wealth can be dangerous. Not evil on its own. But whether it's money or any manner of other things, it's super easy for them to become what we worship."

"So, what are you saying? I can't be trusted with a ton of money?"

"I'm saying, as your friend, just be cautious. Because this could be an incredible blessing. But at the same time, even good things can become gods."

"Got it. I promise to be very careful. No money gods."

"Very good."

We stepped onto a relatively flat, rocky stretch of shore and dipped our hands in the cold, clear water.

"I think you might be wrong about Bob," she said. "I don't think he actually loves money."

"Why not?" I looked at her with probably too much of a grimace.

"Because otherwise, why would he give so much away to a grandson he barely knows?"

"I don't know. Guilt?"

I picked up a few more smooth stones and flung them one by one into the middle of the river.

"I've never met anyone who seems to have it all together," I said, looking at her. "And seems so…I don't know, peaceful, I guess."

"Who, Bob?" she asked.

"No! *You.*"

"Thanks, but I don't know about that. I'm insecure and anxious. Selfish and materialistic. And I can be irrational. The only thing 'together' about my life is Jesus, whom I'm trying to follow in my very feeble, messed-up way."

"You do talk about Jesus more than anyone I've ever met. Like, *way* more."

She laughed. I really loved making her laugh.

SEVENTEEN

B ob's endless trail had already shown us some stunning vistas of America—but I-70 may have been the best so far, as it meandered alongside and back and forth across the Colorado River. We were mesmerized by the craggy mountainsides with their broad legions of evergreens standing at uniform attention. There had been plenty of days when I was sick of driving Betsy Ross, but this wasn't one of them.

Amelia kept taking videos of the naturally sculpted landscape as we slowly wound our way through the mountain passes. At one point, enraptured by the encompassing beauty, she read aloud from the Bible in her lap:

"'*For ever since the world was created, people have seen the earth and sky. Through everything God made, they can clearly see his invisible qualities—his eternal power and divine nature. So they have no excuse for not knowing God.'*"

Everything with her always seemed to come back around to God. And I didn't really know what to do with that. It was kind of awkward, I guess, but I don't know why.

The relative green of the Colorado River–nourished mountains slowly gave way to the alien brown barrenness of eastern Utah. It had its own rugged beauty, but it was rather desolate and foreboding. The change in landscape mirrored my plunging mood when late in the afternoon Betsy suddenly began lurching and sputtering. Then I noticed black exhaust smoke in the sideview mirror.

I slowed way down, but every mile just felt like I was probably making the problem worse. I took the next possible exit to seemingly nowhere. We rattled into a small town and Betsy gave us just enough juice to make it to a repair shop.

If Amelia shared my alarm, she didn't show it. Her sunglasses hid her eyes, but she seemed to be looking at the floorboard—and her lips were moving.

"What are you doing?"

"Praying," she replied.

"Good. We're probably going to need it." Again, awkward, but I guess we had nothing to lose by her firing off some prayer flares.

A jolly, middle-aged mechanic with "Mike" stitched to the front of his coveralls met me in the shop's postage-stamp parking lot.

"That thing is *awesome*," said Mike, shaking his head as he ogled Betsy Ross.

I don't think he was joking.

"I've always wanted to see one of these in person."

"*Why?*" I said with a grimace.

I grew restless loitering around the sunbaked vehicle repair shop for the rest of the afternoon. It took forever to get a full diagnosis. And when it finally came, I felt like I'd been kicked in the junk. The repairs would cost over $2,500. Mike said something about the carburetor, and spark plugs, and a couple other vital-sounding things that were way over my head. Frankly, I barely know how to drive, much less anything about the inner workings of motor vehicles. They wouldn't even be able to get started until sometime the next day because they didn't have the right parts or something.

Honestly, I barely heard anything he said past "twenty-five hundred dollars."

Amelia thanked Mike and said something about getting back to him in a few minutes with our decision. I just stared silently into the dusty distance. My mind was a cyclone of panic as I frantically tried to calculate how I would possibly cover the expense.

I walked slowly away from Amelia, into a mostly empty adjacent parking lot, where I got a torrent of profanities out of my system. My heart raced and I took some deep breaths, trying to head off a panic attack. A $2,500-repair bill would essentially wipe me out. I owed my share of rent in a couple weeks, and I had no idea how much longer Bob's trip would take. Even if it was just another two weeks, I wouldn't be able to cover rent plus the RV repair bill with the meager amounts left on my credit cards.

My stomach sank, and I felt a little dizzy. The searing heat did not help, but mostly it was the depressing realization that this short-lived fantasy of seeing all my financial woes evaporate, as well as seeing my financial future totally secured, was about to die a quick, painful death in the Utah desert. This was it. This was where my quest would fail.

Amelia kept her distance for several minutes while I worked out my initial dismay. I could call my California roommates and beg to be late with the rent payment. They would be pissed, and honestly, they'd probably say no. But I didn't really want to have to explain my predicament. I decided to put them off since rent wasn't due for two weeks anyway.

I pretty much hated myself for it, but I decided to take a chance and call Bob. Maybe I would catch him in a charitable mood. Betsy Ross was his vehicle, after all, and this trip *was* his idea. Surely he bore some responsibility for her mechanical issues.

I did not catch Bob in a charitable mood.

He said he was sorry, but as stipulated in our contract, I was on my own for any RV repairs while on the trip. I never bothered checking the contract to verify his claim. It's not like I was going to be able to outsmart a CEO on a contract issue.

"How 'bout some basic compassion then?" I tried. "I'm seriously doing my best to finish this thing, but I'm really gonna be stuck here."

Bob's brief pause made me think I might've plucked a heartstring if he still had any in tune. But then he said, "Compassion's not my natural gift—that was my wife's—but it doesn't mean I don't care."

"Just not enough to actually help me when I'm desperately screwed."

"You'd be in breach of contract."

"*Shit.* Fine. Thanks for *nothing*," I growled, hanging up on him.

I paced and swore some more before finally calming down just enough to rejoin Amelia. I was out of options. I'd have to eat this repair cost and then rob a bank or something to finance the rest of this godforsaken road trip.

I entered the tiny repair shop waiting area where a lonely oscillating fan on the counter futilely tried to move the air. The mechanic finally saw me through the window and waved me into the garage. I reluctantly gave him the green light to do whatever had to be done.

We had to spend the night at the Rusty Clif Motel—the only place within decent walking distance of the repair shop. I don't know whether the name referenced the local topography and "Cliff" was misspelled, or if Clif was a dude with tetanus issues. Either way, the missing "f" annoyed me. Weirdly, our room had one queen-size bed, and one twin. I took the twin. It was as craptastic as it sounds.

I slumped in a cracked plastic chair inside a nearby laundromat, whining to Amelia about how long the repairs were taking. How they were probably just jacking up the labor cost to rip me off more. How this delay was setting us back three days, maybe more.

She didn't even look up from folding her clothes as she said, "Time is an illusion. It's just a bunch of numbers that make people stressed."

Utterly bored, I stared at the TV hanging a bit askew on the wall. Fox News was on, with some alarmist footage of the George Floyd protests. My blood boiled for the protesters. I *so* wanted to be out there with them, marching in solidarity. This was a true *moment*. A long overdue reckoning. And I was missing it. Stuck in RV-repair purgatory.

Sometime later in the glacially slow, scorching hot afternoon, Bob called. I still smarted from his unwillingness to help me in my desperate circumstance, but I had nothing else to do besides waiting for my clothes to dry, so I answered the phone and stepped outside the laundromat.

Bob had seen some George Floyd riot footage too.

"Where's the justice in these punk looters torching people's businesses?" he wondered.

"Extreme situations require extreme measures," I said.

"It's because of *that* kind of Marxist BS that this country is screwed," he said.

"How else can you demand change?" I asked. "When the racism is so rampant and it's so deeply entrenched that black people can't get justice, how else are you supposed to get it?"

"You don't have a clue how hard it is to build a small business. Behind every one of those stores in flames is someone who scrimped and saved and worked their butt off to build a dream.

And they lose everything in one night because of someone's supposed anger that has absolutely *nothing* to do with that business owner. How exactly does that bring any justice to the situation? These looters are pathetic, ignorant lowlifes."

"Well, it's a small price to pay. Police brutality is the real crisis."

"It's *not* a crisis. It's isolated cases of idiot officers. In a population of three hundred twenty-five million, you're gonna get some idiots now and then. The Left tries to make it a crisis to feed this racial grievance industry. I mean, it *is* a lucrative business, you understand."

"Yeah, well, so is the conservative grievance industry." I was proud of my semi-burn, but Bob ignored it.

"It also just causes people to judge an entire group by the actions of its worst members."

I couldn't tell if he was talking about black people, white people, or police officers, but I didn't ask him to clarify.

"America is a deeply racist, sexist, heteronormative country where people of color and women are disadvantaged at every turn. White guys like you start on third base in anything you want to accomplish. That's how you became super rich. You're the ultimate example of white privilege."

"You've really fallen for all the left-wing propaganda, haven't you? White privilege is a myth, Tom. It's an excuse for people not to apply themselves. Go to rural West Virginia and ask those folks how well white privilege has worked out for them. If privilege is inherent to the white race, why are there any poor white folks?"

I was frustrated that a quick answer eluded me. But I was tired. And it was really hot.

"I don't know, I guess it's complicated. People get into drugs and stuff. There are a lot of factors. Bad healthcare, you know..."

"Oh, it's complicated now? I thought white privilege was the blanket boogeyman. The reality is, everyone born in America, no matter how poor, has privilege. It's called *American* privilege. Just by being born here, you have a leg up on most of the rest of the world, and that reality should be celebrated for how unique it is."

I laughed the most scoffing laugh I could muster.

"See? You laugh, and that's the problem. Half the country doesn't believe American privilege is real."

"Because it's *not,*" I snorted, "it's a *mirage.*"

"Well, I guess you're gonna have a heck of a conundrum on your hands if you get your inheritance then, huh? How to live with the guilt of millions of dollars that someone else earned for you. *That's* actual privilege. How will you ever live with yourself? Look, you want poor people to have more money; you want justice, racial reconciliation, and a healthy climate—believe it or not, so do I. We just have very different paths to get there. That used to be called political debate. But now, if your tribe doesn't get their way, they just want to burn everything down. By the way, you talk a lot about justice like it's the ultimate righteousness, but when you want to release criminals and defund the police, you're denying justice to countless other victims who aren't on your priority list. Like it or not, part of justice is *criminal* justice."

"First things first. You have to defeat the bigots."

"Oh yes, the bigots. There's so many now," he said with biting sarcasm. "Way worse than the dogs and water hose days of the sixties. We haven't made any progress at all. We can't have a productive conversation when your side calls us bigots all the time."

"Geez, you poor, right-wing victims. For people who make fun of the Left for victimhood all the time, you sure whine about being oppressed a lot, especially about Trump being oppressed. God, it's gross."

"Because the media *does* oppress him! Relentlessly!"

"Because everyone who doesn't have their head up their own ass understands clearly that Trump is an existential threat to America. He makes everyone unsafe."

"But to you, *everything's* unsafe when words are violence. When you've gotta go get counseling after you learn in class about how someone was mistreated three hundred years ago."

"You can't deflect away the fact that Trump is a raging psychopath who only cares about himself."

"Let me get this straight: after four years of you commies blaring this crap on an hourly basis, your big plan for getting rid of Donald Trump and course-correcting America is the *white* geezer, Joe Biden? The guy who did the eulogy for his best pal, Senator Byrd, who literally used to be in the KKK? Great plan."

"He's not my first choice, but you know, whatever it takes. Desperate times—"

He cut me off with, "Call for *sane*, well-*reasoned* measures. Remember that. By the way, where does morality come from?"

"I don't know... societal forces... the white patriarchy."

"So, morality is subjective?"

It felt like a trick question, but after giving it the briefest thought, I replied, "Yeah, probably. Basically, yes."

"If morality is subjective, then how can injustice be an issue?"

"Well... at least I care about injustice. It's much worse to claim to have strong morals and not care about injustice."

"I *do* care about injustice."

"How?"

"I support many causes with my financial resources. I just don't blare it from the rooftops because my Judeo-Christian moral code teaches me not to."

"So, you give money to soothe your conscience. That's an easy way out because it's not hard to donate money. I've been to protests. I've been part of sit-ins. *That* takes effort."

"Let me ask you this—does the phrase 'all lives matter' bother you?"

"Of course. It's a total racist dog whistle."

"Or maybe 'all lives matter' just bugs you because you don't actually believe they do. If you're pro-abortion, that means there are some lives you're okay with throwing away. 'All lives matter' is actually the more open-minded position."

"God, you people are all about protecting the unborn because there's no downside. It's easy to care about them because you don't see them. You don't have to deal with them. Try applying your super-holy, pro-life stance to African Americans, immigrants, the poor, people in prison, and then get back to me."

He challenged me to be able to say "*all lives matter*" out loud. I challenged him to say "*black lives matter*" out loud. Neither of us caved.

I reentered the dingy laundromat and landed hard in an uncomfortable metal chair with ripped vinyl padding. "I can't believe the party that's obsessed with individual freedom is so restrictive about what a woman chooses to do with her own body. As a woman, doesn't that just totally piss you off?"

I didn't anticipate Amelia's silence and I wondered for a second whether she had her earbuds in. She finally glanced up from her book.

"Um...well...I understand your frustration," she said hesitantly, "but actually, I'm rather surprised that the side that seems to be about protecting the vulnerable, taking care of the oppressed, you know, doesn't also stand up for the unborn. They're the *least* able to protect themselves of anyone on earth, right?"

"Oh, geez, I should've seen this coming..."

"I've read the numbers: something like six hundred thousand babies were aborted last year in America. Six hundred thousand kids who will never get to kick a football. That's rather ghastly."

I hated that Amelia seemed to be more on Bob's side on this, but I didn't feel like letting her in on my disappointment. I closed my eyes and exhaled my frustration.

She tried to cheer me up with the fact that it was teatime. Since we couldn't access Betsy Ross to make tea, she suggested we walk a few blocks to some drink place she'd discovered. I wasn't really in the mood but figured it might beat sitting in the hotbox laundromat.

It was a lengthy, sweaty walk to get to this place called Swig. Its drink menu had way too many options and I was too numb with boredom and depression to care, so I just lazily told Amelia to make it two of whatever she wanted.

We sat at a table on the shaded patio and drank some kind of Dr. Pepper with a coconut-berry infusion. Amelia was delighted with her choice. She'd apparently never had a Dr. Pepper before.

Prompted by my bad mood, I brought up BLM and the riots. Wasn't it really twisted, I wondered aloud, for us to be sitting in the shade sipping cold drinks in a town that seemed so disconnected from the reality of this historic riots movement that we were totally missing? It seemed immoral for us to be sidelined from this moment. From our vantage point, you would never even know that such a racial reckoning earthquake was going on.

As usual, Amelia listened patiently to my venting. But sometimes her earnest silence annoyed me. I guess I wished I got more cheerleading and active agreement from her. I tried goading her into an opinion on the BLM movement.

"I'm sorry, I don't suppose I know enough about the organization, or the context, to have much of an opinion."

"I don't think you need context to know which side to be on here."

"Well, since I can't authentically know the experience of a black person in America, I don't feel it's wise to really weigh in on the subject."

I almost retorted that that was a cop-out, but I stopped myself. She was trying to cheer me up with teatime at Swig after all, so I finally concluded I should stop trying to ruin it.

After spending a second night in the janky Rusty Clif Motel in no-man's-land, Utah, I awoke extra early, about to go out of my mind with eagerness to hit the road. As soon as mechanic Mike released Betsy Ross with a clean(ish) bill of health, I popped in the video to get Bob's rambling over with about our next destination—Promontory Summit. Bob looked pale and a little gaunt onscreen. He winced as he shifted his weight in his easy chair. I remembered his cancer diagnosis and felt a brief pang of compassion. But the pang didn't linger, because of his refusal to lend me a helping hand with the RV repairs. And because of our BLM exchange the previous day. And then because he almost immediately launched into a tangent on government healthcare.

"The other day I was waiting on my chemo treatment to start—I'm getting excellent care, and I'm really thankful for that."

He glanced into the camera sincerely.

"And I was just thinking, 'Thank God,' right? Because if I was at the mercy of almost any other healthcare system in the world, I'd probably be toast right now, a man my age. But—this might surprise you to hear me say out loud—I'd be fine with a universal healthcare system *if* it worked. That's an enormous *if*. See, for me, it's all about things that work well. If you could make a system that worked just as well as what we've got, and still created the financial incentive to attract the best and brightest to the medical profession—and if the care worked every time and was widely available, and if it was actually nice, not like the VA—then sure, I'd be for it. Oh, and if it wouldn't cost a giant chunk of taxes out of every paycheck. But see, that's simply not possible, so I'm against even trying. Why would you want to replace a system that works, even though it's expensive and full of problems, with a system that's way worse from the get-go? It drives me out of my mind that Bernie and all these socialist boneheads never bother to explain that the healthcare is not *and can never be* free. It's just paid for in a different way—skimming it right off the top of your paycheck. Where's the logic in compulsory spending on a garbage product, especially when it has to do with your health?"

While Bob adjusted himself in his chair, I muttered at the screen, "It wouldn't cost so much if rich guys like you paid your fair share."

Startlingly, Bob resumed as if he'd heard my comment. "And in case you're one of those who think guys like me don't pay my fair share of taxes, let me assure you, I pay *way* more than my fair share."

I wanted to punch a hole in the screen in the middle of his smug, naïve, elitist face. But then I wouldn't have a way to watch his dumb tapes.

EIGHTEEN

I practically peeled out of the parking lot—as much as you can in an RV anyway. I had blind determination to make up for all the lost travel time. I was sick of Betsy Ross. Sick of the road. Sick of not knowing how many more stops lay hidden in Bob's sinister box of tapes.

My paranoia resurfaced that there was no pot of gold at the end of Bob's malevolent rainbow. What if this was all just an elaborate ruse, concocted by an eccentric rich white dude who was several cards short of a full deck? Maybe this was some sick way of getting back at his daughter for cutting him out of her life and raising me as the anti-Bob—a fatherless, godless, progressive socialist.

I maxed out Betsy on the interstate heading northwest through the heart of Utah. I figured she could handle it with the expensive new innards. We forged ahead for five-plus hours, through Salt Lake City, bending around the Great Salt Lake, until we abandoned civilization once again for a remote rocky desert spot called Golden Spike National Historic Site.

"This is some serious bullshit," I declared as I pulled into the abandoned visitor center parking lot.

According to Bob's video, I was supposed to be wowed by the monumental achievement that took place at this site on May 10, 1869. The driving of the final spike that marked the official completion of America's first transcontinental railroad. The spot where the Central Pacific building east from Sacramento and the Union Pacific building west from Omaha were fused together after six years of spectacular expense and prodigious construction effort. Bob said it was the internet connection of its day—that it transformed America and changed the world. That it united our nation like never before, and represented a stunning feat of engineering and physical labor. That this was a largely unappreciated site of significance, perhaps the most important American site west of Independence Hall.

I felt none of his preordained awe.

Instead, I felt more exhausted than ever. And angry. I left the engine running and rushed out the door without saying anything to Amelia. I did a quick 360-degree survey of the landscape. Nothing but an unending dusty palate of brown and beige in every direction. Bland, depressing sagebrush with some stretches of wild green grass tossed in to speckle the monotony.

I wandered around the parking lot, shaking my head, almost trembling with growing fury, and not sure what to do with my rage. I hated feeling stranded in the middle of nowhere. It picked at one of my deepest, darkest phobias. The past couple days made me feel stuck in quicksand, unable to advance Bob's scavenger hunt from hell.

I trudged over to a brown slatted fence jutting out from the right end of the visitor center. The fence didn't extend far, so I walked across some patchy grass and stepped around the end of the fence. There was railroad track running parallel to the back of the visitor center, which I guessed was the big-deal famous spot I was supposed to fawn over.

A tall, gray-bearded park ranger ambled out of a maintenance-looking building on my left and we both looked at each other in surprise.

"Hello," he said flatly.

I just briefly raised my hand in reply. I was in no mood for chitchat.

"Sorry, sir, but the visitor center is closed."

"It's fine," I said dismissively.

The park ranger tried to make small talk—where I was from, where I was headed—but he soon took the hint from my abrupt answers, told me to have a nice day, and retreated through the door from which he'd emerged.

I walked slowly back around the fence to the parking lot. Amelia met me halfway, carrying the printed page of whatever drivel Bob wanted me to read.

"Uggghhh," I groaned as she held the page toward me.

Bob wanted me to know about some 1800s guy named Theodore "Crazy" Judah, an engineer who surveyed and mapped the western route of the first transcontinental railroad. Bob said it was Judah's obsessive drive that ultimately spurred private businessmen and the federal government to go all-in on finally building a railroad that stretched across the entire continent. Judah apparently wrote a short book called *A Practical Plan for Building the Pacific Railroad*. He printed the book at his own expense and gave a copy of the plan to every member of Congress. I stared at the page Amelia handed me. It was an excerpt from Crazy Judah's plan.

I finally summoned the bare minimum motivation and began reading aloud, but Amelia stopped me.

"What?" I protested.

"Aren't you supposed to read this on the actual site?"

"Geez," I said too harshly, "this is close enough. The guy said they're closed anyway."

"*Okay*," she said tersely.

I glanced at her and she seemed to have more to say, but she refrained and I didn't inquire.

"I just wanna get this over with," I said.

"Fine."

"'*It is the most magnificent project ever conceived,*'" I read without enthusiasm. "'*It is an enterprise more important in its bearings and results to the people of the United States, than any other project involving an expenditure of an equal amount of capital. It connects these two great oceans. It is an indissoluble bond of union between the populous States of the East, and the undeveloped regions of the fruitful West. It is a highway which leads to peace and future prosperity. An iron bond for the perpetuation of the Union and independence which we now enjoy.*'"

I remembered feeling some faint goosebumps when I read stuff at the first couple stops on the trip—and how I'd get a minor thrill when Amelia got a major thrill from hearing me read. Now I felt nothing. A sudden, deep sadness enveloped me.

I thrust the page back toward Amelia as if she was the secretary of this charade. After a brief pause, as if she wasn't going to accept the page from me, she took it and glanced over it.

"You missed a line," she said.

"Whatever."

"No, you did. Just one more, here at the end."

"Who cares?"

"I do."

"It doesn't matter. Why do you care?"

"I'm sorry—you must do it right. I won't sign off on this page unless you've done the whole thing. Every word. That's what you're contractually obliged to do. We can't have traveled all this way for you to cheat, even if it is just a few words."

We stared into each other's eyes for several seconds. The usual warmth and gleeful humor in her eyes had, at least temporarily, diminished. She was serious. It was a showdown of sorts, with only the sound of the wind whistling across our sagebrush surroundings.

I blinked first, of course.

"Shit," I said as I snatched the page back from her. My eyes fell to the bottom of the page, and I forced out the last line to satisfy her demand: "'*Little plans have no magic to stir men's blood. Make big plans—Daniel Burnham.*' Who the hell is Daniel Burnham?"

She pulled out her phone and began typing.

"You don't have to look him up," I said, rolling my eyes.

"Daniel Burnham was a famous nineteenth-century American architect," she read aloud before I cut her off.

"Let's just get out of here."

I already had my seatbelt buckled by the time Amelia stepped inside and closed the door behind her. I jerked Betsy into drive, and the abrupt movement threw Amelia off-balance. She steadied herself on the back of the front passenger chair.

"It's going to be alright, Tom," she said in a calm, reassuring tone.

I didn't believe her. I roared the engine across the parking lot, but Amelia stopped me before we made it to the exit toward the highway.

"What?" I snapped.

"Where are we going? You don't know your next destination."

My shoulders slumped and my head fell back against the seat. She was right. I sighed and threw Betsy reluctantly back into park. Then I unbuckled in a huff, turned on the TV, pressed play on the VCR, and collapsed into the couch. As Bob's face flickered into view, I didn't think I could take it anymore. I didn't really hear any of his setup, but my brain melted down when I heard him say "Grand Canyon."

"Oh my God," I said, burying my face in my hands. "That's at least another entire day!" I yelled, punching the side of the kitchen counter with my right fist. It hurt. The sharp slam startled Amelia.

I lunged forward from the couch and ripped the videotape from the VCR. My sudden move caused a string of black tape to remain caught in the machine, but I just dropped the tape to the floor and stepped back into the driver's seat.

I surged out of the parking lot, and we rocked and swayed as I wrangled Betsy far too recklessly back onto the deserted highway. Amelia got out of her seat and very carefully removed the dangling videotape from the VCR's mouth. In my peripheral view I saw her coolly wind the unraveled tape back into the cassette and place it in the box. Then she returned to the passenger seat and buckled her seatbelt.

We'd been on the road less than five minutes before I heard a disturbing, consistent *whomp-whomp-whomp* sound. As soon as I could, I pulled off on a decent-sized shoulder and rushed outside to investigate.

It was a flat tire on the driver's side.

I smacked Betsy's hull with the palm of my hand. I unleashed a primordial yell at the very top of my lungs. It actually hurt my throat a little. I spotted a red-brown rock about the size of my fist nearby. I rushed over, bent down, grabbed the rock, and flung it as hard and far as I could into the relentlessly cheerless landscape off the highway.

I determined to quit. In that moment, I didn't really feel I had an alternative. Bob won. He got the better of me. The road, the RV, his conservative diatribes, and the expense was all too much for me to handle. I couldn't just keep taking these hits, spending money I didn't have, without any real proof that it would all pay off.

I stomped back into the RV and announced my decision: "I quit."

"What's wrong now?" Amelia asked as I grabbed my phone from the console and rushed back outside. She followed me out with, "What do you mean you quit?"

I didn't answer her as I'd already dialed Bob. The moment he answered, I said, "I quit."

"Quit what?" he asked as if he didn't know.

"This whole…whatever this fucking trip is! I can't do it anymore. I'm stuck in the desert—the middle of nowhere. I've got a flat now—on top of the thousands of dollars of repairs I *just* got done. I'm completely broke. I can't afford to finish this. Especially never knowing how much of it is left. There was probably never going to be any money prize at the end of this shit show anyway."

Bob chuckled his condescending chuckle. I despised it when he did that.

"Well, I guess you're just gonna have to exercise a little faith," he said.

"Oh, screw that, man!"

As I paced through the gravel behind Betsy, I glimpsed Amelia waving down a pickup truck that approached from behind us. The truck pulled off the road, stopping in front of the RV.

"Alright, just calm down now. Take a deep breath," said Bob.

"No! I'm not gonna take a deep breath. This is it. I'm done. I'm quitting. This is officially me breaking out of the deal. I don't want to do this anymore. *You win.* Congratulations."

The driver got out of the pickup and conversed with Amelia. It was the park ranger from Golden Spike. Together, they examined the flat.

"It's not a game," said Bob.

"Like hell it's not! And the joke's on me. You're probably not even rich. Just some bitter, lonely old bastard getting some sick kicks out of lecturing a millennial."

"Well, you probably got the 'lonely old bastard' part right. Believe what you want about it, but it's not a game on my end. It *is* a sort of challenge, but I'm not playing games. I never said it'd be easy. But there *is* a lot of money with your name on it, as long as you complete the job."

"What part of this do you not get? I don't want to complete the job anymore. I am quitting the job. It's *over*."

I hung up on Bob and was a nanosecond from spiking my phone into the simmering gray asphalt of the highway, but I managed to resist the powerful urge.

I plodded back inside the RV without talking to Amelia and the ranger. It was lazy and irresponsible of me, but I didn't care. I just didn't want to deal with it. Mom says I do this sometimes when I don't want to face something—I try to ignore it to make the problem go away. I dropped my phone on the console, then laid flat on my back on the couch with my left arm over my eyes to seal out any sunlight.

After several minutes of welcome solitude, I heard Amelia enter.

"Are you alright?" she asked.

I just shrugged my shoulders.

"Well, that was Ben, the park ranger who stopped to help. He's called a roadside assistant service for us. Should be here within half an hour."

I wanted to say "thanks" and tell her how relieved I was that help was on the way (because I really *was* relieved). Instead, I thrust out my right hand with a thumbs-up.

I fished in my duffle for my cigarettes and went outside again. I didn't tell Amelia where I was going, because I didn't know myself. I walked maybe fifty yards down the road from the RV. There wasn't a tree in sight. I finally just sat in the dirt with my back against a wooden fence post and smoked. A hot breeze blew the smoke back in my face.

Eventually, the roadside assistance truck came and went, but I didn't budge from my spot in the dirt. I guess they changed the flat tire and I guess Amelia paid for it, since my wallet was in the front pocket of the jeans I was wearing.

I silently drove us back toward Salt Lake City. I didn't have a plan—I had just quit the trip, after all—but it was getting late, so I figured we needed to eat and find a place to park Betsy Ross for the night. Beyond that, I presumed I'd ditch Betsy somewhere and work out a way back to northern California.

As the sun faded, we happened on a Love's Travel Stop north of Salt Lake City. Still without conversing, we went inside the Love's and ordered from the Subway sandwich counter.

As we unwrapped our sandwiches in the parking lot, I finally said, "Thanks for taking care of the tire thing."

"You *do* realize you can't actually quit this trip, right?" she asked before taking a bite of her all-veggie sandwich.

I winced and leaned my head to the right skeptically. I took a huge bite of my sandwich instead of answering her question. So, she answered for me: "Because *we* have a deal. You and I, remember?"

I sighed and took an extra-long sip of my soda.

"So, you *must* finish this to honor our agreement," she continued. "Sorry to be so blunt, but we signed a contract of our own."

I don't think I'd heard her sound so emphatic before—even a little intimidating.

She was right, of course, but I was frozen in denial. We'd been traveling so long together; it was easy for me to forget about our deal. And it was easy to forget that she was now free to bail on it at any time, and I would *still* have to pay her tuition. Her reminder made me feel guilty for snapping at her all day. She didn't have to be here at all. She *chose* to hang out with this loser.

I let my sandwich dangle in my right hand at my side and leaned my head back against Betsy's door. I was trapped. There was no way out. The irony struck me that *I* was the only one to blame for not being able to quit Bob's road trip. Because *I* had been so desperate for Amelia to come along. And now I couldn't quit because *I* owed her.

I suddenly recalled Bob saying, "Your word is worth way more than any inheritance." And I really hated that his words were loitering in my head like that.

"I know. You're right," I relented. "I mean, it sucks, but I guess I can't quit."

"You can do this, Tom." Her intimidating tone was gone.

"Can I?"

"You've come so far already."

"Not far enough. Sorry I've been such an asshole the past few days."

"All is forgiven."

"Just like that?"

"Yeah, just like that."

She grinned at me, and I managed a half grin in reply.

Since it was so late, we decided to risk staying the night in the Love's parking lot. It was *way* better than the Rusty Clif Motel.

Before bed, Amelia said she looked up what happened to Crazy Judah. It took me a moment to remember who she was talking about. Finally, it came to me—the transcontinental railroad guy. She said he died of yellow fever while crossing the isthmus of Panama in 1863. He was apparently only thirty-seven years old. He never even got to see the completion of the dream he had spearheaded. His was a big plan—and it had more than enough magic to stir men's blood.

Amelia added that no one even bothered to invite Crazy Judah's widow to the Golden Spike ceremony.

"Damn—that's cold," I said. "They must've been Republicans."

That made Amelia giggle. She was really what made the trip tolerable.

NINETEEN

The Arizona wilderness managed to be even more barren and menacing than Utah's. I mean, there is a rough-hewn appeal to it, I guess, but now that we'd had problems with Betsy Ross, I had constant anxiety about breaking down in the middle of literal nowhere. We rarely saw other vehicles on Highway 89. If Betsy had any mishaps on this route, we'd be stuck forever, wasting away to skeletal remains like desert victims in cartoons.

At some point in the afternoon, Amelia informed me that we'd entered Native American reservation territory. As far as I know, we were still in it when we stopped at another Subway—not because we couldn't get enough of Subway; it just appeared to be the only option in the somber town.

After we'd eaten our sandwiches in the parking lot, I gathered our trash. As I turned to walk to a trashcan that was just outside the Subway entrance, a beat-up, navy-blue pickup slowed to a stop in my path. The driver's side window descended, and a Native American–looking man scowled at me. His face was wrinkled and stern as he stared me down for an uncomfortably long moment. I paused in my tracks and noted the apparent displeasure on his stoic face. I also noticed a similarly scowling woman in the passenger seat. She stared me down too.

I was about to walk around the bed of the truck and continue on my way to the trashcan when the man spoke in a gruff voice.

"Do you need a mask?"

I wasn't exactly sure I'd heard him correctly, so I said, "I'm sorry?"

"I said, *do you need a mask?*" The man raised his voice and his eyebrows, emphasizing the seriousness of his question.

My mind raced, trying to decipher what he was getting at. Finally, I realized that I looked like a threat to his community the way I was callously walking around maskless. I cursed myself for not having my mask on, especially since I'd just been wearing it a few minutes earlier inside the Subway. I'd only tossed it in the RV while we ate outside. Amelia and I never wore them around each other inside the RV.

"Uh, no," I finally stammered. "I've got one. It's uh, it's in my RV there."

"Well, I suggest you put it on, then." He sounded and looked like he meant business.

"Yes, okay, I was going to." He started rolling up his window as I quickly added, "I was just throwing this stuff away."

The man shook his head disgustedly and the truck rumbled slowly away. I wanted to chase him down and explain that I wasn't what he thought I was—some privileged, white, mask-hating Trump worshipper. That I was actually just the *opposite*. I was on *his* side. I believed in masks and quarantining and all of that generally. I wanted him to understand that I was not *that kind* of white guy. I was a Bernie campaign staffer, for God's sake.

Instead, I just continued my insensitive, maskless walk of shame across the cracked parking lot to the trashcan and back, vowing to myself never to be so callous ever again.

The mask confrontation made me think of Bob. I was putting off pleading with him to let me recant my "I quit" declaration. I couldn't procrastinate any longer. I had to see if he would take me back, especially since we were over halfway to the Grand Canyon.

Bob answered his phone with a sharp, almost yelling, "Hello?" There was a terribly loud motor noise on the phone that almost drowned him out.

"What's that noise?" I shouted.

"My lawn mower," he replied. "Here, hold on a second…"

I heard some metallic jostling sounds, and then the motor noise ceased.

"There," he said, "That better?"

"Yeah. You mow your own lawn?"

"Oh yeah."

"I thought you'd have a whole team of lawn guys or something."

"Nah. I like to mow. So, what's going on? I didn't figure on hearing from you today. I thought you quit."

"Yes. But, uh…"

"You had a change of heart?"

"I guess you could say that."

"Well, twenty-five million dollars has a tendency to do that," he laughed, which I resented because to me his laughter always sounded like *I-know-way-better-than-this-idiot* laughter.

"So, can I still finish the trip?"

"I don't know. Can you? Yesterday, you made it sound impossible."

"Yeah, I mean, I haven't figured out how I'll be able to do it yet." I hesitated before adding, "But I guess I'm gonna try to come up with something."

"Well…that gives me some hope for you, son. There you go— resilience! Sometimes in life, you just can't take no for an answer. Gotta just figure it out."

I closed my eyes and rolled my tensing neck. *Geezers and their freakin' tough-as-nails crap.*

"I just didn't know if I was allowed back in after I quit like that."

"I haven't ripped up the contract yet. I figured I'd hear from you eventually. Where are you today?"

"Somewhere in Arizona," I replied with zero enthusiasm.

"Okay. Well, I reckon you're over halfway done now, so you just might make it after all."

I guess that was his version of encouragement, but I was stuck on him saying *"halfway done."* If I was really only halfway, I might hurl myself into the Grand Canyon.

"So what have you learned so far?" While I was still fixated on the dread that I would be doing this trip forever, he added, "Anything?"

"Uhh…I don't know. I've learned this is a damn big country."

"Well, that's something, I guess. Anything you've extrapolated from that, or…?"

I really didn't know what he was fishing for.

"Like what?" I made the mistake of asking.

"Maybe like learning to appreciate different points of view? America's natural beauty? Our unique history?"

I made a skeptical sort of snorting noise. "I've learned some very *selective* history."

"How do you figure that?"

"Come on, it's a propaganda tour. The MAGA tour. You haven't sent me anywhere that shows the US in a negative light."

"There's no point in dwelling on the bad stuff, 'cause I know you got plenty of that at commie college. By the way, I'm curious—did you ever pause to question anything you were fed in college? When you learned about the glories of the Soviet Union, did anyone ever question Stalin? Have you ever read any Solzhenitsyn? If not, that wasn't a class—that was a pep rally."

"I got the other side of the coin in college. The stuff that your generation sweeps under the rug to maintain power. You see

American history as this glorious past to be proud of, and I just don't see it that way. Like, at all."

"But you refuse to see *any* of the good. You can't change the past, so why keep on prosecuting it? We should appreciate the good parts, try to learn from the bad stuff, and do better going forward. I mean, that's *life*, basically. Where does wallowing in shame get you? Nowhere productive. It's paralyzing. A nation can never thrive on shame."

"It's your sunshine-and-rainbows-version of America that makes it so paralyzing for the marginalized."

"Really? You can look at America as glass-half-empty, which seems to be your socialist view, or glass-half-full. Here's the reality—this glass-half-empty, perpetual-victim, loathing-and-revenge politics will eventually cause America to fall victim to despots, and it will speed up the decline of what makes America exceptional."

"Oh, geez, why do you right-wingers always get high on this America is *so* exceptional crap?"

"Because it *is*! When did patriotism become a vice? Look, America has always been for optimists. I'm no psychiatrist, but I learned from my wife that the glass-half-full view is the only way to live. Her instinct was to always look for that silver lining, to search for a positive in every situation. She was the Sherlock Holmes of finding silver linings." He grew quiet for a moment, then added, "There was no silver lining when she died, though."

I don't think I've ever had a glass-half-full view of anything in life. Yet, I hated Bob pegging me correctly. Silver linings about America, though? No, he couldn't be right about this. America had way too much baggage. Still, there was the tiniest sliver of me that was curious about what he said he learned from his wife, that "the glass-half-full-view of life is the only way to live." It annoyed the hell out of me that Bob could be right about anything. I pulled myself out of this thought spiral and resisted. I couldn't let him wear me down.

"How can you call your country great when it's still so racist? And…and…" I tried to come up with some quick examples, "it invaded Iraq to find weapons of mass destruction, that—*oops*— didn't exist? When it uses the CIA to jack with so many other countries? When it has the wealthiest population in the world, yet old people can't afford their prescriptions? I mean, it sent you to Vietnam as a teenager!"

"Well, now, you're right about Vietnam," he said, which had to be the first time he'd ever said I was right about anything. "Look, if anyone should be disillusioned about America, it should be me after going through that. When I was rotting in that jungle, I *hated* Uncle Sam for putting me there. But then I remember the one time at Christmas they let us make a phone call back home. I waited in line two hours for my turn. We each got sixty seconds on the phone. I talked to my mother first, then my dad. I'll never forget it, he said, 'You look after yourself now, son, make sure you get back home in one piece.' And I said, 'Yes sir, I will.' And then— even though I can probably count the number of times we told each other 'I love you' over the years on one hand—real quick, because we were running out of time, he said, 'I love you son.' And he said that with such confidence, I remember, that it really stuck with me. And I carried that around with me every day for the rest of my tour."

The stressful week and restless sleep had probably weakened my emotions. As Bob talked about his dad, I felt the sting of tears trying to form in my eyes.

"That was a small thing, but it helped me get through," continued Bob. "I decided I had to stay alive because there was life worth getting back to. I realized that America—the people—hadn't sent me to Vietnam. It was wicked, corrupt men in our government who put me there—namely LBJ. That sixty-second phone call with my parents reminded me that America, for all its faults, had more potential than anywhere on the planet. And *that's* what I had to get back for—not a promise, but the *potential*. See, people used to understand that America was about the potential. Why else would black soldiers volunteer to fight in the Civil War and two world wars? What else would compel them to do that? It's not like most of them had a good situation to come home to. It was the *potential*. Anyway, somewhere along the way, folks started confusing the potential for a guarantee. See, that's the great lie of socialism: that it can guarantee stuff for people, that it can guarantee happiness. The Founders knew better—life, liberty, and the *pursuit* of happiness. 'Cause there are no guarantees in life. Period."

He always had to bring things around to socialism. It really pissed me off. I was about to give him an earful about it, but then I saw the same pickup truck from earlier heading slowly in our direction through the parking lot again. I had been milling around outside Betsy while I talked to Bob, still maskless. I didn't want any more trouble, so I told Bob I really had to go and escaped inside the RV just as the truck slow-rolled past us.

Bob's call rankled my mood again. Even this deep into the journey, he still knew how to get under my skin. How could a man of his age and stature be so wrong on all the issues, and be so confident in his wrongness? I also didn't like how unprepared he always made me feel. I hated to admit it, but he was right that I'd never really had to defend my beliefs. I'd always just run in circles of people who believed the same things I do. We ranted and made arguments to each other, but there was never any real pushback because we essentially agreed with each other.

Late that afternoon, we drove past a Trump 2020 billboard, which was all the impetus I needed to ask Amelia point-blank, "Let's say the election's tomorrow and you can vote. Are you voting Trump or Biden?"

She apparently finished the sentence she was reading in *To Kill a Mockingbird*, because several seconds passed before she looked up from her book with crinkled eyes.

"Are those my only two choices?"

"Well, yeah. They're the candidates."

"I guess I'd have to say neither, then."

"Why?"

I *had* to know.

"Well…I suppose I prefer my heads of state to be able to speak in complete sentences." She looked at me. "So, that disqualifies both candidates in my view."

It was not the answer I expected, so I laughed.

"But say you were *forced* to choose between those two. Who would you pick?"

"I…I don't know," she said, sounding a bit exasperated. "Why are you so desperate to know?"

"I'm just curious."

"I'm sorry. I've tried to avoid talking politics with you because it obviously means a lot to you, and I want to be polite."

"So, does that mean you're a Trump person?"

"No! I don't know. I can't vote here. But since you keep badgering me about it, I can say, with all due respect, that I'm *not* a socialist. But I don't go around saying I'm conservative or Labour Party back home either. I don't want to be tethered to *any* political party. Defending freedom, and justice, and standing up for basic rights—that's what I'm interested in politically. And I suppose I always considered that very American."

"Alright," I said. "Finally! A spark of political passion from Amelia."

She shrugged and looked down at her book again. She barely had time to read another sentence before I added, "You know, I guess I'm just a little surprised because, well, you're a kind, loving person. And ... basically socialism stands for minorities, you know, the oppressed."

She looked up from her book again, her brow wrinkled.

"Does it? That's simply the marketing campaign. Where are the world's socialists when it comes to China's treatment of the Uighurs?"

I didn't know who the Uighurs were, but I didn't admit it.

"China has them in actual concentration camps, right now," she added. "And Western governments simply yawn and get back to their tea. Curious, isn't it? And wrong."

I liked her fervor and felt I was finally getting somewhere.

"I come by my anti-socialism honestly, because we had an immigrant woman called Adriana from Romania who went to my church when I was growing up. And there were many Sunday lunches at my grandparents' house where she told us horror stories from communist Romania before she fled."

"You sound like Bob now," I retorted. "I get exhausted with this notion that socialism equals communism. It doesn't. Don't we have a responsibility to do more than just say 'here you go, here's some freedom, good luck making a living?' If a society has the wealth and means to help its citizens, shouldn't we do that?"

"Perhaps."

"Perhaps?" I raised my voice indignantly.

"I've just never thought of it as fully the responsibility of government. Besides, if you want to have a quality welfare state, don't you have to foster the freedom that allows a society to produce enough wealth so it can pay for all the welfare?"

"I...uh...sure," I conceded. "I guess."

"Ultimately, I see it as the church's responsibility to care for the poor. Because that's what scripture mandates. Jesus said—"

"Here we go," I interrupted sarcastically.

"Jesus *said*," she repeated over my interruption, "true religion is caring for orphans and widows and keeping yourself from being corrupted by the world."

"What is that? What are you doing? Why do you do that all the time?"

"Do what?"

"Bring Jesus into everything. It's like a coping mechanism or something. Some people use drugs. Some drink. Some quote the Bible like you do, I guess."

"Beg your pardon?"

"Is it part of your dad-abandonment complex or something?"

"What?"

"This religious shield you hide behind."

"I'm not hiding behind anything."

"Yeah, maybe you use Jesus as this imaginary perfect replacement for the father you never had."

"I'll ask you to check yourself, Tom," she fired back, raising her voice. "His is the name above *all* names, the one which, like it or not, you will eventually bow down to according to scripture. For your own sake, his is not a power you want to treat lightly or shake your fist at."

I'd clearly gone too far (again). I drove in reprimanded silence for a moment before she continued.

"The gospel of Christ is truth. It's the power of God at work, saving everyone who believes. It's simply terrible manners for you to attack me this way, besides. If I knew you were a devout Buddhist or something, I would never think to insult you that way— that your faith was just a balm to fill the hole left by your missing father. And even if it were, what's wrong with that? It's much better than wandering through the hopeless void being bitter and cynical at everything. Christianity makes an easy target, I suppose. I suspect there's something about it that hits a person between the eyes and makes them very uncomfortable, so they lash out. Jesus is not a neutral figure. The mere mention of his name instigates a response. To some it's a swear word. To others—to me—it's salvation."

There was a confident edge to her voice that made me feel raked across the coals. An odd sense of guilt and shame engulfed me, like I was a kid in the principal's office, knew I was in for it, and had no one to rescue me. I wondered again how I'd stumbled across this person. She was unlike anyone I'd ever met.

I drove quietly for a while, letting the dust settle from her rant. I considered a joke to try to salvage the situation. I started to open my mouth, then reconsidered. Then I reconsidered again.

"So, then...does that mean you'd vote for Trump?"

She sighed heavily, shook her head, and stared out her window. My joke did not land, and I felt like an idiot. For good reason.

TWENTY

We spent the night in a crowded RV park near Grand Canyon Village. If it wasn't for a lot of people wearing masks, you could almost believe the world was back to normal. And how I wanted it to be. Sometimes it felt like COVID had changed everything, and I hated it. I hated the constant uncertainty and despair. I hated walking on eggshells, fearing I'd contract it at any moment. I hated the not knowing when, or even *if*, life would get back to normal. I hated all the stupid conspiracies about treatments. Maybe being there, surrounded by people trying to vacation in spite of all the uncertainty and despair, should've boosted me with hope. But I found it all very surreal.

Amelia seemed her usual, cheery self in the morning, which surprised me because we'd barely spoken the rest of the evening after I'd insulted her devout faith. By the time I woke up, she had apparently already walked to a store because she unloaded a plastic bag with a small carton of eggs, a loaf of bread, and orange juice. She made eggs and toast for us. Her kindness in doing so, and her sunny disposition as she went about the task, baffled me. How could she serve me like that after how I'd treated her the past several days? Why did I always end up trying to push people away? I needed to figure out how to make it up to her and redeem myself.

As usual, video Bob told me way more than I needed to know about Grand Canyon history, including how President Theodore Roosevelt first protected it by declaring it a national monument in 1908. Bob made it extra clear that even though he applauded Theodore Roosevelt's work in helping establish America's National Park system, he drew the line there. He did not condone Theodore's overall approach to being president.

"Teddy Roosevelt is a fascinating character," noted Bob, "but he changed the presidency for the worse and there was no going back after that. He was our first progressive president."

"What's wrong with that?" I muttered to the TV screen, cutting my eyes toward Amelia. "I like him already."

Bob went on at length about how Theodore Roosevelt's ego and lust for power caused him to swell the presidency. Then Woodrow Wilson took that ball and ran with it, he said, growing the executive branch far beyond how the Founders envisioned it.

"And it hasn't stopped growing since," said Bob. "Calvin Coolidge was probably the last guy to actually try to trim it back. Dadgum Roosevelts—closest thing America's had to a royal family. They were progressive to their core, which also means they were *arrogant*. Thought they knew best how to run everyone's lives, and Democrats have been trying to one-up them ever since. It's really disgusting."

I was on the verge of unleashing a snarky tirade back at the screen, but I glanced at Amelia and the calm, innocent look on her face as she ate her toast made me resist the urge. I like to think that was progress on my part.

I don't have much to compare it to because before this trip I'd barely been anywhere, but the Grand Canyon is the most amazing thing I've ever seen. For once in life, something actually lived up to the hype.

It was like looking out over an ocean of meticulously sculpted rock that stretched on forever. Every time I thought we'd surely discovered the definitive stunning angle, the next bend in the walking trail would reveal an even more mind-blowing vista. I was entranced by the endless layers of flat-top peaks and jagged valleys, with their seemingly limitless shades of brown, red, and gray. I couldn't stop staring at it. Amelia seemed equally enthralled.

While we paused at one alcove, silently taking in the view, she tilted her face toward the sky, closed her eyes and murmured something. I think she was praying again. Sometimes, in spite of what I'd said to her the day before, I was kind of jealous of her faith. I kind of wished I had something like that to latch on to, instead of feeling as alone and vulnerable as I constantly did. I felt those things less being with her, though.

We leisurely walked the paths along the South Rim. It was hot, but the steady wind made it bearable. Amelia read aloud from the National Park brochure as we walked. She was especially curious about an endangered bird, the California condor, one of the rarest birds in the world, and (as she read) the largest land bird in North America, with a wingspan of up to nine and a half feet. She thought it would be amazing to get to see one, but I didn't think she should get her hopes up.

Two hours flew by, and I barely noticed or cared. I actually felt myself starting to relax after the strain of the past week. The canyon views were hypnotic enough to make me almost forget why I was there.

"This is the most I've seen you smile all week," Amelia remarked. "Dare I say you're enjoying yourself?"

"I might be. I'm not sure what this strange sensation is," I replied sarcastically.

We found a picnic table with relative shade and sat for a while. I was surprised by Bob's choice for the required reading given his anti-Teddy Roosevelt rant from the video. It was part of a speech Roosevelt made about the Grand Canyon on his first trip to Arizona in 1903:

"In that canyon Arizona has a natural wonder, which, so far as I know, is in kind absolutely unparalleled throughout the rest of the world. I shall not attempt to describe it, because I cannot. I could not choose words that would convey or that could convey to any outsider what that canyon is. I want to ask you to do one thing in connection with it in your own interest and in the interest of the country—to keep this great wonder of nature as it now is… Man cannot improve on it. Not a bit. The ages have been at work on it and man can only mar it. What you can do is to keep it for your children and your children's children and for all who come after you, as one of the great sights which every American, if he can travel at all, should see. Keep the Grand Canyon of Arizona as it is."

I slid the page and a pen across the table to Amelia.

"It's a metaphor, isn't it?" she asked as she signed her name.

"What is?"

"Protecting the Grand Canyon sounds like a metaphor for protecting your Constitution, your freedom," she replied, handing the page back to me.

I was a little jarred by her comment. I scanned Roosevelt's words in light of her conjecture. I'm not sure her assessment was accurate. But maybe.

Amelia suddenly snapped her head around, distracted. She stood up with a start.

"What's wrong?"

"Oh my gosh, I see one!" she declared.

She sprang off her bench and jogged toward the nearest rocky ledge, which didn't have any railing, of course. I instantly thought,

This is how it happens—this is how people somehow manage to fall to their deaths at the Grand Canyon.

"See what?" I called, jumping up from the table to follow her.

"The California condor!"

She whipped out her phone and ostensibly began recording, panning from left to right in what I assumed must be National Geographic–worthy footage. I arrived at her side and could hardly believe it—she was right, it was unmistakably the California condor, with its dark reddish head and bright white triangles under its enormous black wings.

"Oh my God!" I said. "That's really it!"

"It's incredible! It's a miracle!"

The majestic bird dipped and soared over the Canyon in front of us, like a death-defying circus performer giving us a private show. After about a minute, it glided down and away from us, farther into the Canyon until it was out of view.

Amelia excitedly examined her phone for the footage. Then her face fell into a pained expression. Suddenly, she laughed rather maniacally.

"Nooooo!" she cried. "Nooooo, I can't believe it!"

"*What?*"

"I didn't get it!"

"What? How?"

"I don't know! I thought I hit record, but I guess it was still in photo mode. Oh, I can't believe it."

I patted her back, which, like mine was damp with sweat. "Nice try. So close."

"But I had it," she said, still laughing and shaking her head. "I totally had it."

"It was definitely the California condor," I said as if that was any consolation.

It was a beautiful, amazing sight. But it was one of those fleeting moments that, despite Amelia's best effort, couldn't be captured. Like a lot of moments in life, I guess.

To my surprise, there was enough cell phone coverage on the South Rim for me to call Bob. When he answered, I told him I didn't have him being a National Parks guy on my bingo card.

"Why not?" he asked.

"I thought you didn't like big government programs and stuff."

"I don't. But within reason, protecting certain National Parks is a good and proper function of government."

"Huh," I said, feeling almost stumped. "I think we might've just agreed on something."

"What—that some things may be worth preserving?"

I mentally froze as I calculated his question. Were we talking about the same thing? Or had he switched over to that metaphor Amelia had detected? I decided not to probe.

"Yeah…I guess so."

"Huh. Maybe we should hang up while we're ahead then," he joked.

"Probably a good idea," I said, hoping to escape early for a change.

"Hey, one thing before you go," he said. My heart sank and I braced myself for an onslaught of lib-bashing. "I was thinking about Betty today. It's our anniversary. You never stop missing a person like that, even after they've been gone twenty-five years. Really wish you could've known her."

He paused and I couldn't tell if he wanted me to say something. But I didn't know what I could possibly say.

"Believe me," he continued, "she was the *much* better half."

I believed him.

"Anyway, I just thought I should tell you that if you ever get around to thinking about getting married someday, make sure you're best friends first."

His totally random advice perplexed me. Finally, I just said, "Okay... I'll, uh... I'll keep that in mind."

TWENTY-ONE

By the next afternoon we were in the wilds of northern Nevada when we paused for teatime at a remote rest stop. We were slowly making our way toward the extreme southern tip of Washington (aiming for some site related to the Lewis and Clark expedition). We took our tea outside, stretching our legs in the breezy parking lot.

I watched a guy with long graying hair don his helmet and straddle his gleaming motorcycle. He had tattooed biceps busting out of a sleeveless shirt. His motorcycle started with a low growl, then he roared out of the parking lot and back onto the interstate. Sometimes I'd notice a random older guy like that and wonder if he could be my dad. I shared my dumb observation with Amelia.

"That wasn't him," she deadpanned, "He's too cool."

I grinned at her. "That hurts. Wow. Could've been *your* dad, then."

"Maybe. Although he didn't look like a Jared to me."

"Your dad's name is *Jared*?"

"Yeah, Jared Hughes."

"At least you have a name to go with yours."

"Sorry."

"Nah, it's fine. I'm used to being a literal bastard. It's all I know."

Amelia almost spewed her tea laughing. I laughed too.

"I've always struggled with forgiving my dad," Amelia admitted. "It's a real test of my Christian faith, I suppose. Ironic, isn't it? Forgiveness is at the core of our faith. It should be a little easier for me to figure out."

"Forgiving dads is uniquely hard, I guess. I know my mom never forgave Bob. I never really thought he deserved her forgiveness. Maybe your dad doesn't either."

I thought I was being semi-profound, affirming her bitterness toward her dad, giving her permission to hate him.

"Oh, I could never say that. I can't sponge up God's grace then refuse to give a drop to Jared Hughes. Jesus told a whole parable about that."

I didn't understand her level of faith. Not that I wanted it, but even if I did, it didn't seem attainable to me. Yet somehow, being around her made me feel less hopeless all the time. Less hopeless, that is, until that night, when we collapsed on our respective beds after the longest day of driving of the whole trip. I felt myself fading fast when Amelia's voice broke through the hum of the AC.

"Have you ever considered how going to sleep every night is a kind of rehearsal for death? Maybe that's why we tend toward melancholy at sunset."

Her stark observation woke me up a little—and made me squirm a lot.

"Uh, *no*. That's really dark—you doing okay back there?"

"Yeah, I'm fine."

"I've never really thought about it. I try *not* to think about it actually."

"It's a nightly reminder of our mortality."

"I don't really want to be reminded."

"So you just avoid thinking about death?" she asked.

"Doesn't everyone?"

"What if you died tomorrow? You never think about that?"

"My mom warned me about that when I was a kid. She said it's a classic church trap, when they're trying to convert you."

"Ohhh. No. No trap here. I'm just honestly asking."

"I don't know. I guess I'd wonder what the hell was that all about? Sure seemed like a waste."

"Tom, that's quite bleak."

"Well, you asked."

"Thank you for being honest. Well, just remember, morning is different. It's new life. It's a reminder of the reality of the resurrection. 'Weeping may last through the night, but joy comes with the morning.'"

I grinned to myself in the dark. She really couldn't help herself when it came to the faith stuff—it just came gushing out all the time. She apparently cared about the state of my soul. I loved her for it. And I was really desperate to tell her. There was no way that she loved me the same way—but I was desperate to have *some* special status with her to cling to. Like a total dork, I suddenly blurted, "So…can I be your best friend?"

I hoped the ensuing silence was her considering my out-of-the-blue proposal. But the silence was long enough that I wondered if she was asleep.

"I suppose you already are," she replied finally. "Because I don't really know many other Americans yet."

"So I've got a head start."

"Yes."

"That's good. I'm a progressive—I like head starts." I paused, then added, "That's a progressive joke that Bob would like. Or maybe not."

She gave me a polite laugh at least. I don't know if she said anything else after that because I fell asleep.

TWENTY-TWO

"It took Lewis and Clark a year and a half to make it from St. Louis to the Pacific Ocean. Can you imagine?" asked the wobbly image of Bob from the TV screen. He was leaning toward the camera, elbows on his knees, wearing a cap with an American flag on it. "What an American story! A year and a half of walking, canoeing, riding horses, and sleeping outside all the time. Now *that* was some grit. Can you imagine pushing toward something day after day, no matter the elements, without a clue how long it's going to take you to get there?"

"Uh, yeah," I said to the screen, "I can imagine that."

I smirked in Amelia's direction, but I don't think she found it as cleverly humorous as I did.

"You know what phrase pops up over and over in their journals?" asked Bob onscreen.

"No, Bob, I do not," I said, "but I can't wait for you to tell me!"

I was already feeling sarcastic that morning.

"*We proceeded on.*" Bob leaned back with a satisfied grin and slapped his right knee with his right hand. "*We proceeded on,*" he repeated. "Isn't that great? Most of the time, that's the only choice you have with all the twists and turns in life. Are you gonna stop and have a pity party because you can't see where the trail leads? Or are you going to proceed on?"

Neither of us wanted to leave the RV park we'd lucked upon. It was no-frills, but it didn't need any because it faced the intoxicating view of the Columbia River as it merged with the Pacific Ocean. It was Amelia's first time seeing the Pacific, and she was captivated by its endless shimmering blue.

Our destination was only about a mile up Highway 101 from the RV park. So, after finishing Bob's video midmorning, we walked along the highway through a cold, fall-like breeze to a place called Station Camp. Part of Lewis and Clark National Historical Park, it was where Lewis and Clark apparently camped for several days when they first reached the Pacific Ocean in November 1805. Station Camp was barely a spot in the road—only a Bob-level history nerd would send someone there.

"This is it?" I asked incredulously when we arrived.

Amelia didn't answer as she surveyed the scene. It was kind of a drab site, with a handful of info markers and a few Chinook canoes that had seen better days. Fortunately, we still had a full view of the Columbia and the Pacific; otherwise, the only thing that saved the site aesthetically was a tiny gray church with a sign to the left of its door that said St. Mary's McGowan. Amelia loved it, of course, and had me snap a few photos of her standing on its front steps.

Bob's required reading included excerpts from the journal of William Clark. The last part of my reading was a curious line from a letter Clark wrote to Toussaint Charbonneau, the man who joined the expedition as an interpreter with his wife, Sacagawea, and their newborn son:

"'Your woman who accompanied you that long, dangerous and fatiguing route to the Pacific Ocean and back deserved a greater reward for her attention and services on that route than we had in our power to give her at the Mandans.'"

I asked Bob about it when I called him that afternoon. He seemed surprised and enthused by my inquiry.

"Sacagawea may be the most remarkable aspect of the whole expedition," he said. "Because she endured all the hardships with a baby on her back the whole time. That is unreal. I guarantee you only a woman could do that. A man wouldn't have lasted half a day carrying around a baby out there."

I hadn't pegged Bob as having even an ounce of feminism in him. I had him on speaker just because I was still feeling sarcastic and wanted Amelia to hear everything so I could make reaction faces at her.

"A man's *got* to have a great woman to help him navigate life's journey," he continued.

And just like that, he flushed away his flimsy feminist credit. I shot an exasperated look at Amelia.

It seemed to me like he thought Sacagawea's greatest accomplishment was assisting these uppity white guys who got all the credit for the big adventure. Amelia had done some googling before we walked to Station Camp and informed me that Sacagawea was captured by a rival tribe as a child, maybe as young as twelve. Even worse, Sacagawea's "husband," Toussaint Charbonneau, took ownership of her either by winning her in a game or buying her from the tribe that kidnapped her. Regardless, she wasn't even his only wife—he was already married to a Native American woman when he acquired Sacagawea. Plus, he was probably at least twenty years older than her.

When I mentioned those creepy details to Bob, he basically shrugged them off.

"You don't think that's disturbing and gross?" I asked.

"Of course that aspect of her story is disturbing and gross! But that doesn't diminish what she accomplished on the expedition except to make it even more remarkable. Look what she overcame!"

"Yeah, by *force*. She probably didn't have a choice thanks to her pervy white husband."

"Oh, gosh... again with the perpetual victimhood. And again with pointing out that only white guys are evil. Look, if there's one irrefutable lesson from all of history, it's that humans are equal opportunity offenders when it comes to evil."

"Yeah, well, what about the fact that Clark brought along his slave?" I felt smart throwing out that tidbit, even though I'd just learned it via Amelia's googling. "They had like thirty guys on the expedition, but he still had to bring a personal slave."

Bob made what sounded like a frustrated chuckle. "See, there you go again with your notion that the story of America is only about slavery and oppression. It blinds you to the achievement of something like the Lewis and Clark expedition. You can't see the forest for the handful of rotting trees."

"But the Right just wants to clear out the rotting trees and go about business as usual."

"You know, it's so ironic that the generation who has the best situation, racially speaking, in the history of this country are now whining about race the loudest. They never suffered a fraction of what their ancestors went through, yet *they* want reparations."

I grinned at Amelia—I'd wound him up for sure—but her face maintained a look of concern as she listened in.

"Makes me sick," continued Bob. "Seriously, how are you supposed to heal a nation's racism wounds by dividing everyone up into white people, who are the guilty bad guys no matter what, and people of color, who are innocent victims no matter what? How does that heal anything?"

"One could say your strong denials of racism, and constantly diverting, you know, indicate *guilt*."

Amelia's eyes widened at me in what I read as her indication that I'd gone too far.

"I don't understand why racism and social justice is such a hang-up for Republicans," I added.

Bob did his edgy laugh again. "Social justice," he repeated with more than a dash of sarcasm. "The real fighters for social justice were the folks who fought in the Civil Rights movement, because they actually had something on the line. Your generation..." he paused, I guess searching for the right harsh words, "is the wussiest, most spoiled generation in history. You're afraid of a conservative speaking on your campus, and you need safe spaces to help you cope with having your feelings hurt. Halloween costumes and words trigger you, make you curl up in a ball. You think you're working for justice while you slowly kill freedom. I mean, it's *sick* and *embarrassing*. Trying to cancel people for having a different point of view? It's the new McCarthyism. And if you don't know who McCarthy was, that's part of the problem."

I couldn't remember exactly who McCarthy was, which annoyed me a little.

"Your generation is too foolish to realize you're peddling poison," he added. "You idiots canceled John Wayne, for goodness' sake! God almighty, what happened to the tough, hardy people this country used to make? We're in a unique time now. I don't know how you develop resilience and a people with grit without having to face hardship. What we're seeing is the result: a spoiled rotten, entitled, bratty people who, instead of counting their blessings, think they're oppressed. If China or Russia invaded tomorrow, they'd take our blue cities without having to fire a damn shot, because our pansy, pampered men would be most concerned about not spilling their lattes as they retreated."

It was my turn for a sarcastic laugh. Amelia cringed and shifted nervously on the couch as if she might flee the scene. But she stayed.

"I think you're just pining for an America that never really existed," I said.

"You're wrong. You couldn't know anyway because I actually lived it."

"Well, you lived in ignorant bliss then—ignoring all the systemic wrongs and steamrolling minorities. Now my generation is finally trying to fix and improve things, and you're terrified of change."

"I give up. So many of us tried, but you lazy, ungrateful babies ruined a great nation. The sick irony is, you actually think you're making it better. But good luck with your no-absolutes thing. You won't be free like we were, and you're going to suffer for it. I'm tired, and I'm gonna go be with Betty sooner than later. God, we failed to teach you. We were just as selfish and stupid as your generation, I guess, just in a different way. And a lot of us snapped out of it eventually when we realized we have it pretty good here. Others never figured that out, and just screwed around and invented new ways to tear down the nation that gave them everything. People like Bill Clinton dodged real service, sat around here and smoked dope and chased skirts while we bled in the mud in Vietnam. And then they dare to call themselves public servants. And the Bidens…they make me sick. They're so deep in bed with China, they wake up in red pajamas. They've never served anything other than themselves. Corrupt as hell, and there's not a darn thing we can do about it anymore. Meanwhile, your side just worships these creeps."

"So…it's Bill Clinton's fault the country sucks?" I asked sarcastically.

And for the first time of the entire trip, Bob hung up on me.

I looked at Amelia with a mix of mischief and amusement, shook my head, and shrugged. She returned my look with a furrowed brow and pressed her lips together.

"What?" I asked defensively.

"You were badgering him a bit, weren't you?"

"The frickin' geezer had it coming. God, you heard him flying his true bigot colors. He called us the worst generation in history. That kind of arrogance takes balls coming from an old white guy from the capital of the Confederacy."

"Tom, he's clearly hurting. It almost sounds like he's in mourning for America or something. He's also your grandfather."

"No he's not. Not really. Why the hell are you defending him? He's a rich, bitter, asshole."

"Who's willing to give you a fortune in spite of the fact that he vehemently disagrees with everything you believe."

She was serious, but I also detected compassion in her eyes. She had my attention—especially since no one had ever used the word *vehemently* in a sentence aimed at me.

"I don't know," she continued, "I just think perhaps you should be a bit nicer to the man who's poised to make you spectacularly rich."

I regretted my harsh tone toward her (again). Maybe she had a point, but I certainly wasn't going to call Bob back and apologize.

That evening we walked across the highway to sit on the rocks and watch the sunset over the water. The sky was clear and the sun an intense orange as it lowered itself beyond the Pacific. We sat quietly at first, absorbed by the sun's commanding performance and the way it turned the kinetic water a cool shade of pink.

"I can't believe I've made it coast to coast. That's a major item checked off the bucket list. Thanks for that, Tom."

"No, thank *you* for tagging along."

We watched the sun until its last golden band disappeared below the seemingly infinite deep. Then Amelia shared what I guessed she'd been mulling through the afternoon since my tense conversation with Bob.

"America is unique in the history of the world, you know? Never has such a diverse people made such a mixed nation like this. Really, it shouldn't have worked—it's actually a miracle that it's worked as long as it has."

I slowly nodded, thinking carefully through her words, and mostly agreeing.

"Why do you think that is?" she asked.

"What do you mean?"

"Why do you think America has succeeded, relatively speaking, for so long?"

"I mean, I'm not sure it's succeeded for anyone other than the wealthy. But if I had to come up with reasons, I guess it's a ton of land. Natural resources—although stolen from Native Americans, of course. Plus, slave and cheap labor."

She shook her head before I was even done with my answer. "I don't think so. It's your Constitution. Your Declaration of Independence. And your Bill of Rights."

"This, coming from a *British* person."

"Yes. I realize," she said, smiling and nodding.

"Oh my God," I said, "you're one of them. You're an *America* fan. You're an America groupie. You want to make America great again."

"Go ahead, make all the fun."

"But why do you *love* it so much?"

"Why do you *hate* it so much?"

"I think maybe you just love the idea of America more than the reality," I said.

"The idea is the whole point, and it's a *good*, noble idea."

"But that's easy for you to say. You don't have to share a country with all these evil, dumb Trumpkins."

"They're not evil, and they're not dumb," she said calmly. "They're your fellow countrymen who disagree with you on government policies. If you really want to persuade them, which is a lot of what politics is as I understand it, no one's ever going to agree with you while you're insulting them. Love is the ultimate persuader. Right now, people don't seem very interested in persuading though. Only interested in pummeling."

I didn't argue with her any further. I basically dismissed her patriotic gush as the musing of an America fangirl being in America for the first time. But for some reason, her saying that "the idea is the whole point," wedged itself in my mind. I'd have to let that one steep for a while, like a cup of Amelia's beloved tea.

When we made it back from our sunset viewing, Amelia casually gestured at the words in chipped, yellow paint tattooed on the back of Betsy Ross.

"So *that's* where 'Corps of Discovery' comes from," she said. "Lewis and Clark."

"Huh?"

"That's what their expedition was called—the Corps of Discovery."

"Oh. Yeah." I said, almost as if I already knew that, but I didn't. I'd forgotten the words were even back there. I probably would've gone the whole trip not knowing what it meant if it wasn't for Amelia. I marveled at what a miserable voyage this would be without her.

Before going to bed, I borrowed Amelia's phone to check my email, which I'd neglected for over a week. I dreaded what unpaid bills might be lurking in the inbox. I'd been trying not to think about my money crisis, but I couldn't put it off forever. I would either have to beg my housemates for an extension on my rent payment, or beg Mom for some money. There was no guarantee Mom would have any extra to lend me anyway.

I was distracted from my money woes when I spotted an email from Nick Douglas, a friend from my Reed College days. I hadn't communicated with him in a couple months at least. It was a rather urgent-sounding email asking me to call him. So, I did right away.

I shouldn't have called him.

TWENTY-THREE

The night air was chaos to the senses. As soon as I stepped outside, I heard random pops, metallic clashes, and what sounded like small explosions echoing through the streets. I heard the undulating chants and yells of a crowd. A low, smoky haze hovered eerily over the pandemonium, punctuated by the intense red and blue flashing lights from police vehicles. The pungent air reminded me of the smell of fireworks after launch. A few blocks ahead of me, a multistory building was on fire. I suddenly felt uneasy about wading into the protest and leaving Amelia behind in the RV. But she didn't want to join me.

Nick Douglas was nowhere to be found, of course. He hadn't been very reliable when we were friends in college. Now, he wasn't at the park where he'd said he would be. I'd called him three hours earlier, just after Amelia and I watched the sunset near Station Camp. Nick breathlessly told me that the revolution was in full swing in downtown Portland and that I had to see it. Our time had finally come, Nick said—they were battling the police violence and systemic anti-black racism. It was a historic moment, and I was missing it watching the sunset like some retiree.

Amelia had no desire to go to Portland for the protest. She objected, more than once, that she had a bad feeling about it.

Her "bad feeling" wasn't a strong enough deterrent for me. The lure of this historic BLM movement was too much for me to resist. I pled my case.

Finally, reluctantly, she gave in. But she insisted she would stay in the RV.

It was nearly midnight by the time we rolled into downtown Portland. Nick said I could meet up with him at Keller Fountain Park. So, I picked an empty side street nearby and parked Betsy Ross.

"Be careful," Amelia said with concern in her eyes as I stepped outside.

After waiting half an hour for Nick, I gave up on him and walked cautiously toward the din and the haze. Dark-clad figures darted around me seemingly from all directions. I couldn't tell what they were rushing toward. I felt like the chaos was starting to envelop me a bit, so I quick stepped out of the street toward the sidewalk on my left. I accidentally collided shoulders with a scrawny guy dressed in all black and wearing a skeleton mask that covered his whole face. He shoved me hard with a gloved hand. I almost tumbled to the street but clumsily maintained enough balance to stay on my feet. I finally made it to the curb and stepped onto the sidewalk.

From my slightly removed perch, I could see what appeared to be soldiers in riot gear. It looked like tear gas canisters were going off, but I couldn't tell if they were coming from the soldiers or the crowd. Even in the darkness, there was enough light from the fire, flares, and cop cars that I could tell this was Antifa.

Suddenly, the Antifa crowd roared and a portion of them surged toward a section of the soldiers. It was a raw, rabid, brutal attack—unchoreographed and out of control. It was impossible to tell exactly what was going on.

I didn't know how to feel. These black-clad warriors were supposed to be my cohorts, my colleagues in the wider movement for justice. But seeing them up close, it felt less like we were on the same team. Most of them looked like they were cosplaying some live-action version of an apocalyptic video game. I watched a small group with baseball bats bashing in the windows of a cop car. Another group was busy using a barrel of some kind to break the clear plexiglass side of a bus stop shelter. A few others used their weapons to smash up an ATM outside a bank. In theory, I loved their antifascist/anti-Trump zeal. But in person, there was more of a vicious, primitive hive-mind vibe. This seemed more about crude, random destruction than protesting for meaningful social change. I understood the concept of needing to make a splash and rattle the nation out of its lethargy to stop police violence and racism. But observing their method in real time, I was suddenly less convinced.

I heard what sounded like gunshots, followed by another roar from the crowd. Maybe the soldiers fired rubber bullets—I couldn't tell. But the largest section of the crowd suddenly scattered toward me like a lava flow. Not wanting to get swept into their retreat, I began jogging back in the direction of Betsy. Someone running past me clipped my ankle hard, which sent me sprawling forward, and I skidded on the pavement, scraping my arms and knees.

I glanced up from the pavement to see a small group veer down the side street where Betsy was parked. I jumped to my feet and sprinted after them. Seconds later, I rounded the corner to find seven or eight masked figures rocking the RV and beating the side of it with their blunt weapons. I continued my sprint toward them, yelling, "Hey!" as if that was going to stop them.

I shoved the first person I came to away from the RV. Out of nowhere, from behind me, an object slammed into the right side of my head and ear. I don't know what it was— it felt like some sort of heavy, rubber hose. The blow knocked me to the street again. My ear rang sharply, and for several seconds I felt like I might pass out. I think one of the attackers threw a bottle, or maybe a bag, of some kind of liquid at the RV, because I felt the residual spray on my face and neck.

With my ear still ringing, I pulled myself up on all fours and looked up as one of them bashed the back window with a thick chain. Somehow, the window didn't break. Afraid for Amelia, I rushed the person with the chain in the blindest rage I've ever experienced, tackling them to the pavement. My boorish tackle knocked their mask and hoodie askew enough for me to see long, neon-green hair and part of their face—I think I tackled a woman. She swung and kicked wildly at me, continuously yelling, "Bitch!"

At least two of her pals dragged me off her, and another one punched me above my left eye. I heard Amelia scream, "Tom!" and glimpsed her rush out the door toward me, but another loser ran across her path and knocked her to the street.

Swinging my elbows desperately and making minor contact with my attackers, I clambered to my feet and surged toward the person who knocked down Amelia. I kicked him as hard as I could, catching him mostly in the calf. He stumbled enough to allow me to connect one solid punch on the left side of his masked face. It felt like I broke my right hand. My punch knocked him to the ground, but it was the last blow I landed as his gang quickly swarmed me. I could no longer tell who was beating me.

I heard Amelia desperately yelling "stop" to no avail.

They hit me everywhere—face, neck, ribs. A stomach blow knocked the air completely out of me, and I crumpled to the street with gasping, sputtering breaths. I managed to clamp my arms around my head and just hoped the rain of blows would stop.

When they finally did, I opened my right eye to see the green-haired woman slap the RV one more time with her chain.

Finally, the band of goons trotted away. I tasted blood in my mouth and felt it trickling down both sides of my face. Amelia rushed over and knelt beside me. She put her right arm under my neck and helped me sit up. She held me against her for a moment. I felt her whole body trembling. In between her sobs, she said, "You're bleeding."

She helped me to my feet and together we limped back inside the RV. She closed and locked the door behind us. I collapsed on my back on the couch. Amelia found my towel and her hands still shook as she pressed it tight above my left eye. She wet some paper towels with bottled water and dabbed the rest of my face, and then my knees and elbows.

"I'm sorry," I said. "I'm so sorry for bringing us here. *So* stupid."

She lifted the towel for a moment, then clamped it back down.

"We need to get you to hospital."

I tried to sit up, but she resisted my movement with her left hand.

"Stay still. I've got it. I'll drive."

"But…" I started to protest.

"I'll figure it out," she said, moving past me into the driver's seat.

After a couple minutes, I felt Betsy slowly lurch forward and we were moving. Then I heard Amelia's phone giving directions. She drove excruciatingly slow and ran over multiple curbs trying to make turns. But she persevered and got us to the nearest hospital.

On the way, my head throbbed and my entire body ached. I was still in shock from the attack. It was so nonsensical. I thought of the footage I'd seen of the Charlottesville riot three years earlier. I had been incensed by the racist, right-wing reprobates dressed up like dweeb warriors in their football helmets and homemade shields. I *hated* them. Our attackers also turned out to be violent assholes, just in different uniforms, but with the same homemade dork weapons. Even though they were supposed to be on my side of vital issues, it didn't matter because their bloodlust apparently overruled their claim to desire justice. I realized that those Charlottesville neo-Nazis and Portland's Antifa were just different sides of the same degenerate coin. And that realization led to another disquieting thought—that if Antifa didn't actually represent me on the Left, then maybe those neo-Nazis didn't really represent someone like Bob on the Right either.

Amelia escorted me inside the hospital, but they wouldn't allow her to stay due to COVID protocol. I got five stitches to close the gash above my left eye, which was swollen like a boxer's. Miraculously, I didn't have a concussion. Neither was my hand broken. A nurse cleaned the rest of my cuts, bandaged me up, and sent me on my way with a couple ice packs.

By the time I got back to Betsy, it was almost 3:00 a.m. I found Amelia asleep on the couch, but she stirred when I entered. She sat up and I sat beside her. She clicked on a light and examined my face, then hugged me. I hugged her back and we held each other as she began to cry.

"I've never been so scared," she said.

"Me neither. I'm sorry. I'm so sorry."

Eventually, we loosened our embrace, but I kept my sore right arm around her. She leaned against my chest and continued crying softly. She still had blood on her T-shirt, which I assumed was mine. She had strawberry scrapes on her hands and knees. We sat quietly for a long time. The stillness finally allowed me to begin winding down from the night's adrenaline spike. Amelia wiped at her tears, and I hugged her closer with my right arm. I wanted her to feel safe again. I'd taken her perfect sunset evening and turned it into a nightmare.

When she stopped crying, she lifted her head and sat forward a little on the couch. She clicked off the light, but I didn't want her to go. Slivers of white light from the harsh parking lot lamps shone around the window shades and onto her face. I almost overthought it, but then acted on impulse, leaned over, and kissed her cheek. She grinned but didn't look at me. I hesitated a second before kissing her cheek again, a bit longer this time. I'd wanted to do that basically every waking moment of every day since I'd met her. She glanced at me. Her eyes, even in the dim light, melted me. I guess I thought her wordless glance indicated a go-ahead, so I pressed my luck and kissed her cautiously on the lips.

I finally felt her kiss me back, and I thought my heart was beating loud enough for her to hear it. I couldn't believe this was really happening. We kissed with increasing passion. I pulled her closer to me on the couch and ventured putting my left hand on her waist.

She suddenly broke away and stood from the couch. She raised her right hand to her forehead in distress. "No. I'm sorry, Tom," she said shaking her head. "I'm very sorry. I should *not* have done that."

"What? There's nothing to apologize for…"

"This is all wrong. It's not fair to you. I'm exhausted and I've had a lapse in judgment. I'm *so* sorry."

Before I could protest or say anything to convince her otherwise, she went to her bed and closed the divider. I pulled out the couch, converting it to my bed, and laid down with one of the ice packs on my forehead. *What just happened?* It was the most thrilling and fleeting moment of my life. I was flooded with hope that this meant she had at least an inkling of the feelings for me that I'd give anything for her to have. Was it just the heightened trauma of the night? Was it the fact that I tried to defend her and took a severe beating for it? Surely she wasn't just sympathy-kissing me, right? I had to know, so I lay awake for the next hour, tortured.

Why had she stopped? What did she mean that she "shouldn't have done that"? Then I recalled the weird phrase she'd used that time when she told me she couldn't be with me—*"unequally yoked."* She couldn't love me because I was a heathen, but I didn't know how not to be one.

When I woke up the next morning, I was utterly disoriented. My watch said 8:37 a.m., but in my fogginess, I didn't know if I even had the right time zone. It felt stuffy in the RV. It finally struck me where we were—still in the parking lot of the hospital in Portland.

I winced as I swung my feet to the floor. Every slight movement was going to be painful for a while. In the daylight, I realized how scraped up my arms and knees actually were.

The divider to Amelia's cabin was open. I leaned forward and glanced through her cabin to the bathroom, but that door was open too. She wasn't there. Then I saw all her stuff packed and neatly piled by the door.

I had just finished finding and downing some Advil when she opened the door.

"I hope I didn't wake you."

"Nope."

She sat in the chair opposite the couch and leaned forward in an earnest posture with her elbows on her knees.

"Tom…this is really hard. And odd, I know. And I sincerely don't want to disappoint you. But…I'm leaving. I can't finish the trip with you."

"What? Why?"

"I think you know."

"But…that was great. Right?"

I shifted forward on the couch and sort of gestured with my sore right hand, really wanting to reach out and take her hand. But I stopped short.

Amelia looked at the floor as she said, "No, I let you down. I crossed a line. I'm sorry, I had a moment of weakness and I let my emotions get the better of me. I just can't go on traveling with you with *that* hanging in the air."

"But nothing happened. No lines were crossed. I mean *something* happened. But it was just…it was amazing, but…" I stammered because I was panicked. I felt the same, sharp, heart-ripping desperation I'd felt way back in Philadelphia when I tried to figure out how to get her to travel with me. But this was a thousand times more desperate now that I actually knew her. I didn't want to lose her because she was hands down the best thing that ever happened to me.

"I feel awful. I failed you. I knew better, and I screwed up anyway."

"It wasn't a screwup, though! But if that's what we need to call it for you to stay, then…"

"I'm *not* staying, Tom. I can't. I made up my mind. I've already ordered a ride. It should be here any minute."

This was a nightmare. I could *not* do this trip without her. I fumbled for reasons she shouldn't go. I almost blurted something about her not needing to prove her religious conviction to me any further—I got it, loud and clear, she was devoted to God—but I didn't.

"What if I doubled your payment?"

Our eyes met briefly, but she quickly looked away.

"No, Tom. It's not about that. You have a lot of stuff you need to figure out, and…you need to finish this on your own in order to do so."

"No, I mean, let's figure it out together."

She grabbed her backpack and small suitcase. "I'm going to wait outside."

I rushed after her into the parking lot.

"Please don't go. I don't want to do this without you." She didn't answer my plea, but I could see tears in her eyes, glistening in the morning sun. "*Please,*" I added desperately.

We saw a car approaching. My stomach knotted up. "Amelia, I'm begging you."

She finally looked at me, wiped her eyes, and smiled.

"Tom, please remember this—God loves you, more than you can imagine. He sees you and *knows* you, and he wants you to know him."

The car stopped in front of us, parallel to Betsy. Amelia embraced me quickly—so quickly that I didn't have the chance to hold her like I wanted to. Then she picked up her baggage and moved swiftly to the back seat of the car. I stood there, numb, with the RV door agape behind me.

Just like that, Amelia was gone. And I was destroyed.

Her parting words reverberated in my mind, and it made my eyes sting. Maybe it was the fact that I didn't really have a father to speak of, or whatever, but I longed to be truly known and loved. Like everybody, I guess. I was desperate to be told I was good for something and had a purpose. If her god was real and could do that, then I was ready for him to speak up.

I pulled myself back inside the RV and shut the door. I could instantly tell it sucked being in there without Amelia. I slumped behind the wheel. Then I pounded it a few times in a brief rage (with my left hand, since my right one was too bruised).

I finally cranked the engine because I didn't have a choice. I was out of money and couldn't think of any other option than driving home to beg Mom for a loan to get me through the rest of this diabolical trip.

It was the saddest drive of my life.

TWENTY-FOUR

It was a three-hour drive from Portland to my quasi-hometown of Aberdeen, Washington. I spent the first hour or so excoriating myself for kissing Amelia. I couldn't help replaying the wonder of it in my mind. Yet, if I'd just had an ounce of self-control, she would still be in her seat beside me.

The dread of seeing Mom later distracted me somewhat. I mean, it would be good to see her, of course. But I dreaded pulling up in the RV and having to deal with her shock and likely scorn at me for having met Bob, accepting his offer, and all the rest.

Since college, I'd been home less and less. Part of it was busyness and living far away in California. Part of it was that I kind of had a slow-growing resentment toward Mom. I appreciated all she did for me, raising me on her own and everything, but I resented the fact that she largely gave up in life. She'd dropped out of college, got pregnant with me, and basically used it as her excuse to never have to strive to do better than the bare minimum. She's so smart, and I knew she could've done much more (and I think deep down she knew it too). I resented her for being a little low-class. I don't know; the older I got, the more I found her kind of embarrassing.

Every time this resentment reared its head, I'd feel guilty, and I always came back around to feeling sorry for her because she'd been through so much. I mean, she carried the guilt of her own sister's death, and to some extent, she felt responsible for her mom's death too. That had to be an insane burden.

I tried to time my arrival after Mom was home from work. I guess I thought that would be a less shocking scenario for her, because I could hopefully make it inside the house and prepare her before she glimpsed the RV. That was my brilliant plan, anyway… which totally failed because we pulled up to the house at the same time—her into the driveway and me along the curb at the edge of her perpetually dingy front lawn.

I bolted outside as fast as I could, but Mom was already out of her car, staring at Betsy Ross, slack-jawed with bewilderment, hands raised in utter confusion. "What the hell?" she yelled.

"It's okay, Mom," I said, holding both hands up as if I was trying to stop her from attacking me.

"What the *hell*?" she repeated with louder desperation as she crossed the yard toward me. When she got close enough for a good look at my still swollen left eye and stiches, she exclaimed, "Oh my God! What happened?"

"Calm down, Mom, please. Everything's fine. I can explain."

"No you can't," she said, practically hysterical. "There is *no* way you can explain all this."

She gestured frantically with her hands, I guess grasping for which explanation she needed more urgently—my injury or the shocking presence of Betsy.

"Wait, he's not…is he in there?" she asked, pointing at the RV.

"Who? Bob?"

"My father."

"Yeah, *Bob*. No, no, he's not in there."

"How are you on a first name basis with him?"

It took a *lot* of expedited explaining. She tried to absorb what I was saying, but she was clearly shell-shocked. The RV was a wild intrusion from her former life, like seeing a ghost or something. After the bulk of my rapid-fire explanation, she snapped out of it enough to give me a hug. I hadn't seen her since Christmas.

She was not happy about Bob's "scheme" as she put it. "Only *he* would come up with something like this," she said. She was also pissed that I did not consult her about it first.

"Yeah, what would you have told me, Mom? *Don't* try to go for the twenty-five million dollars?"

"Well, *maybe*. There's always strings attached with people like him. Wait, so you've been talking to him, like, regularly?"

"Yeah," I replied with a shrug. "I have to—it's part of the deal."

"This is so messed up."

"I know, believe me."

"Has he mentioned any inheritance for me?"

"Uh…no." I totally should've seen that question coming. "I mean, not yet, anyway."

She shook her head sarcastically. "Of course not."

She opened the RV door and stepped inside. I stuck my head through the door, watching her glance around in awe.

"This is *sooooo* trippy," she said.

After examining the interior front to back, she stepped back outside with tears streaming down her face.

Eventually, Mom calmed down and stopped crying. She ordered from my favorite burger joint and even splurged to have it delivered. As we ate at the same small, beat-up, round wooden table I grew up with, she reminisced about our old times together. She was obviously dodging any talk of Bob. Mom never liked to talk about hard stuff.

When we were almost done eating, I finally had an opening to force the issue, since it had been gnawing at me for most of my trip.

"Mom," I started hesitantly, "did you never...I mean, surely you must've wanted to, like, make up with Bob at some point. Why didn't you just..." I did a terrible job trying to form my inquiry.

"No. I mean, he was totally in the wrong."

"But..."

"I've told you before, he basically said he wished I was dead. So, I made myself dead to him."

"Don't you ever wonder what might've been, though? Like, things could've been maybe a little easier for us."

"Come on, we didn't have it so bad, did we? We managed. We had an adventure."

"I guess you could call it that."

"Besides, I don't think you'd really get along with him anyway. You don't know what a hardcore Republican he is."

"Actually, I kinda do."

"I can't believe you've actually been talking to him. I just..."

"Well, it's mostly arguing if it makes you feel any better."

"Sounds on-brand for him."

"I just don't get...you never felt like reaching out? *Ever?*"

Mom got up from the table and started clearing the takeout trash. I could see her jaw muscles twitch, which meant she was getting irritated.

"Why does this matter to you all the sudden? What's he been telling you? Is he trying to get you to feel sorry for him or something?"

"No," I interjected, defensively. "It's not like I'm on his side."

"Because remember, *he's* the one who wished I was dead. And, honestly, I half wished *he* was dead a lot of times. We weren't exactly close, even before my sister..." she crammed wrappers and cartons in the trashcan and swallowed hard. She was trying to ward off tears again. "He *always* liked Christine better. We were never going to be able to have a normal relationship again. How could we? He would always blame me for Christine's death. For Mom's too. He called a couple times over the years, but I just never answered."

It was news to me that Bob had ever reached out to her. "You never told me that."

"There was no reason to. I don't wanna talk about this."

"Okay, sorry I asked." I wasn't really sorry.

Eventually, she returned to the table and told me about her latest boyfriend. Some guy named Derek. I knew I'd forget his name almost as soon as she mentioned it, because her boyfriends were all basically the same brand of loser.

That night, I lay awake for a long time in my old bedroom, thinking about how to ask Mom for the money I needed before she left for work in the morning. I hadn't brought it up the rest of the evening because she'd been so upset talking about Bob.

I slept 'til 6:30 a.m. but couldn't sleep in. So, I took my cigarettes out onto the back patio. I sank into a rickety lawn chair and had just lit up when the sliding glass door opened and some dude, presumably Derek, stepped outside. I glanced briefly at him, and he gave me a nod. I didn't nod back.

"Those things'll kill ya," he said as he pulled out a cigarette from his own pack and lit it.

He was wearing a rumpled T-shirt, jeans, and some kind of work boots. Maybe he worked in construction? I didn't really care—I was mad that he'd invited himself onto the patio with me.

Derek drew on his cigarette a couple times before saying, "Your mom's a lovely woman."

I cut my eyes at him.

"I don't want to hear that," I said, disgusted.

I stood abruptly and went back inside. I continued through the living room, out the front door, and into the RV, where I could smoke in peace away from freakin' Derek.

I left the RV door open while I finished my cigarette. Derek's presence screwed my plan because I didn't want to ask Mom for the money with him around. I didn't even know how much money I needed to beg her for. I was just desperate to get back on the road and get this over with.

I flipped open the box of VHS tapes and found Amelia's copy of *To Kill a Mockingbird* sitting on top of the pile. I picked up the paperback, which had a bulging envelope wedged in its pages. I opened the envelope to find it stuffed with cash. Hundreds of dollars at least. There was a handwritten note at the front of the stack, which read:

> "Dear Tom, This is what's left of my wedding ring money. Please use it to finish your journey. Maybe you can pay me back when you complete it and become Daddy Warbucks."

There was a smiley face after "Warbucks." It was signed "Amelia," and in case there was any doubt, she included a Bible verse reference—Proverbs 15:16.

My heart soared—just sheer elation. I was so relieved that I kept miscounting the money and had to start over. There was over twelve hundred dollars in the envelope. Surely it would be enough to see me through. It would have to be. Amelia had saved me.

I made a rush of saying goodbye to Mom. I think she was annoyed by my hurry, but I assured her I'd call soon. As I tried to get out the door, she added, "Hey, when you talk to him again, could you ask about my inheritance? You know...find out if there is one?"

"Geez, Mom. Don't go quitting your job just yet."

"But...will you ask?"

"Yes, okay, I'll ask."

It bothered me that this was such an urgent priority for her, but I didn't linger on the thought because I had to get going. I was flying high on the renewed energy of Amelia's wild generosity. Of course I would pay her back, every cent, plus crazy interest. Maybe I'd even double what I'd promised her. I felt desperate to do something amazing for her for once.

TWENTY-FIVE

Without Amelia, there was no more smartphone for navigation. So, it was back to the old-timey atlas to plot my next course: east across the width of Washington, slicing through northern Idaho, plunging into a marathon slalom across southern Montana, a southeasterly slide through the northeast corner of Wyoming, and finally into the Black Hills of South Dakota. It was two extremely long days to Mount Rushmore—a slog of time to miss Amelia.

Being back on the open road without her was just about unbearable. It felt like I was cheating by making my way through a stunning medley of new states without her. I lost count of how many national forests I traversed on the route to South Dakota. She would've adored them.

I missed everything about her and our easy travel companionship. I passed many hours racking my brain, trying to figure out how to be with her again, how to get her to trust me, longing for her to take a chance on feeling for me the way I felt about her. I was so relieved to have an excuse to see her again to pay her what I owed. It didn't necessarily have to be done in person of course, but I had no intention of taking care of it remotely. The prospect of seeing her again was the extra motivation I needed to press on toward Bob's infernal finish line. Yet, by myself, with all that time to think, I felt my old anxieties shoving their way back in, trying to haunt me.

When I stopped for the night near Missoula, Montana, I pulled out her bed and decided to sleep on it, as if that could make me feel closer to her or something. Naturally, she'd left her sheets neatly folded. I began reading her copy of *To Kill a Mockingbird* until I finally got drowsy.

On the video, Bob talked about the construction of a secret room at Mount Rushmore that was started but never finished. He said it was the dream of Rushmore's sculptor, Gutzon Borglum, to include this room known as the "Hall of Records." Located behind the sculpted heads of Washington, Jefferson, Theodore Roosevelt, and Lincoln, it was to have been built into the mountain as a sort of shrine to America. It would contain copies of the nation's founding documents and tributes to famous Americans who made lasting contributions to the country. Borglum even sketched out a grand staircase that would allow visitors to access the room. But, Bob said, Congress tightened the money flow for Borglum's bonus project, World War II broke out, and the Hall of Records was never completed.

I briefly got my hopes up that Bob had arranged for me to visit this secret, unfinished room.

"I checked into maybe paying to complete it myself," said Bob onscreen, "but the Park Service won't let me."

He said back in the 1990s, Gutzon Borglum's family partially fulfilled his dream by having copies of the founding documents sealed in a titanium vault at the base of the opening to what would've been the Hall of Records room. Bob said it's better than nothing.

"This way, if the Marxists ever succeed in melting down our founding documents, a freedom seeker wandering through the rubble of liberty might find these documents at Mount Rushmore, and they can create a new America based on the original."

I thought it was bleak of Bob to ponder such an unlikely scenario, but I guess knowing that copies of the founding docs are in a secret vault at Mount Rushmore gave him some peace of mind that his way would ultimately win or something.

Bob read aloud the Gutzon Borglum quote, which he said is etched on the granite capstone covering the titanium vault:

"*Let us place there, carved high, as close to heaven as we can, the words of our leaders, their faces, to show posterity what manner of men they were. Then breathe a prayer that these records will endure until the wind and rain alone shall wear them away.*"

Bob said Borglum didn't live to see Mount Rushmore finished and that his son, Lincoln Borglum, took over the project, completing it seven months after his father's death in 1941.

"Imagine dreaming something so big that you never get to experience it," said Bob. He shook his head and glanced past the camera with a far-off look in his eyes. "Dreams are important, but they can derail your life if you're not careful. The dreams that really last are those that aren't just for you—dreams that reach beyond yourself."

The National Memorial Plaza at Mount Rushmore was crawling with people. I had not seen so many people wearing Trump attire anywhere else on my whole journey. Other than that, the view was spectacular.

I arrived midmorning and quickly made my way through a pavilion lined with all fifty state flags, which led to the Grand View Terrace. The iconic carved faces of Washington, Jefferson, Theodore Roosevelt, and Lincoln appeared, vivid and bright, the white-gray rock almost gleaming against the perfectly blue-sky backdrop. I was kind of fascinated in spite of myself. I couldn't stop staring at the presidents' faces, earnest and rather solemn, gazing into—what? America's past? America's future? Amelia would've been spellbound by this place. Knowing how much she would love it kind of made me love it a little. Yeah, I'm sure the carbon footprint of blasting and chiseling out a mountainside was atrocious, but it was truly a work of art.

I hiked the Presidential Trail—a paved, rock, and eventually boardwalk pathway that wound past mammoth boulders and towering pines, leading partially up the mountain for a closer view. I made it to the farthest point of the trail nearest the presidents' faces, which ended in a wooden-railed cul-de-sac. Then that uncomfortable feeling hit me that I'd almost forgotten about—without Amelia, I'd have to find a stranger to witness my required reading.

I glanced around at the smattering of people milling about the boardwalk and pausing at the railing for photos. I pulled my printout from the back pocket of my jeans and somehow, I guess due to my sudden nerves at the prospect of having to recruit a stranger, I fumbled the page and it fell to the boardwalk. A strong gust of wind then blew the page beyond my reach. Alarmingly, the page sailed swiftly toward the wooden railing, but just before it slipped underneath the slats, a sneakered foot stomped on the paper, saving it from gliding down the mountain. The man who saved the page bent over, picked it up, and glanced around for the owner. He was a tall, paunchy, middle-aged guy wearing the infamous solid red "Make America Great Again" hat. His white T-shirt featured a photo of Joe Biden with his hands on a woman's shoulders, seemingly sniffing her hair, and a caption that said, "No hidin' from Joe Biden."

I stepped toward the man, our eyes met, and he grinned as he handed me the page.

"Thanks a lot," I said.

The MAGA man half-turned to walk away and I hesitated, my heart pounding, then I desperately said, "Excuse me ..."

He paused and faced me again.

"Would you mind, uh, I've got to do this assignment of reading this thing aloud and having someone sign off on it. Would ... could I ... would you mind me reading it to you? It will just take a minute."

The man crinkled his brow momentarily as my oddball request registered, but then gave a slight shrug of his broad shoulders and replied, "Sure."

So there we stood, facing each other rather awkwardly—I in my mask, he in his red MAGA hat. And I began reading:

"'The union of these four Presidents carved on the face of the everlasting hills of South Dakota will constitute a distinctly national monument. It will be decidedly American in conception, in its magnitude, in its meaning and altogether worthy of our country... The fundamental principles which they represented have been wrought into the very being of our country. They are steadfast as these ancient hills... The progress of America has been due to the spirit of its people... If coming generations are to maintain a like spirit, it will be because they continue to study the lives and times of the great men who have been the leaders in our history, and continue to support the principles which those men represented... This memorial will be another national shrine to which future generations will repair to declare their continuing allegiance to independence, to self-government, to freedom and to economic justice. President Calvin Coolidge, August tenth, 1927, excerpts from his speech at the opening of the work on Mount Rushmore.'"

"Calvin Coolidge, right on!" said MAGA man with a grin. "Great president."

I had no clue whether Coolidge was a great president or not—I didn't even know which party he was from (though based on Bob's fandom, I assumed Republican). I recalled Bob mentioning in his video that Calvin Coolidge was the only US president born on the Fourth of July. Bob seemed to think that was cool.

"Apparently, Coolidge was the only president born on the Fourth of July," I uttered.

"Nice," he said. "Well, happy early birthday, Cal."

"Right," I said with a slightly nervous chuckle.

"Should we sing happy birthday to him?" he asked with a straight face.

I looked at MAGA man with probably too much alarm in my eyes. Finally, he broke into a grin and said, "Just pulling your leg."

I nervously chuckled some more. I wondered if MAGA people have a sixth sense for sniffing out Bernie Sanders/Joe Biden supporters. Could this guy tell I didn't know how to interact with him?

Before he could get away, I pulled the pen from my pocket, pulled off the cap, and held the pen and paper toward him. "Would you mind signing this?"

"No prob."

He took the pen from me and set the paper on top of the wooden railing as a writing surface. Fortunately, he didn't ask any questions about my "assignment" or the stitches over my left eye. When he was done signing, he handed me the paper and pen and I read his signature: *Clint Hedges.*

"Thanks, Clint."

He stuck out his right hand, as if it was a dare. I definitely hesitated for a moment. I was a long way from the nearest hand sanitizer. But, to get it over with, I finally shoved the pen in my pocket and shook his hand. His grip was tight, and I'm pretty sure he infused our shake with an extra vigorous pump or two.

"And you are?"

"Oh—Tom."

He finally released my hand. "Okay, Tom. Have a good one."

"You too," I said and then breathed a sigh of relief when he departed down the path.

I continued along the Presidential Trail loop back to the main plaza. I paused at the ledge above the amphitheater for one last, long gaze at the rock faces of the presidents. As I did, I realized I honestly didn't know much of anything about those men. Before my visit, if anyone had asked me which presidents are on Mount Rushmore, I would've maybe guessed Washington and Lincoln but drawn a total blank on the other two.

When I got back to Betsy Ross, I decided against calling Bob right away because, even though it already seemed forever ago, our last call ended with Bob hanging up on me. So, I checked the video instead. After discovering where I was headed, however, calling Bob couldn't have discouraged me more.

I had to go to a farm outside of some place called Fish Creek in Wisconsin. It sounded *very* far away. But the worst part was that Bob said I had to work at this dairy farm for three days. He said America was first built by farmers and that my generation is way too far removed from "the land." He said I needed to get my hands in the dirt to truly appreciate America's incredible abundance. Of course, he also added the jab that, "It'll make you appreciate the muscle behind the milk in your lattes." Bob—always with the jabs. And I don't know what he had against lattes.

I wondered why the hell I had to go all the way to Wisconsin for this three-day thrill fest, and he eventually got around to an explanation. The farm apparently belonged to a guy named Burt Schaefer, who was the longtime dairy provider for all of Bob's Liberty's stores. Bob said that Burt was a ninety-one-year-old Korean War veteran and that his daughter ran the dairy operation now.

I clicked off the TV and collapsed on the couch in temporary despair. All my good vibes from the morning spent in the crisp Black Hills breezes, the pines, the clear sky, and warm sunshine were forced out of me like a squeezed balloon. I felt some rage bubbling up and thought about punching something, but my hands were still too sore from the Portland rumble.

My mind spiraled downward and I didn't have Amelia there to help pull me out of the freefall.

I stopped for the night at a Jellystone RV park outside Sioux Falls. After dinner, I took a deep breath and finally called Bob. I forgot about the time zones—it was almost 10:00 p.m. at Bob's house. He sounded tired when he answered.

"Sorry, I guess I'm calling kinda late," I said.

"Well, I'm still up watching the news. Same old dumpster fire as usual." He cleared his throat before continuing. "Every night it's like I've got a front-row seat to the end of the republic."

I tried to think of a reply, but he didn't give me a chance to respond anyway.

"These damn Democrat governors would rather keep people locked in their homes, crush every small business, and wreck the whole economy instead of trusting folks to make their own commonsense decisions. What a nightmare! You've got cities burning with all these race riots. One presidential candidate hiding out in his basement 'cause his brain short-circuits every time he's in public. Then on top of all that, we've apparently got a lot of folks who think that a *boy* who thinks he's a *girl* is an *actual* girl and should get to use the girls' restroom and compete with them in sports. It's sick! But this is where we are. We think basic fundamental biology is just a state of mind. Man, we've lost it. We've totally lost it. I don't recognize this country sometimes."

"What happened to America being for optimists? Isn't that what you told me?"

The lengthy pause made me think maybe I'd finally stumped him.

"It still is. But...even optimists have bad days. I don't know," he mumbled a bit, "I'm rundown and tired. They say my cancer has spread. Guess the chemo's not working."

"Oh...uh...I mean, wow, that sucks."

"Yeah. Yeah, it sucks bad."

I considered changing the subject by telling him about Portland and how I punched a couple Antifa people. I thought that might cheer him up some. But I stopped short.

"Sometimes...well...sometimes I don't know if I really love this country anymore," he said.

I could barely believe my ears.

"I mean, I love what it *was*, what it used to be," he continued. "See, people didn't used to be such babies. People were tougher. People weren't glued to their phones. We cared about the country. And we didn't get offended by every little slight. We didn't have our feelings stuck out so far that they're guaranteed to get stomped on. Next-door neighbors were Democrats and Republicans, but they could still be friends, because they knew about manners and they didn't question that each other loved America. When did loving America fall off the radar for Democrats? When's the last time you heard a Democrat mention the Constitution? You're a Bernie guy—you know he doesn't give a flip about defending the Constitution. None of 'em talk about it. They scoff at it. It's just an obstacle in their never-ending quest for control. If a conservative brings up the Constitution, the Left calls it racist. All I know is, America was more free. The Bible was respected. Church was respected. Maybe you weren't a believer, but you respected it. I don't know...I guess I love what America could still be, but I just have a hard time believing there's much of a chance anymore. I'm just afraid … I'm afraid we may be past the point of no return now." I had plenty of pushback, but it felt like it would be punching down. I'd never heard him sound defeated. He sounded just as disappointed in America as I felt, except we had totally different reasons for feeling let down.

I finally told him that I'd completed the Mount Rushmore leg, but I guess he felt too beat down to expound on the merits of Mount Rushmore. When I said I was on my way to Wisconsin, he said he'd let Burt know to expect me.

"Burt Schaefer is one of the good guys," he said before we hung up.

I decided to sleep on Amelia's bed again. As I took off my jeans, I found the page with the Coolidge quote and Clint Hedges's signature, which I'd forgotten to return to the folder. I glanced over Coolidge's words again and one line stood out to me: *If coming generations are to maintain a like spirit, it will be because they continue to study the lives and times of the great men who have been the leaders in our history, and continue to support the principles which those men represented.*

I thought about those words in light of Bob's depressing rant. I *hated* to admit it, but if I was honest, Bob knew history and I didn't. I only knew some fragments of history that I'd been told from one perspective, and I didn't really know the principles that Coolidge referred to. What if those principles *weren't* simply devious right-wing talking points as I'd assumed?

I realized that ever since I'd been politically conscious, around halfway through high school or so, I'd always thought of myself as a Democrat—a progressive, a socialist—before thinking of myself as an *American*. For the very first time, I wondered if I might have that backward.

Another disorienting realization quickly followed: I'd never really considered the possibility that Bob was right about anything when it came to America. What if he was? What if Bob was right that the Constitution and all the rest might have come from a motivation of best intentions? What if it was just that people simply screwed everything up and twisted the principles because that's what people do?

It did not feel great to have everything I thought I was sure of called into question. And I didn't like it, but Mount Rushmore hammered home the fact that there was a *lot* I didn't know. I wondered how it was possible for two people to grow up in the same nation and have such completely different understandings of it. To me, Bob's America was an alternate reality version that I was only tangentially familiar with through legend and social media clips.

As my head hit the pillow, an image from many states ago lurked in my mind—the statue in Tuskegee of Booker T. Washington lifting "the veil of ignorance" from the newly freed slave. I had an unsettling thought: What if *I* was that slave, intellectually at least, bound by what I didn't know? And an even more frightening thought—did that make Bob my veil lifter? I wasn't ready to give him so much credit.

It took me quite a while to fall asleep after that.

Thunder woke me up way too early the next morning. It wasn't raining yet but looked certain to be soon. The dark gray sky mirrored my gloomy mood. I didn't want to face the nine-hour drive ahead of me. But I forced myself outside to unhook Betsy before the sky opened up, and I finished just as fat drops started pelting me.

I only had my own thoughts to entertain me on the dreary, wet interstate, and they weren't entertaining. A "Minnesota Welcomes You" sign was proof of my slow progress, and it didn't do much to cheer me up.

I brooded over the reality that Bob's manipulative road trip was causing me to question my own assumptions and convictions. I barely knew what to believe anymore. I felt lost and the despair scared me. I had always thought political action was the answer to pretty much everything. Surely things would be better if Biden was elected president. I was pretty confident he would win. But then what? It's not like he would be able to set things right and keep them that way. There would always be another election, always another Trump. Where was it all going? Would it ever end in peace? Both sides were relentless. Politics was an unwinnable game. Thinking about the pandemic, Biden and Trump, the election, and beyond, I just felt staggeringly hopeless.

What was wrong with me? If I couldn't wake up every morning ecstatic over a $25 million inheritance, then I was way beyond repair. Fact: the money would be nice in many respects, but it couldn't fix my life in ways I wanted it fixed the most. It couldn't buy me Amelia's affection. It couldn't fix Mom and wean her off her loser boyfriend habit. It couldn't win me friends who liked me for *me*. It couldn't write my play and finally finish my degree. It couldn't buy me an ounce of genuine hope.

As I crept toward Bob's inheritance, I had a heavy, sick feeling that it really wouldn't change much—I still basically hated myself. *Is this all there is?* Those dark thoughts spawned darker thoughts and soon I contemplated something that hadn't stalked me in weeks. I could just save myself a lot of trouble and find a deep ravine to drive into.

My ringing phone suddenly sprang me from the thought prison. It was Bob. He sounded less tired, like a night's sleep did him some good, but his tone was serious from the get-go.

"Tom, I uh…I'm sorry for how I sounded last night. That wasn't helpful."

"Uh, that's okay," I said with basically zero sincerity.

"I wanted to apologize, but that's not the only thing I need to apologize for."

"Okay," I said curiously.

"I need to admit something to you. It's the fact that I have resented you, unfairly, because…well, you're a flesh-and-blood manifestation of the deepest regret of my life, which is my failed relationship with my daughter. My lack of forgiveness. My pride. My neglect. I mean…you wouldn't believe the regret. Then I read those blogs you wrote and the desperation to try and rescue you just boiled over, you know? I felt like I had to try an intervention. So, I hoped this road trip would open your eyes, and be a sort of conversion for you. At least put a major dent in your left-wing worldview."

He paused and, in my discomfort and rising emotion, all I could muster was a jokey interlude. "Well, I'm not gonna vote for Donald Trump if that's what you were hoping for."

He skipped past my statement without acknowledgment, which was probably for the best.

"You're a product of the environment you grew up in just as much as I am. You make your stand from where you sit. By that I mean, you growing up on the West Coast, of course you believe what you do—it's all you know. We don't get to choose what we're born into, but it doesn't have to define us forever. We *do* get to choose what we do with our circumstances, and that's one of America's greatest gifts."

Distracted by the call, I let my speed dip down close to fifty. A guy in a pickup truck roared around me in the passing lane, blaring his horn.

"But I screwed up," Bob continued, "because I should've led with this—you have *so much* potential, Tom. You need to know that your life has meaning and purpose. God put you here for a reason. Don't ever doubt that."

My chest tightened and my eyes filled with tears.

"Determine what that purpose is, and then lean into it," he said. "Work really hard at it." After a few seconds, he added, "Did you catch all that?"

"Yeah," I finally managed. "I got it. But..." my voice shook a bit as I squeezed out, "where the hell was all this ten years ago when I really needed it?"

"I know. I...I don't have any excuse. But are you hearing me? I'm trying to say sorry now." He was interrupted by a rough-sounding coughing fit. When he'd recovered, he added, "I know it's too little too late. But I'm trying to apologize."

"Well, I mean, I guess...thanks."

"By the way, this inheritance, you're free to do what you want with it. It'll change your life. But please understand this—it will *never* be your most valuable resource. Your most valuable resource is *time*. Lincoln said, 'Time is everything. Please act in view of this.' Remember that. Don't waste it. Don't be greedy with it. Spend it wisely. Spend it on the right people. Do better than I did with time. I spent way too much of it on my business and not nearly enough on my family. I thought I was doing it *for* them—and I *was*—but it wasn't what they needed most from me. A person who gets to be my age and says he has no regrets is a lying fool. I have a lot of regrets, but one dwarfs them all—being such a stubborn SOB that I didn't move mountains to reconcile with your mother."

"Why did you never apologize to her?"

"I was too stubborn. I thought she was in the wrong, and I didn't know how to start. I mean, how do you even begin to apologize for essentially telling your own daughter you wish she was dead? How do you even start to undo that damage? Then time moves on, and before you know it, two years snowballs into twenty-five, and you have totally separate lives."

"Well, can you just try telling her all of this sometime?"

"I hope I can," he said.

And I think he meant it.

TWENTY-SIX

Burt Schaefer's dairy farm was ridiculously picturesque. Lush green pastures, surrounded by a forest of bushy, billowing trees packed so tightly together that from a distance it looked like one giant continuous wall of shrubs. The main house was white, two-story, with a red roof that almost matched the red of the huge main barn. A silver-domed silo and white wooden fencing completed the quaint scene.

I arrived at dusk and was shown where to park between the house and barn by a guy named Don. He was a tall, sinewy, mostly friendly man of very few words. He looked to be maybe in his late thirties or early forties, but his weathered face, arms, and hands indicated a life of way more work than I was familiar with. I never learned his exact job title at the Schaefer dairy operation, but he seemed to know everything about every aspect of the place and was apparently assigned to babysit me for my three-day farming crash course.

Don said he'd see me at 4:30 the next morning, and I'm sure I stared at him blankly for an overlong moment trying to determine whether he was joking. I decided he wasn't, and the prospect of getting up before 4:30 cast an even drearier pall over my next three days.

The first morning, I stumbled into the barn by 4:40, according to my watch. Don was already there, along with at least a dozen cows. He didn't say anything about my lateness, so neither did I. The cows just stared at me creepily with their big, bulging, paranoid eyes.

Apparently, the cows had to be milked first thing in the morning. I expected Don to start hooking them up to some milking contraption, but it turned out *I* was the contraption.

"Grab that stool," Don said, and I followed his gesture to retrieve a stool that was sitting in front of one of the stalls. "You ever milked cows before?"

"Nope."

He replied by nodding his head as if to say that's what he suspected, and I interpreted it as resignation that he had his work cut out for him dealing with such a noob.

Don showed me where to set the stool and he placed a bucket beneath the cow. He briefly sat on the stool, demonstrating how to squeeze the teat to release the milk. He kept saying the word "teat," and I really wished he'd just go with "udder." I'd know what he meant. I wanted to be just about anywhere else in the world than there, touching that *thing*. Don made it all look very easy, of course.

I glanced around the stall to see if there were any rubber gloves or anything that might provide a protective layer between me and the cow's business. But it was too late—Don was already up from the stool and ready for me to get in there. So, I clenched my teeth and got in there. Then, once I finally sort of got over my squeamishness and squeezed hard enough to get some milk out, I proceeded to squirt milk pretty much everywhere except into the bucket. Don grimaced and had to keep reinstructing me as to the proper grip and pull technique. The way he described it made it sound so simple. But it was not simple for me.

When Don finally said I was done with the first cow, I stood and wiped my sweaty brow with the bottom of my T-shirt.

"You don't have to wear a mask for my sake. I mean, since it's just you and me out here. I don't have any symptoms."

"Okay," I said, stuffing my mask in the left front pocket of my jeans.

"And the cows don't have COVID as far as I know," he added dryly.

I thought he was joking about the cows but really couldn't be sure. I had no clue whether cows carried COVID. Now I had something else to worry about.

I got marginally better at milking, but it took forever. Turns out cows are super high maintenance. You have to do *everything* for them. I had to clean their stalls and spread fresh straw for their bedding. I filled up their troughs with water and filled buckets with feed. After just a few hours of these chores, I couldn't fathom why anyone would choose this life on purpose.

Don would set me up with a task and leave to work on something else for a while, then reappear to assess and correct whatever I'd screwed up. He was one of those unintentionally intimidating guys who seem to know everything manly men are supposed to know how to do. He reminded me of a nicer version of some of the guys Mom dated over the years. They always seemed to be blue-collar types who knew how to fix cars and replace drywall and other stuff I knew nothing about. I always had this fear of being found out by these guys, that they'd discover how mechanically incompetent I was. One summer when I was fourteen, I remember one of Mom's live-in boyfriends trying, impatiently, to show me how to mow the lawn. He was exasperated because I couldn't keep our ancient, dilapidated mower running. I'd mow like, two feet of grass before the mower died on me again. He kept trying to show me what I was doing wrong, something about a throttle, but I just couldn't grasp what he was talking about. Eventually, he snatched the mower from me, thrust his beer can into my hand, and with a flurry of expletives, restarted the mower and finished the job himself. It made me feel so dumb.

Around eleven o'clock, Don finally mumbled something about lunchtime. He said he'd see me in an hour, climbed in his truck, and drove away. I scarfed a couple PB&Js in the RV, then set my watch alarm and passed out on the couch for half an hour.

When Don returned, I finally asked him if he knew when I was supposed to meet Burt. He said Burt was visiting his wife, Marie, who was in the hospital recovering from hip surgery and that he should be back sometime that afternoon. While I had Don in rare speaking mode, I tacked on a question about the Schaefer dairy operation being a lot smaller than I imagined. Don grinned at my naïve notion.

"This isn't the whole operation," he said. "This is the original Schaefer family farm." He nodded toward the house, "That's the original house Burt grew up in. Of course, they refurbished and added onto it over the years. But the main dairy's over near Egg Harbor, and the ice cream factory's in Green Bay."

With that mystery cleared up, Don went back into silent mode, and we started moving hay and doing an assortment of other hardy chores that thoroughly kicked my ass.

Around 4:30 p.m., when I thought we should be wrapping up for the day, I had to milk all the freakin' cows in the barn again. Don must have been weary of my sluggish pace and ready to go home, because he ended up milking most of the remaining cows. The way he tackled the task on top of all the other labor of the day reinforced how pathetically lazy I am.

When we were *finally* done and exiting the barn, Don said, "Looks like Burt's back home." He nodded toward a gray sedan in the driveway. "You can go on over and meet him if you want. Just ring the doorbell. He's probably in his office."

My whole body ached as I dragged myself inside the RV. I figured my muscles were atrophied from driving thousands of miles. It felt like I hadn't worked out in ages. Fortunately, Don had helped me hook up Betsy Ross to water, so I took a lukewarm shower and changed into some semi-clean clothes before walking over to Burt's house.

When Burt Schaefer answered the door, I was surprised by his robustness. He was tall, with a head full of light gray, almost white hair, and a full, closely cropped white beard. He wore navy-blue Velcro sneakers and a short-sleeve button-down shirt tucked tightly into khaki pants that were pulled up a little high and cinched with a black leather belt.

With a wide smile, he welcomed me inside his cozy home that smelled somewhere between a bakery and a florist. He moved slowly but fluidly, I thought, for a ninety-one-year-old. I followed him into his office on the back side of the house, and the first thing I noticed was a simple framed quote on the wall to the right as I entered. Burt invited me to sit in the chair in front of his desk and before I did, I leaned closer to the frame and silently read the quote: *"When a nation goes down or a society perishes, one condition may always be found—they forgot where they came from.—Carl Sandburg."*

"I bet Bob sent me all this way just to see this quote, didn't he?" I asked, only partially joking.

"I'm sorry?" Burt replied, cupping his right hand up to his ear. Then I noticed he wore hearing aids.

I tried again with more volume. "I said, I bet Bob sent me all this way just to read that quote."

"Oh. Well, I don't know about that. Although I bet Bob would appreciate that quote. I think he wanted me to tell you about my politics."

"Okay," I said, with an eager inflection, trying to be nice even though I was way too tired for a political lecture.

"See, I was a lifelong Democrat, until, oh, twenty years ago I guess."

"What happened?"

"Well, I changed my registration to independent."

His long pauses between statements made me feel like I had to urge him on. But maybe that was just his ninety-one-year-old speech pattern.

"What made you switch?"

"That was quite a drastic change for a Schaefer, you see. Our family were loyal Wisconsin Democrats—going way back to the Progressives, the Wisconsin Idea, and the whole thing. You know, concern for the common people, workers, and all that."

I nodded with as much sincerity as I could muster with my fatigue.

"But the Democratic Party left *me*, you see. I should've seen the train coming. It started with all these regulations. You wouldn't believe what we have to deal with trying to run a dairy farm. When I was growing up in the Depression, we thought we needed all these government regulations because the situation was so bad. That's what government had to do to pull the country out of the mess. At least, that's what we thought. But later, when I started running the farm, I realized most of the regulation is just a bunch of nonsense. Of course, my daughter has to deal with all that nonsense now."

Burt spoke slowly, sincerely, but with an even, pleasant tone. He was utterly calm as he talked politics, which was kind of refreshing.

"So, it started with all their rules. Then the party's priorities started to get crazier and crazier. They started making abortion a top priority. Well, I don't believe in that. I'm a traditional Presbyterian, all my life. So, when the party became radical for abortion, I said that's not for me. I used to go to the town halls, and call my representatives, you know, and tried to raise my objections. But it became very clear that we weren't on the same page anymore. Letting boys into girls' restrooms and that kind of nonsense. That train just kept on moving and I just couldn't be on it. They didn't seem to have room for old Democrats like me, anyway. I guess I was the last of what they would call a pro-life Democrat. You don't hear of those much anymore. Now, that doesn't make me a Republican. They've got plenty of knuckleheads on that side too—President Trump, I mean, what a national embarrassment. There are good people in both parties; it's just hard to find them. I had to be an independent and just vote for people and everything on a case-by-case basis."

I tried to grin politely. He grinned back as he added, "Things change. People change. By the time you're my age, who knows? The parties may completely swap what they're for and against. History's funny like that. Politics is complicated. Your generation is smart, though. You'll figure it out."

I almost instantly liked Burt—and not just because he was the only old person I'd ever heard call my generation "smart." I liked that he was able to talk about politics without blowing a fuse.

He soon changed the subject to how he met Bob at a trade show "eons ago," they hit it off right away, and he said that's how he became Liberty's dairy supplier.

"Even though Bob's a hardcore Republican?" I asked.

"Oh, sure. That was alright. That didn't matter so much back then. We're Americans, aren't we? We can do business together no matter how we voted. I didn't even know he was Republican until we'd been friends for a while."

He got around to talking about his dairy cows, and we briefly discussed how my day had gone. He got a good laugh from my description of my milking incompetence.

I wasn't sure how much meeting time with Burt I was supposed to put in, but exhausted and starving, I decided to excuse myself.

"Thanks for stopping by," he said, in a very neighborly fashion, as if we were already pals.

On day two, milking was only slightly easier, but no less gross. The chores seemed to take forever and were even harder on my sore body. It was hot and humid even with dense clouds blocking the sun most of the day. By noon, my shirt was drenched in sweat. Don showed me how to bushhog a field on a tractor, and it took me three hours to get it done.

Time seemed to move differently on the farm—as in glacially slow.

It started raining just as Don and I left the barn after the day's second milking session. Don wasted no time leaving in his truck. I was about to climb into the RV when Burt stepped out his front door and called to me, "Tom! Do you drink coffee?"

"Of course!" I replied over the sound of the pattering rain.

With our mugs full of steaming coffee, Burt and I sat in glider rocking chairs on the wide, covered back porch that ran the length of his house.

"That's the first rule of farming," Burt said just after we were seated. I looked at him expectantly. "You always have to have a pot of coffee on." He took a slow sip, then added, "Some people don't believe in afternoon coffee. They're weirdos."

The rain escalated to a steady, heavy shower, punctuated by periodic low-rumbling thunder. Beyond the porch, directly in front of us, was Burt's vegetable garden. He was glad for the rain and told me about the broccoli, carrots, lettuce, and peas that were about ready to be harvested.

"Don takes care of most of the hard stuff for me now," he said.

I asked how his wife was doing and he said she'd had a good day. If all went well, she would get to come home in a couple days. He said they make him get all suited up in COVID protective gear just to visit his wife in her room for a few minutes. Then he told me about the long driving trips they still go on every year and how he does *all* of the driving.

"Next year, if COVID goes away, we're planning to drive to Vermont to try to join what they call the Two-Fifty-One Club. You know what that is?"

Of course, I did not.

"That's where you visit all two hundred fifty-one towns in the state. We've been doing it for several years, so we've only got seventy-six left to go."

"How long will that take?" I asked.

"No idea," he laughed. "That's just part of the fun."

I watched the rain, and listened to it, smelling the swirling scents it stirred up from the pasture, trees, and garden. In the tranquility of that place, you could almost forget there was a pandemic terrorizing the world. I kind of felt guilty for enjoying the comfort of it so much. Then I had the disorienting feeling that, perhaps very soon, I could find somewhere like this, a quiet haven of my own, and buy it if I wanted to. *If Bob's check clears*, I thought.

That night, I fell asleep before 9 p.m.—the earliest I'd gone to bed since elementary school.

By the afternoon of day three, I think Don was having to invent stuff for me to do. After the milking, feeding, and stall work was done, he had me mow the lawn around Burt's house. Fortunately, I didn't struggle with keeping the mower running.

When I finished the lawn around noon, Burt drove up in his car, back from his daily visit to see his wife. He rolled down the driver-side window and asked me what I was doing for lunch.

"I don't know," I said, not wanting to admit that my cupboard was essentially bare.

"Well, hop in. Let's go get a hamburger."

I gladly got in the car.

Burt meandered over two-lane highways until we entered a hamlet called Ephraim, right on the edge of Lake Michigan. The previous day's rain had moved on, replaced by deep blue sky, wispy clouds and clear sun that made the lake sparkle.

Burt parked in a small public lot, and we walked a short distance to an old-fashioned-looking joint called Wilson's just across the street from the lake. We were seated outside, under a red-and-white candy-striped awning. Burt removed his mask, so I followed his lead.

"It doesn't make a lot of sense to me to wear a mask into a restaurant and then take it off once you get to the table, but I'll be a good soldier, I guess," he laughed.

Before our burgers arrived, Burt talked about his combat experience in Korea.

"I was onboard with the mission at first," he said. "Well, it's not like I had much of a choice. I was drafted, you see. But now I'm not sure that war was a good thing at all. I knew it wasn't by the time Vietnam rolled around. I don't want to see communism anywhere. But that reason to fight was just a whole different ball of wax than getting struck at Pearl Harbor."

I nodded along, wishing I could follow him better, but I had only the slimmest understanding of the Korean and Vietnam wars.

"One thing's for sure," he said, abruptly changing topics, "I don't approve of all this trying to cancel people these days. What do they call it ... cancel culture?"

"Yeah," I confirmed with a grin.

"That can't lead anywhere good. Fact is, people say a lot of dumb things. Always have. But it's our Constitutional right to say dumb things. I don't know much about a lot of things, but I know canceling people like that is too close to—or at least it's the same spirit as—the communism that Uncle Sam sent me to fight against in Korea. Anyway, it's un-American."

Our burgers and fries arrived in time to distract Burt from cancel culture. As he added some ketchup to his burger, he remarked, "My doctor told me I should back off having a hamburger once a week. I said to him, 'Doc, I'm ninety-one years old. Maybe we should just not talk about my diet anymore.'"

Burt laughed heartily, and I joined him.

I hoped I'd make it to ninety-one, with Burt's brand of vigor and outlook. I wanted to be driving myself around like him at that age, and maybe even learn to garden.

By the time we got back to Burt's farm, I don't think he or Don had any expectation that I was going to do any more chores. When it was late afternoon milking time, I decided I couldn't abandon Don while I was still around. Those dim cows weren't going to milk themselves. Don seemed pleasantly surprised when I showed up in the barn to help him.

When I'd finally milked my last cow (hopefully forever), Don and I exited the barn together.

"Thanks for your help," he said.

"I'm pretty sure I mostly got in your way," I replied apologetically.

A faint grin formed on his face, but he didn't disagree.

"Well, good luck to you, Tom," he said before climbing into his truck.

That evening, Burt invited me to his back porch, where he showed me how to make homemade ice cream. He didn't believe me when I confessed I'd never had homemade ice cream before.

He had an old-fashioned hand-crank ice cream maker to which we added a canister that he had already chilled (Burt was an ice cream master after all). He showed me how to pack layers of ice and rock salt in the bucket around the canister. I poured in the vanilla ice cream mix that he'd prepared. Then he had me attach what he called the "dasher" to the canister, and it was time to crank. Burt failed to mention that I would have to crank continuously for the next half hour. My arms and shoulders were on fire by the time he casually said, "That's probably good, you can stop cranking."

Burt went inside the house and returned with two bowls, two spoons, and an ice cream scooper. He dipped us two generous servings and as dusk settled over the farm, we dove in.

Somehow, I think all the work I'd put in made it taste even better.

After a couple bites, Burt said, "Mmmm...tastes like freedom, doesn't it?"

"Yes sir," I replied, truthfully, without feeling my usual level of cynicism.

I woke up early the next morning, barely after 6:00—I think that's just what happens on the farm. I suddenly felt free. My three-day stint babysitting cows was finally over. At the same time, as odd as it seemed, I was going to kind of miss it (well, *some* of it).

I checked the tape to see what creative torture Bob had next in the queue, nervous as usual that it would be something outlandish like working on a lobster boat in Maine or something.

"Good news," he said on screen, and I got slight goosebumps. "Your next destination is your last stop…before returning the RV to my house of course."

I yelled, "Yeeeaaahhhhh!" at full blast and pumped both fists in rapid, out-of-control fashion.

Bob said I was to proceed to Abraham Lincoln's house in Springfield, Illinois. I didn't even know Lincoln had a house in Illinois. I paused the video and scrambled for the atlas. By my rough calculation, it looked like I could be there in maybe eight or nine hours. If I got going, that meant I could potentially be done with the whole, insane marathon that very day.

I resumed the video and listened impatiently as Bob gushed about Lincoln.

"Lincoln proved that if you're super smart and eloquent, America can even love a Republican president," he said, chuckling at his own joke. He said that I was to walk from Lincoln's house to the Great Western Depot, apparently the train station where Lincoln bid his farewell to Illinois before his first presidential inauguration. Bob's last instruction was that I was to call him to do my final reading, rather than recruiting someone to listen to me. That made me even more ecstatic about the prospect of the finish line.

I was nearly beside myself as I scrambled out the door to say bye to Burt. I rang his doorbell like a moron, forgetting that it wasn't even 7:00 a.m. yet. Fortunately, Burt was already totally dressed—shirt tucked in, hair combed—ready to take on the world.

"It was really a pleasure meeting you, and I just wanted to thank you for everything," I said.

Burt asked me to hold on and said he'd be right back. I really hoped he wasn't going to find another chore for me because as much as I liked Burt, I was desperate to hit the road.

He returned after a few very long minutes with an envelope, which he handed me.

"What's this?"

"That's your check for all your work."

"Oh, I don't think Bob intended for me to get paid or anything. I mean your ice cream was payment enough."

"Nonsense. Bob may not have intended it, but I do. Honest pay for honest work. No buts, okay?"

Burt was a hard man to argue with.

"Okay," I said, though I didn't feel great accepting it. "Thank you. Very much."

"You drive safe, Tom."

Back in the RV, I practically leaped into the driver's seat and buckled up before tearing open the envelope. The check was for $600—*$200 a day?* It was way too generous considering the wrench I'd put in Don's operation with my ineptitude.

Bob was right—Burt Schaefer *was* one of the good guys.

TWENTY-SEVEN

I waited until I made it onto I-43 outside Green Bay to call Bob. For the first time all summer, I got his voicemail. I left a message, letting him know I was done working at the Schaefer farm and was on my way to Springfield.

Over an hour later, my phone rang, and I answered. It was Kathy Montgomery, Bob's executive assistant whom I'd met at his house that day which now seemed half a lifetime ago. She said Bob had been in the hospital with COVID since Monday.

My mind spun a bit, and I glanced at my watch to confirm what day it was—*Thursday*. That meant he had been in the hospital since my first day working on the farm.

Kathy said Bob had his phone with him at the hospital, so I could call him if I needed to. I didn't tell her I'd already tried.

After she hung up, I panicked a moment, trying to figure out what this would mean for the whole trip. Surely his condition wasn't too serious if she said I could call him at the hospital. But he didn't answer earlier, and he'd already been in the hospital for three days. I quickly tried to call him again, but once more, straight to voicemail.

I took some deep breaths and tried to calm down. Then I felt like a garbage person for worrying about whether his hospitalization would affect me getting the $25 million in a timely fashion. I wished Amelia was with me. I wondered if she was back at school. I would be driving through Chicago later on the way to Springfield. I really wanted to try to see her, but would she think it was too soon? Would she think I was trying too hard? My mind couldn't help returning, again, to that night before she left. Reluctantly, I decided it would be too long of a detour to try to find Amelia, assuming she *was* back in Chicago. So, I pressed on.

I was just north of Milwaukee when I called Mom to let her know about Bob. Her reaction was way too casual.

"Well, thanks for letting me know," she said, almost as if I regularly called to tell her that her father was in the hospital with a deadly illness.

"*Mom...*" I said in kind of a scolding tone, "what if he's...what if it's serious?"

"I...I don't know," she stammered. "What do you want me to say?"

"Well, I mean, he's still your dad."

She giggled sarcastically and said, "I can't believe I'm hearing this from you."

"If there was ever a time that you might, I don't know, consider reaching out...*now* might be the time."

"Look, he made his choice, and I guess I made mine too. There *is* no relationship anymore."

I let out a deep sigh, which I'm sure she caught at least some of over the phone.

"But Mom, you don't want to think about...for your own sake at least...I mean, I think he's actually sorry now."

"Oh my God. He got to you. He brainwashed you into feeling sorry for him, or brainwashed you with his money or something."

"Mom, come on, *stop*."

"No, really—you like him now, don't you?"

"You know what? Maybe I do sometimes. He's not that bad. I mean, he kinda is. I get it—he can *definitely* be a jerk. But he has his semi-decent moments too."

"Okay, I don't want to hear this. You don't fully understand everything that happened."

"I'm sorry, Mom. I'm not trying to upset you."

"Too late."

"I just…you've been carrying this around for so long. And so has he. And—"

"Did you ask him about my inheritance?" she interrupted.

I couldn't believe she brought that up again considering the circumstance.

"No…not yet," I finally admitted. "There hasn't been a good opportunity."

"Well, you promised to ask for me. Don't forget."

Her attitude really bothered me.

"I'm not gonna forget, but I'm not gonna ask him about it when he's in the hospital with COVID, either."

After our call, I fumed for several miles. Before this trip I didn't really care about Mom and Bob's nonexistent relationship. But now I *did* have a sort of relationship with Bob. It was a very contentious, erratic relationship, sure, and he was still a Republican blowhard boomer who drove me nuts, but I also heard cracks in that persona the last time we talked, when he tried to apologize. And I believed him that he was full of regret. Maybe I was wrong to believe him. Maybe he *was* just manipulating me for whatever reason. But I believed him in spite of my cynicism. I actually wanted to believe him. And I was willing to hear more from *that* Bob, the remorseful one. I just thought it would be good for Mom to hear from that Bob too.

Abraham Lincoln's house in Springfield—the only home he ever owned, according to Bob's video—was nothing particularly special. Maybe that's what Bob liked about it. I stood on the wide, red-brick walkway directly in front of the Lincolns' front steps and thought how much cooler, aesthetically, Booker T. Washington's house was than this. Not that there was anything shabby about Lincoln's two-story house—it was just smallish and very boxy. It was painted khaki with green shutters. And of course, thanks to COVID, no one was allowed inside.

The wide streets around Lincoln's house were unpaved, just fine pebbles and dirt. I guess it helped give me a slight feeling of what it may have looked and felt like in Lincoln's day. The Lincolns' old neighborhood was neat and tidy, but it felt abandoned. Knowing that there was a pandemic, and that Bob was in the hospital because of it, made that little corner of Springfield feel especially empty and depressing.

I walked a short distance over the pebble street, which transitioned to red bricks before the Lincolns' neighborhood ended, and like a time traveler I was suddenly back in 2020 Springfield again. I turned left on the sidewalk parallel with South Ninth Street, then turned right on East Monroe Street. At the end of the block, there it was—my last stop—a tiny, two-story red-brick building: the Great Western Depot. There wasn't anything particularly "great" about it. The short walk between Lincoln's house and the Depot seemed too easy, almost like I was cheating on the final leg or something. There had to be some catch. But I tried to brush aside my pessimism and revel for at least a moment in the fact that *I'd made it.*

Above the Depot's entrance was a white sign that read "Great Western Railroad, Springfield, Illinois." The sign was flanked by two long, vertical American flag banners. There was an old-fashioned lamppost on the brick walkway in front of the entrance. On the right side of the building's facade, atop a black flagpole, the Stars and Stripes gently flapped in the casual summer breeze.

I approached a small bench that was facing the street, pulled the folded-up reading page from my shorts pocket, and sat. I took a deep breath, then dialed Bob. I got his voicemail. I sighed, unfolded the sheet of paper, and glanced over it. I closed my eyes. I was so very close to the end, and I couldn't get him to answer his phone.

I tried his number again. This time, after four rings, he finally answered. As soon as I heard his voice, I almost wished he hadn't answered because he sounded absolutely horrible. Even saying "hello" seemed to be a struggle for him.

"So, you're in Springfield?" he inquired. Bob's robust voice was gone, replaced by raspy, wheezing words.

"Yeah. I'm sitting outside the train station now."

He squeezed out, "Good," before a coughing fit. His voice then shook as he forced, "Congratulations," before another cough.

"I'm ready to read, if you're…"

"Yes, go ahead," he said, "I'm listening."

I began reading the brief speech that Abraham Lincoln gave to the crowd gathered at the train station to see him off as he departed for his inauguration in Washington DC:

"*My friends, no one, not in my situation, can appreciate my feeling of sadness at this parting. To this place, and the kindness of these people, I owe everything. Here I have lived a quarter of a century, and have passed from a young to an old man. Here my children have been born, and one is buried. I now leave, not knowing when, or whether ever, I may return, with a task before me greater than that which rested upon Washington. Without the assistance of that Divine Being, who ever attended him, I cannot succeed. With that assistance I cannot fail. Trusting in Him, who can go with me, and remain with you and be everywhere for good, let us confidently hope that all will yet be well. To*

His care commending you, as I hope in your prayers you will commend me, I bid you an affectionate farewell.'"

I had to pause a couple times for Bob to cough—long, wretched, torturous-sounding fits. Near the end, I heard him sniffling and wondered if he was choked up, but his already trembling, short-of-breath voice made it impossible to tell.

"Are you ready for me to do the last part?" I asked. On my sheet, there were a few more lines, separate from the farewell speech. Above those final lines, Bob had written: *Ending of Lincoln's Second Inaugural speech on March 4, 1865.*

"Yes," he barely uttered, "but let's say this part together."

"Okay," I said, with hesitancy, wondering how he would be able to get through it (and whether he had the words in front of him). But as soon as I began reading, Bob chimed in with his brittle voice, and it seemed to me like he was reciting the words from memory:

"'*With malice toward none,*'" we said aloud together, "'*with charity for all; with firmness in the right, as God gives us to see the right, let us strive on to finish the work we are in; to bind up the nation's wounds; to care for him who shall have borne the battle, and for his widow, and his orphan—to do all which may achieve and cherish a just and lasting peace, among ourselves, and with all nations.'"*

I felt a twinge of emotion as I heard Bob strain so hard for breath to finish the words with me.

"Thanks, Tom, for doing this," he managed.

It was the first time he'd said thank you for my effort, as if I'd done all of this for him. From his perspective maybe it *was* for him, but I'd certainly never thought of it that way.

"You're welcome," I said.

Then came the kind of sucker punch I'd half-expected during this all-too-easy final leg of the journey. Even though every word he said sounded like it took enormous effort, he persevered: "Now, I've got one last stop for you."

I squeezed my eyes shut, hung my head, and shook it slowly. *Of course he does*, I thought.

"This one's not far from my house. Kathy will give you directions."

"What is it?" I asked, restraining myself as best I could to avoid letting my burning frustration shine through.

"It's just something you should see. I..." his voice trailed off as he sounded completely out of breath and dissolved into coughing.

I was about to protest that this bonus stop was definitely not in our contract but decided at the last second that arguing with a man who was in the hospital and sounded desperately ill might not be the best look. I simply said, "Okay."

"I'm sorry...you know...this whole project is something I should've started a long time ago. Instead, I tried to cram it all into this crash course for you. But..." He coughed some more. "I just wanted you to like your own country. I figured if you saw it for yourself and heard from someone outside your bubble, you might find out it's not all bad, and maybe it's worth preserving."

I winced at the excruciating effort in his voice. He really had to wring the words out of himself.

Then, with an unnerving sense of finality, he added, "Stay open-minded, Tom. Seek the truth—*the* truth, not *your* truth. We can deceive ourselves so easily."

I finally said, "I'll try to remember that."

"I...well...if things had been different, and you got to grow up knowing your grandfather...I think I probably would've liked to go by 'Grandpa.' Could I hear you call me that? Just to hear what it sounds like?"

"Uh, sure...*Grandpa*," I said.

"Hmm...I like the sound of that," he said.

"Well, I guess I better get going," I said, blatantly brushing past his sentimentality because it made me uncomfortable.

"Okay, see you soon."

I stood from the bench and glanced over Lincoln's words again. I was confused by my emotion lurking over the thought of parting ways with Bob. Why did I feel even slightly bothered by the idea of being rid of this guy who had so annoyed me and turned my life completely upside down over these weeks? I guess, maybe, there's something inexplicable about family bonds. Maybe there's an underlying current even when you're essentially strangers. It was weird, though—he didn't seem like such a stranger anymore.

TWENTY-EIGHT

The sun was well into its descent behind me as I raced eastward on I-72. The end of the quest felt so near, I didn't want to waste time trying to figure out another night in an RV park. So, for better or worse, I kept driving. The adrenaline of nearly completing the journey sustained me through the night across Indiana and Ohio. I got sleepy a few times but was able to slap myself awake. Around dawn, however, exhaustion finally overtook me, so I slid into a rest stop somewhere along the interstate in West Virginia and quickly fell asleep.

My ringing phone jolted me awake and as I groggily answered it, I glanced at my watch, surprised it was already after 9:00 a.m. It was Kathy, informing me that Bob had to be put on a ventilator and, as a result, was now in an induced coma. I barely knew what any of that meant, and my sleep-deprived brain fog didn't help the confusion.

"He's not doing well," she said. "We're very concerned."

I managed to thank her for the update before we hung up. I immediately thought of everything I should've said. Maybe I should've offered to help in some way. What are you supposed to do when someone's in a coma? Did I need to be the guy on watch at his bedside? Did they even allow that with COVID? It was all very deflating.

Nearly seven hours later, I retraced the first steps I'd taken on the road trip—from Williamsburg to Bob's secluded property. It felt surreal turning off the highway onto his winding driveway, through his green fields with their immaculate white fencing. I'd made it, somehow.

The finish line did not feel as celebratory as I thought it would, mainly because of the uncertainty surrounding Bob's condition. If he was healthy and at home, we probably could've had our postmortem on the trip that evening, he could've transferred the money, and I'd be on the first flight out. Instead, I didn't really know how him being in the hospital, and in a coma, would affect things. Part of me was worried that the whole deal could still fall apart.

I slowed Betsy Ross to a stop in front of Bob's fancy garage, which was not open. I turned off the RV and walked to the patio doors, peering inside the house. There was no sign of anyone. I walked around to the front of the house and rang the doorbell. After a few moments, Kathy finally answered the door. She immediately welcomed me inside and was quite friendly and helpful, though she did seem a bit distracted. She talked fast and kept checking her phone during our brief interaction.

While I was outside, I remembered that Bob had two dogs, so I asked Kathy about them. She said they were fine and that her teenagers were taking care of them at her house.

I asked Kathy if there was anything I could do. Her only suggestion was that, if my schedule allowed, I should stay for a few days until Bob hopefully improved and we could get things sorted out. She said I was welcome to any of Bob's guest rooms, but the idea of staying in Bob's sprawling house, alone, while he was in the hospital in a coma just seemed off. So, I told her I'd prefer to just stay in the RV.

She gave me a house key and a key to one of Bob's pickup trucks. She teared up talking about Bob getting COVID.

"Who knows how he got it," she said, daubing at her eyes with a tissue. "He was pretty careful. But I guess it was probably at one of the stores. I told him he should just stop going for a while, but he insisted on keeping up his regular visits."

Before she left for the day, I asked her if I could have my phone back and she immediately retrieved it for me. It was strange to be holding my real phone again. I hadn't been on social media for a month, and honestly, after some initial withdrawal, I didn't really miss it.

After Kathy left, I wandered into Bob's office and studied the framed items on the walls. There was a photo of him with President George W. Bush that I hadn't noticed before. There was the vintage Pepsi machine in the corner that I'd forgotten about. I moved behind his neatly arranged desk and almost sat in his chair, but it somehow felt wrong, so I stopped short.

Laying on the upper right-hand corner of the desktop was the US citizenship test he'd had me take. My score of fifty-three was written in red and circled on the front. I grinned and shook my head. My thoughts and feelings were all over the map about Bob's epic, peculiar journey. Maybe one day I'd be able to catalog all the thoughts and feelings and figure out what it all meant. One thing was certain: I was no longer the same person who took that test.

I stepped out onto the patio and tried to call Mom. I had to leave a message, telling her about Bob being on a ventilator and that I'd made it back to Virginia. Voicemail seemed the wrong way to deliver such a dire update.

After a bunch of fretting and overanalyzing, I finally decided to risk calling Amelia. But she didn't answer. I realized she didn't have the number from my *real* phone, so I texted her explaining.

She called me back right away.

"Hey!" I answered with probably too much enthusiasm.

"Hi!" she said, sounding (fortunately) glad to hear from me.

I explained everything about Bob.

"Oh, Tom, I'm *so* sorry," she said. "The moment we hang up, I'm in prayer for Bob."

"Thanks." I knew she would make good on that.

We fell into what was by our standard small talk. It wasn't too abnormal, but it really made me miss the camaraderie and shorthand we had on the road.

I almost gushed that I really missed her, but at the last moment softened it to, "It's so great to hear your voice."

"It's great to hear you too."

I kept her on the phone by filibustering with tales of my working on the farm in Wisconsin. She laughed and loved the visual of me trying to milk cows.

As I wracked my brain for more stuff to talk about, she asked, "So, what have you learned then?"

"What do you mean?"

"From your journey, now that it's over."

"Oh. Wow. I, uh... I guess I haven't had time to really process everything yet. I don't know."

"I find that difficult to believe. After thousands of miles? All that driving time to think? There must be something."

"Well... okay... how 'bout this? I don't want to be cynical anymore."

"That sounds promising."

"I'm not sure how *not* to be, but I want to figure it out."

"Baby videos and hot chocolate, that's a start," she said, and we laughed. "And *Phineas and Ferb.*"

"Right?" I said. "Greatest cartoon of all time!"

"Of *all* time," she agreed. "Hands down!"

"How have we not talked about this?"

"I don't know!"

We laughed some more, and it was precisely what I needed. It took everything in my power not to beg her to marry me.

Just before noon the next day, I drove one of Bob's trucks—which was easily the nicest, cleanest vehicle I'd ever driven—to the hospital. Visiting the hospital was not my idea. Kathy suggested it. It almost seemed like she *assumed* I would want to. I did not want to. I silently wondered what the point was of visiting someone in a coma, but then I figured it might be awkward if I *didn't* visit him after she'd brought it up. So, I delicately drove his truck to the hospital, paranoid the whole way about getting a scratch on its immaculate navy exterior.

Inside the hospital, I was directed to the ICU wing on the third floor. Only close family members were allowed on the hall. A chatty nurse named Lucy gave me instructions and got me suited up—full surgical gown, gloves, double mask, *and* face-shield. I felt like I might suffocate under the tight masks. Having all that gear on suddenly made me feel like I was in hyper-danger of catching COVID.

As we walked down the short hall toward Bob's room, I asked Lucy how serious Bob's condition was.

"Really critical. Mr. Brock is a very sick man. But I definitely believe coma patients can hear us talking to them, so it's important for you to let him hear your voice. Just keep talking to him. I know he hears you."

She didn't explain how she *knew* that to be true exactly, but it was no use arguing.

I followed her into the room where she said, "Hey, Mr. Brock. I've got your grandson here to see you!"

I took one tentative step toward the bed and stopped.

"You can get closer," Lucy said. "You can get right beside him. It's fine."

I appreciated her encouragement, but the situation looked anything but *fine*. I walked around to the window side of the room, standing between the wall and his bed. It was trippy being in the same room again with the man I'd grown accustomed to talking to on the phone. It was even more trippy that this man was my grandfather and that it was only the second time I'd ever seen him in person.

Lucy took care of her brief nursing duties, then she left and closed the door behind her. It was just me and Bob—completely silent for the first time since I'd known him.

They had him lying prone on the bed, shirtless, with his head turned toward me and the ventilator clasped tightly to his ragged face. He was a ghastly, feeble sight. A lump rose in my throat and I choked it back. He was an old man, but lying there he looked like a helpless child. I felt truly sad for him. Sad about our shattered family. Sad that Mom wasn't there instead of me. I felt like a total imposter, even though, as far as I know, I was his closest living relative besides Mom.

Then my sadness was infused with rage—rage at all the right-wing nutjobs who were hell-bent on downplaying COVID and the pandemic. If they could only see the ravaging effect of this disease on Bob, on one of their *own*. It was devastating.

I didn't know what to say to Bob. But finally, I swallowed hard, and tried.

"Hey, Bob...Grandpa...it's Tom. So, I finished the road trip. Bet you thought I wasn't gonna actually do it. I thought that too...a lot. But, I did it, and, I can't believe I'm admitting this but, I'm glad I went. I'll never forget it. And it would be a lot better if we could kinda talk about this in person, so, you need to get better, okay? Don't be like those progressive pansies you're always railing against." I chuckled. "Don't be a snowflake. Don't play the victim card here. It's time to man up and fight back against this thing. Okay?"

I paused and gazed out the window for a moment, wondering what else I could talk to him about. I felt a little ridiculous. I turned back toward Bob, and as I watched him clinging to life, I considered all that he'd lost, at a relatively young age—a daughter and wife, and essentially his other daughter. I truly felt bad for him about those losses, even if he shared a ton of blame for the "loss" of my mom.

A thought confronted me that when life hangs in the balance, a person's politics quickly fades way into the background, slinking out of the room, embarrassed that it had sucked up so much air for so long. It just did not ultimately matter that much.

I remembered seeing my citizenship test on Bob's desk the previous evening and it made me think of the last question he asked me before I started the road trip.

"Remember when you asked me how I would sum up the American experience in one word?" I asked him. "And I said, 'oppression.' Well...oppression is still part of the equation, but you'll probably be glad to know that after all you put me through on this trip, I'd like to change my answer. The best word is *opportunity*. Opportunity to do better. Opportunity to dream. To believe. Pursue. Build. Learn. Grow. To *love*."

I'm not sure I fully believed my own words, but saying them aloud worked toward convincing me. I *wanted* to believe it was opportunity over oppression. And I wondered if maybe that's a first step toward not being cynical.

"I gotta remind you of your own words now—you told me America has always been for optimists. So, you've got to take your own medicine…now's the time to be optimistic. You're gonna beat this."

I reached for his bare left shoulder with my right hand, but hesitated. I was afraid to touch him even with a gloved hand because of the risk of transmission. But I finally put my hand on his shoulder and gently squeezed.

"See you tomorrow, okay?"

Then I left his room.

Late that afternoon, I made good on Bob's request, the one he'd made on the phone when I was in Springfield about the mysterious bonus stop. I got the address from Kathy and headed out in Bob's truck, still having no clue what the visit entailed.

I turned off the rural highway onto a dirt road, rattling around a bend to some sort of construction company storage area, or truck-hauling operation—I couldn't tell. It was a dumpy, overgrown lot with rock piles, rusty barrels, a bulldozer, and other random construction vehicles. It did not look like I was supposed to be there (the "No Trespassing" sign that I drove past was a strong clue). This had to be the wrong place.

I parked beside a large dumpster and hesitantly got out of the truck. The place seemed abandoned and felt eerie. The eerie vibe wasn't helped by the gathering clouds, which completely blocked out the sun. A cool wind was sweeping out the humidity and dropping the temperature. Light rain speckled my face.

As soon as I stepped around the truck bed, I saw in the weed-strewn field ahead of me why Bob wanted me to visit this place.

It was a mesmerizing collection of giant gray statues, dozens of them, each one a bust of a US president. It was like a quirky, earthbound first draft of Mount Rushmore or something, except *all* the presidents seemed to be there. As far as I could tell, they were assembled in a completely random order.

I approached the one of George Washington first. A dismal, dark gray stain streaked down his face, nose, and chin—as if he'd been bloodied. These were no amateur likenesses. Each one was sculpted in remarkable, accurate detail. And they were huge, at least three times my height. But the busts were weathered and badly damaged, each one with unique, horrific blemishes. Lincoln was in the same row as Washington. Walking around to the back of Lincoln, I found a jagged, gaping hole in his head and a chill suddenly raced down my spine. Most of them looked like they were decomposing, with macabre chunks missing from their face, an eye, or ear.

There were no signs explaining the statues or their shared deterioration. It was a mystery. I had no idea what these were for, where they'd come from, or how Bob knew about them. What havoc had been visited on these once regal men? It looked like some curse had swept over the disheveled field.

Walking through the mystifying garden of cracked presidents, part of me liked seeing the disfigured visage of some of the men I was supposed to hate, like George W. Bush. But mostly I just found it forlorn and haunting, like walking through America's graveyard. I felt like someone from the future, stumbling across the ruins of a formerly grand civilization and marveling at the puzzle of what went wrong.

Once I'd walked past each president, I circled back to George Washington. I stood directly in front of him, pulled out my phone and was in the middle of snapping several photos when Kathy called.

"Tom," she began solemnly, "I'm so sorry to be the one to let you know this...but Bob just passed away."

"Oh my God," was all I managed to reply.

I shouldn't have been surprised based on what I'd seen at the hospital that morning—but I was entirely stunned.

Just like that, Bob was gone.

Kathy's voice cracked as she reiterated her condolences and said she would be in touch shortly to discuss funeral arrangements. I hope that I thanked her, but the rest of the brief call was a blur.

The moment we hung up, the rain fell harder. The drops streamed down the giant ashen faces of the presidents in dark streaks, which made it look like they were weeping. Then I joined them. I stood in the rain, among the battered gray presidents, and felt warm tears slide down both sides of my face.

I didn't cry because I loved my grandfather so much—I hadn't known him long enough to love him. I cried because I *might* have loved him but was robbed of the chance. I cried because people always make a mess of everything and do too little too late. I cried because everyone dies. I cried because the world is so cruel and lonely. And yet, I thought, that didn't account for Amelia.

I finally climbed into Bob's truck trying to calculate what time it was in Aberdeen (as if that mattered). Of course I had to call Mom right away. Predictably, she didn't answer the first time. But I kept calling, and she finally picked up on my fourth try.

Mom didn't say much after I told her the news. Her voice was quiet, but steady, which surprised me because I mostly expected her to melt down. I told her I'd let her know as soon as I had funeral details.

"I'm not gonna go." she interjected.

"*Mom*," I protested. "Come on."

"Tom—"

"What?" I interrupted. "Why wouldn't you just—"

"I'm not going," she said, cutting me off. "End of story. You're just gonna have to deal."

I was mad but didn't want to hang up on her at a moment like that.

"I've gotta go," she said without explanation. So, the call was over, with no closure, no commiseration, no *I love yous*.

That evening, I sat on the patio at Bob's house in lonely silence. The rain clouds dissipated, and a golden sunset was in progress. A sweet, cool breeze blew off the bay in the distance. I decided I would miss Bob. I'd never had another man in my life tell me what to do or give me advice. Even if I thought most of his views were bogus, at least he was trying to instruct me. He was mostly harsh and judgmental, but he made an effort in his idiosyncratic way. It just felt perverse to have all of that suddenly evaporate when it was just getting started.

Amelia texted asking how Bob was doing. I called and filled her in. I could tell she was crying. She always liked Bob more than I did.

TWENTY-NINE

Bob died on a Saturday. The funeral was set for the following Tuesday morning. Per Bob's previous instructions, it would be a small, graveside service with remarks by his pastor only. He didn't want "long, blubbering tributes" according to Kathy. He was to be buried in a small, local cemetery next to his wife and daughter.

The day before the funeral, I drove to Target—the same one where I'd stocked up to begin the road trip—and bought a black suit. Actually, I had to piece it together, so I'm pretty sure the jacket was a darker shade of black than the pants. But it would do. I even found a black tie and shoes. For once, I felt I should try *not* to look like the broke student and starving wannabe playwright that I was.

I had never been to a funeral before. Kathy kindly asked if I wanted to speak at the graveside service. That was a definite *no*. There was a small, covered pavilion at the cemetery, and I had a front-row seat on one of the benches. I was shocked at the number of people who showed up—it had to be a few hundred. A lot of the crowd wore masks, and most stood outside the pavilion, social-distancing themselves in small clusters. I wondered how so many people knew Bob and what compelled them to be there.

There were a couple of hymns, followed by a brief message and prayer from Bob's pastor. I snuck some glances behind me during the service, hoping I might see Mom wander in at the last second. She didn't.

Then the casket was lowered into the ground. And that was it. The harsh reality of the finality of death fairly terrorized me. What was this all about? Did anything matter? I so wished Amelia was there to talk my ears off about Jesus and God and new life, so I could at least feel some vicarious comfort.

I felt completely out of place, not knowing anyone other than Kathy, until Rosa Felix Young and her husband approached me. They'd flown in from Florida the previous day. She reiterated what a great man Bob was and asked how the rest of my trip had gone. Later, I saw Ferguson Hill and met Laura, his wife. Burt Schaefer even made it with his daughter. They drove all the way from Wisconsin—Burt emphasized that he did most of the driving.

I didn't want to stay mad at Mom for stranding me at the funeral, so that night I called her.

"I made it to the airport," she explained, "but I couldn't go through with it. So, I got drunk instead."

I closed my eyes, shook my head, took a deep breath, and silently counted to ten. What was I going to do with her? She was even more of a mess than me.

"Mom…I don't want us to end up…can we please just swear that we will *never* end up like you and Bob?"

"Honey, we *won't*," she said. "And…I got to talk to him before he died."

"What?"

"After you told me he was in the hospital, he finally called me."

"Really?"

"Yeah. He tried to apologize, and…"

"And did you accept?"

"I think so."

What a typical Mom answer, I thought.

The next afternoon, I had an appointment with Kathy and three lawyers to sign papers and finalize the portion of Bob's will pertaining to me. It finally seemed real. I was actually getting the $25 million Bob indicated in our contract. Kathy pointed out that Bob apportioned me several million dollars more, so that the take-home amount after "Uncle Sam's sick grave robbery" (as Kathy said Bob had phrased it) would be an even $25 million. Betsy Ross was also willed to me if I wanted her. I said yes without really thinking it through.

Mom also got $25 million, so I was essentially getting money that would've gone to her sister. Bob willed his house to Mom too. I had no idea what she'd ultimately do with the property, but it was hard for me to imagine her ever living there again.

"Your grandfather was a very generous man," offered Kathy.

I nodded politely. A lot of people said that about him. It's not that I didn't believe them. I just couldn't really work out the dichotomy of his alleged generosity and his nonexistent relationship with Mom and me. People are complicated, I guess.

"Okay, there's one more thing he left to you," Kathy said.

I followed her down the hall. Behind Bob's desk, she knelt in front of the safe that was in one of the cabinets beneath the built-in bookshelves. She checked a card she'd brought from her office and carefully dialed the combination. I really hoped my money wasn't inside the safe in the form of gold bars or something. The safe opened on her first attempt and she pulled out an old-looking scrapbook.

"Here you go," she said, handing me the scrapbook without explanation.

"Thank you," I replied with a puzzled look.

"You're welcome," she said and left me alone with it.

I set the thick book on Bob's desk. The cover was a faded red and it made a crackling sound as I opened it. Inside, the pages were gray, a bit like construction paper. Turning the first page, I found photos interspersed with ticket stubs, brochures, and other travel paraphernalia. The first photos were of Mom and Christine, elementary school age, in Washington, DC. There was a shot of the whole family on the steps of the Jefferson Memorial. Bob was wearing a tall, dorky baseball cap in the photo. A photo on the opposite page showed Bob (with actual hair) and Mom inside the RV, making faces at the camera. Everyone looked happy. I'd never seen so many photos of Mom with her sister and parents—tragic images of what might have been.

Turning the pages, I found the family at the Grand Canyon, then Independence Hall in Philadelphia. Mom and Christine grew in the photos, their clothes and hairstyles changing with each trip. There were photos of them at Mount Rushmore and Gettysburg, shots of them eating at picnic tables with Betsy Ross in the background. There were lots of photos of my grandmother, always beaming, usually with an arm around one or both of her daughters. There was one from the inside of the RV with Bob behind the wheel, relaxed joy on his face, apparently in his element.

Then Mom and Christine had the look of gangly teenagers on top of Pikes Peak. The next page found them standing with slumped shoulders and sullen faces in front of a locomotive at Promontory Summit. Then they were in swimsuits, on a beach, adjacent to photos of a Space Shuttle launch at Cape Canaveral. And that's when it hit me like the kind of giant wave that used to knock me over at the beach when I was six years old. My head, shoulders, and arms suddenly felt numb.

I sat in Bob's desk chair and put my head in my hands as the realization coursed through me that I had been to *each one* of the specific places in the scrapbook.

I flipped ahead to confirm my epiphany—there was the family at Lincoln's home and the Grand Western Depot, Lewis and Clark's Station Camp, and even Tuskegee, Alabama, and the statue of Booker T. Washington lifting the veil of ignorance.

I leaned back in the chair and stared at the ceiling in wonder… my grand tour of the US had not simply been Bob's quirky effort to teach me to love America. That was part of his agenda for sure, but perhaps more than that it was a trip down Bob's memory lane. "Corps of Discovery" wasn't just the whimsical name of his RV. His *family* was the Corps of Discovery. In his outlandish, flawed, all-too-human way, he had tried to make me part of that Corps, and maybe relive the best moments of his life in the process.

Turning the scrapbook pages, I realized I was holding Bob's map of lost treasure.

That evening, I went for a long walk around Bob's property and discovered he had a small dock on his inlet of Chesapeake Bay. I sat on the end of the dock and basked a while in the warm mid-summer breeze. For a few minutes, I actually felt relaxed and my usual swirling anxieties stilled.

In my relatively chill state, without even trying to think about it, I suddenly knew how to finish the play for my thesis project. The floodgates flung open in my mind and there was such a gush of ideas and inspiration that I was afraid I wouldn't be able to capture it all before I forgot it. I wondered why I hadn't thought of this before—the answer was to toss the garbage first act I'd written and start all over from scratch. The new play would be about Bob and me and this insane road trip. It would be about family and Amelia. About Right versus Left. Belief and cynicism. Love and emptiness. Oppression and opportunity. It would be about America.

I couldn't get back to the house fast enough to get started.

I went on a total writing binge, working almost nonstop. I wrote mostly at the table inside the RV since it seemed only appropriate. I ate and slept only when I absolutely had to. I didn't shave for a week and my stubble sprouted into a scratchy, ungainly mess. It was a feverish writing sprint like I'd never done before. I was afraid to stop for almost any length of time, afraid I would lose the inspired momentum.

I wrote in longhand, filling a few legal pads that I found in Bob's office. When I finished those, I resorted to printer paper from Kathy's office. I rewatched Bob's VHS tapes, sometimes pausing and rewinding to jot down his exact words. Kathy came to her office a few times during the week, but otherwise I had no distractions. The words simply tumbled out and my cramped right hand could barely keep up.

I started on a Wednesday, and as darkness fell the following Monday, I finally wrote the words "END OF PLAY." I was exhausted and exhilarated, but I couldn't stop yet—I had to type it up. It struck me that I could now afford to buy any computer I wanted. But I didn't want to waste time on that. Desperate not to lose momentum, I called Kathy, and she said I could use the laptop on her office desk. I told her she was a lifesaver.

Twenty-four hours later, I finally finished typing. The only thing it lacked was a title. I kicked around jaunty variations on *Road Trip*, but nothing felt right. I stepped out of the RV with the last cigarette in my pack and paced around the outside of the house while I smoked. When I saw the setting sun casting its amber glow on the US flag affixed to Bob's front porch, I knew I didn't need to overthink the title anymore.

I hurried back to the laptop and typed: *American Inheritance*.

I wasn't as mad at America anymore. For whatever reason, one's homeland is an integral part of human experience. My homeland was vast, and beautiful, and terrible, and messy, and virtuous, and greedy, and generous, and deceptive, and truly phenomenal. I was an American, and I was much more okay with that than when I started the journey.

After sleeping for what felt like a day and a half, I printed out a copy of my play from Kathy's printer and set it on Bob's desk. I don't know why I did that exactly, but it just felt like the right thing to do. I helped myself to a Pepsi from Bob's vintage machine, snapped off the cap, and held out the bottle toward Bob's desk chair.

"Here's to you, Bob," I said aloud. Tears filled my eyes without warning. "Thanks for the inheritance. I have no idea what I'm doing. But I'll try to figure it out."

Then I took a drink, turned out the light, and returned to Betsy Ross.

The ending I wrote for my character in the play hadn't happened yet. I didn't know, of course, whether my ending would work out in real life the way I conceived it. But there was only one way to find out.

THIRTY

One night during my playwriting binge, I flipped through the file of selected readings that Bob gave me for the stops along the journey. The words that stood out to me that night were the ones I'd read in Philadelphia—Benjamin Franklin's words from the end of the Constitutional Convention:

> "For having lived long, I have experienced many instances of being obliged, by better information or fuller consideration, to change opinions even on important Subjects, which I once thought right, but found to be otherwise. It is therefore that the older I grow the more apt I am to doubt my own judgment, and to pay more Respect to the Judgment of others."

Bob's road trip may not have had the total conversion effect on me that he hoped it would. But the Benjamin Franklin quote reminded me where Bob's shrewd plan *did* make its mark: I was much less confident than ever that I had all the answers (political or otherwise). After thousands of miles, the only thing I was more certain of is that I did not know as much as I thought I did. In a strange way, there was some comfort in knowing I didn't have all the answers—there was less pressure to be right all the time.

From the start of the journey, I thought Bob was off-the-charts arrogant, but it turns out I was too. I had never given humility much thought, but the trip across America humbled me. I bet it would humble anyone who tried it.

It slowly hit me that this inheritance would completely change the course of my life. I was officially part of the 1 percent that I had been taught to loathe, and I didn't know how to feel about it. Obviously, I was ecstatic about removing the paralyzing weight of my student loan debt. I was also relieved that Mom would be financially free and secure. Other than that, it was bewildering and overwhelming in a different way from being broke. Suddenly, I was free to do basically whatever I wanted. That prospect made me feel guilty and exhilarated at the same time. And really scared. I had no idea what to do with my life when the option was *anything*.

The last thing Bob told me in our final conversation was to seek the truth. So, I got started by filling up Betsy's tank and hitting the road again. I drove toward the best version of truth, beauty, and goodness that I knew—she was in Illinois.

I did not even begin to understand everything that Amelia was convinced of when it came to her faith. But she seemed on to something. She seemed to have found some truth. There wasn't an end in sight to the pandemic, America was a political trainwreck, and city streets were roiling in protest, yet Amelia somehow exuded peace and purpose in the chaos.

I wasn't convinced yet, but she had me Jesus-curious.

Regardless, she made me want to do better, and I needed that in my life. I also owed her tuition money, and I couldn't wait to make good on my promise.

As I got back on the familiar interstate, freed of any agenda other than seeing Amelia again, I felt almost giddy. At this rate, I thought, I might even try having Bob's glass-half-full view of America. Who knows? It could be a game-changer.

The next day, appropriately enough, I found myself on a street named Washington. From there, I turned right on a College Avenue, which led me into the quaint, wooded campus of Wheaton College. I drove past a manicured lawn on my left that held a granite sign declaring, "For Christ and His Kingdom."

This must be the place, I thought.

Ahead on my right was a grand red-brick building with white columns and a sign labeling it the Billy Graham Center. I remembered Amelia mentioning Billy Graham, so I took it as a literal sign that I should turn into the parking lot adjacent to the building.

I didn't tell Amelia that I was on my way. I hoped to surprise her. It was almost noon, and I hadn't planned any further than simply getting to her campus. I grabbed my mask from the center console and stepped out of the RV. That's when I heard her lovely voice ring out.

"*Tom?*"

I looked up to see Amelia, smiling, backpack over her shoulder, descending a short flight of steps from the building toward me.

"It's not going to be easy to park Betsy Ross around here," she said.

I just smiled. I was sure she was right, as usual.

ABOUT THE AUTHOR

Nathan Nipper is the author of the novel *Life on Christmas Eve,* which debuted at number one on Amazon's holiday fiction bestseller chart in 2021. He also wrote the 2014 award-winning nonfiction book *Dallas 'Til I Cry.* He lives with his family near Fort Worth, Texas.

Connect with the author at
www.nathannipper.com.

Made in the USA
Middletown, DE
30 May 2024

55055030R00179